THE GHOST
AND THE MOUNTAIN MAN

HAUNTING DANIELLE

THE GHOST
AND THE MOUNTAIN MAN

USA TODAY BESTSELLING AUTHOR
BOBBI HOLMES

The Ghost and the Mountain Man
(Haunting Danielle, Book 27)
A Novel
By Bobbi Holmes
Cover Design: Elizabeth Mackey

Copyright © 2021 Bobbi Holmes
Robeth Publishing, LLC
All Rights Reserved.
robeth.net

ISBN: 978-1-949977-64-6
(A)

To all the essential workers who've been on the front lines during the last year.
Thank you.

ONE

He stood on the sidewalk, ignoring the persistent morning rain, and focused his attention on the house across the street. He had almost missed it, almost walked right by. Looking at it now, he realized it was both familiar and almost unrecognizable. It was the trees; he decided. Not only more trees than he remembered, but much larger. And the neighboring houses—so many houses.

If not for the large sign posted in front of the house, he might have kept walking. It hadn't been there during his last visit. The sign said he had arrived at Marlow House. He continued to stand on the sidewalk, losing all track of time, something he did all too frequently.

Finally, the rain subsided. He glanced to Marlow House's mansard roofline and noted the position of the sun, surrounded by dissipating rain clouds. A few hours earlier he had witnessed the sunrise while standing on the pier. That was where he had spent last night.

When first returning to Frederickport, the car he had been following turned a corner, disappearing from sight. The unfamiliar sights had distracted him—many new buildings. And the roads— now all paved. Once he found the pier, it had been the touchstone he needed to convince himself he had indeed returned to Frederickport. It simply was not the Frederickport he remembered.

It wasn't that he hadn't tried to go home before. Yet each time he ventured back toward civilization, something new frightened him. First it was the horseless carriages that increased in numbers, followed by paved roads, and later more of those carriages, in unimaginable shapes, going terrifyingly faster and faster.

He might have remained in the mountains if he hadn't seen Alex. Of course, he didn't immediately recognize him. Not only was Alex older, but he dressed differently. Once recognition dawned, he had impulsively pulled the trigger, sending off a flurry of bullets. They had miraculously missed their target. He wasn't sure if he felt relief for not killing Alex or angry it wasn't finally over.

Since it was three against one, he had thought it prudent to flee, yet he hadn't gone far. After the failed shooting, he hid in the bushes, spying on the three for a few hours before he decided it might actually be the ideal time to return to Frederickport, while Alex was in the mountains.

Unfortunately, finding his way back to the road took him longer than he had expected, and when he finally got there, he saw Alex again, this time getting into a vehicle with his friends. Instead of retreating into the mountains as he had done countless times before, he followed Alex's car, keeping a safe distance behind to avoid detection. But when he reached Frederickport, the unfamiliar sights distracted him, and Alex's car disappeared around the corner.

He hadn't intended to confront Alex, but now he stood in front of Marlow House. What would Anna think of all this? How had they explained his disappearance? The more he looked back on all that had happened, the angrier he became. He could no longer hide; he needed to face Alex and tell Anna what kind of monster she had married.

About to step off the sidewalk and head across the street to Marlow House, he paused when movement to the right distracted his attention. A vehicle drove up Beach Drive. It slowed in front of Marlow house. Something flew from the car toward the house, flying over the fence and landing on the walkway. A newspaper, he guessed. The car then continued on its way.

After the vehicle drove up the street, he stepped off the sidewalk, on his way to Marlow House. He thought briefly about the newspaper—assuming that was what he had seen fly from the car—and marveled at the expert throw yet wondered briefly if it had landed in a dry spot or in a puddle left behind from the recent rain. It really didn't matter. Alex would not have time to read the newspaper.

ON SUMMER MORNINGS Danielle enjoyed her coffee with Walt on the back patio. But this August morning rain kept them inside, not an uncommon occurrence for Oregon. Instead of the patio, they retreated to the parlor, each bringing along a mug of hot coffee. Walt carried a plate with a cinnamon roll. Danielle had claimed she didn't want one, insisting she needed to cut back on sweets. Yet once in the parlor, she helped herself to some of Walt's cinnamon roll. He didn't object, knowing there was more in the kitchen. Plus, after last week's misadventure, he was simply grateful to be sitting in his parlor, out of the rain, and with the woman he loved.

Danielle hadn't changed out of her flannel pajama bottoms and T-shirt she had worn to bed the night before. But she had taken the time to weave her dark hair into a French braid, a slight change from the fishtail braid that had once been her trademark hairstyle.

Already dressed for the day in casual tan slacks and a pale blue polo shirt, Walt sat next to her on the parlor sofa. In one hand he held his mug of coffee, and on his right knee he balanced a plate with the half-eaten cinnamon roll.

"You're reading too much into this Brian and Heather thing," Danielle said, resuming the conversation she had started with Walt in the kitchen just minutes earlier.

"Perhaps, but you weren't with them up on the mountain. The pair got rather cozy," Walt said before taking a sip of his coffee.

"Sure they did. Goodness, poor Heather must have been terrified after waking up tied to a tree and those crazy wannabe witches. And I can't imagine how Brian is absorbing all this."

"He seemed perfectly fine with it last night," Walt reminded her. "And then he goes home with Heather." He chuckled and took another sip of coffee.

Danielle rolled her eyes. "Why do people always say women are the gossips? Sheesh. Just because Brian stopped by Heather's house on the way home from here doesn't mean he went home with her in that way. Perhaps she was just nervous about going home to a dark house. I certainly understand that, especially after being kidnapped and almost killed."

Walt reached over and gave Danielle's knee a pat and said, "We will see."

"Anyway," Danielle went on, snatching a pinch of Walt's cinnamon roll and popping it in her mouth. "Brian is too old for her. My dad would be about his age if he were still alive."

"If you will recall, the last man Heather dated was about Brian's age," Walt reminded her.

"True, but the idea of Brian Henderson and Heather Donovan in a relationship is ridiculous."

"There is one way to find out," Walt said, setting his cup on the coffee table. "We could see if his car is still over there this morning."

"You would really go out in this rain just to spy on our neighbor? Seriously, Walt, I am surprised at you."

Walt laughed. "In case you haven't noticed, it's not raining anymore. But I'm not talking about me going outside."

"I'm not going outside."

"And I never suggested you should. But there is someone who was out there earlier this morning who might tell us something." Walt looked over to the windowsill where Max lounged.

"Max," Walt called out. The cat looked up to Walt; their eyes met. Danielle watched the pair in silence. After a few minutes Walt chuckled, took a sip of coffee, and Max went back to napping.

"Well?" Danielle asked after a few moments. Walt pulled off a hunk of cinnamon roll and put it in his mouth.

"Well?" Danielle repeated.

Walt looked to Danielle and asked, "Well, what?"

"What did Max say?"

"You said you weren't into gossip." Walt took a sip of coffee.

Danielle groaned. "Okay, I am curious. What did Max say?"

"He watched the sun come up this morning, perched in one of the trees by the garage. He had an unobstructed view into Heather's driveway."

"And?"

"His car was still there," Walt said.

"Really?"

Walt nodded. "Really."

"How long was it there?"

Walt shrugged. "I'm not sure. Max came in when the rain started. It was still there then."

"Wow." Danielle leaned back in the sofa, considering what Walt had just told her. "Brian and Heather? A couple?"

Walt shrugged. "Or perhaps you were right."

"How so?"

"About Heather being nervous going home after dark, considering everything that's happened. Perhaps Brian stayed over there as a friend."

"Yeah, sure," Danielle scoffed. "A platonic sleepover. I don't think so."

Walt arched his brows. "Really? Not possible? Didn't Chris sleep over here while I was up in the mountains? Is there something you need to tell me?"

"Walt!" Danielle gasped.

Walt laughed.

Danielle's brief outrage dissolved, and she let out a sigh. "One minute you're suggesting there's something going on between Brian and Heather, and the next you're saying there's nothing going on."

"Oh, there is definitely something going on. What exactly, I'm not sure. But we will see."

Danielle's cellphone rang. She stood up and retrieved the phone from the nearby desk. Before answering, she glanced at the caller ID.

"Good morning, Chief... No, no plans. We're hanging out here today. Walt's just glad to be home... Certainly... I hope it's nothing serious... Okay." Danielle disconnected her call and returned the phone to the desk.

"What did the chief want?" Walt asked.

"He has to work today, and his sister agreed to watch Evan. But she got sick about an hour after the chief dropped him off. He asked if Evan could spend the day with us. I said sure. He's going over there now to pick him up and then bring him here."

"I hope it's nothing serious," Walt said.

"The chief feels it's food poisoning. Sissy ate some sketchy leftover seafood late last night."

"Is Eddy coming too?" Walt asked.

"No. He's spending the weekend with a friend. It's just Evan." Danielle glanced down at her pajamas and said, "I should probably change my clothes before they get here."

"Why don't you finish your coffee first?" Walt suggested. "You have time."

Danielle sat back down and took another sip of coffee.

They chatted a few minutes longer before Walt asked, "I wonder if the morning paper is here yet."

Danielle stood up.

"Where are you going?" Walt asked.

"To check if the paper's here."

"I didn't mention that so you would get the paper. Let's finish our coffee, and I'll get it," Walt said.

"I already finished my coffee." Danielle leaned over and gave Walt a quick kiss on the lips. "Let me go see if it's here, and while I'm gone, please finish that cinnamon roll, will you?"

Walt chuckled. "This morning you told me you didn't want one."

"Exactly. I've eaten half of yours. I can't resist those things. We really need to stop buying them."

Walt reached up and gently looped a finger in Danielle's collar and pulled her to him. He brushed a kiss over her lips and whispered, "Not happening."

"But I have no willpower," Danielle whispered back.

Walt chuckled and kissed her again. With a sigh, Danielle stood up after Walt released her collar, preparing to bring in the newspaper. While doing so, she paused a moment and glanced at what remained of the cinnamon roll. She reached down to snatch a bit when Walt swatted her hand away.

"No more. I'll be your willpower," he told her.

Turning from the sofa empty-handed, she grumbled, "You aren't trying to help me. You just want it for yourself."

"True," he said and then picked up the remaining piece of roll and ate it.

TWO

O n her way to the front door to pick up the newspaper, Danielle glanced up the stairs and wondered briefly if she had enough time to run up to her room and get dressed before the chief showed up with Evan. Perhaps. But first, she would get the newspaper for Walt.

A moment later she pulled open the door, expecting to find her front porch empty except for the possibility of the newspaper if the delivery person had tossed it that far. Instead, she looked into the bearded face of a strange man.

"Oh…" She startled, her eyes momentarily widening.

The beard obscured the man's face, and at first glance one might assume he was older because of his gray hair and beard, but his eyes were those of a much younger man. Danielle looked him up and down, noting the worn boots, denims and faded flannel shirt. His floppy leather hat resembled a cowboy hat, yet not one she had ever seen sold in western stores.

"I was just getting ready to knock," he explained. "Who are you?"

"Um… who were you expecting?" Danielle asked.

"I'm here for Alex," he told her.

"Alex? I'm afraid you're at the wrong house."

The man frowned and turned briefly, pointing to the sign out front. "It says Marlow House. This is Marlow House, right?"

"Yes, it is, but there is no Alex here. If you explain why you believe he's here, perhaps I can help you."

"Because it's his home," the man snapped.

"I'm sorry, but no Alex lives here." Danielle glanced over her shoulder to the parlor door, wondering if she should call for Walt.

"Who are you?" he demanded.

She briefly considered not telling him. After all, he was the one who had come knocking on her front door. But considering the large sign she had installed in her front yard, he already had the name of her house, and anyone with minimal computer skills could search Marlow House, Frederickport, and come up with dozens of articles about her. Plus, she was curious why he expected to find this Alex living at her house.

"I'm Danielle Marlow, and this is my home."

"Danielle Marlow? You're related to Alex? Why are you lying to me? He told you to lie, didn't he?"

"Um... I honestly have no idea who this Alex is. I should get my husband," Danielle suggested.

"If you won't let me talk to Alex, then let me see Anna. She's here, isn't she?" he demanded.

"Anna?" Danielle frowned.

"Stop this nonsense! If you won't let me see Alex or Anna, then let me talk to the old man. Is he home? I bet he'd be interested to hear what I have to say. If you won't let me in, I can always go to his office and tell him. Alex can refuse to see me, but it won't keep his secret. You can tell him that! He might as well see me now, because I'm not going away. You tell Alex that!"

The sound of the front gate opening interrupted their conversation. The man glanced behind him while Danielle looked in the same direction. Coming through the gate was Chief MacDonald and Evan. While Danielle hadn't initially felt threatened by the unexpected visitor, his tone and insistence that he had to see this Alex, and his obvious belief she was lying to him, had made her uncomfortable.

"Oh, look, it's Police Chief MacDonald," Danielle said loudly, feeling a sudden flood of relief.

The man looked back to Danielle. With a snarl he said, "You tell Alex I'll be back." He turned abruptly and rushed down the walkway, past the chief and Evan, disappearing to the street.

"Odd greeting," MacDonald said as he walked up to Danielle, Evan by his side.

"Did you get a good look at his face?" Danielle asked when the chief reached her.

"Who was he?" Evan asked.

"That's what I would like to find out," Danielle said.

"Who was who?" the chief asked.

"The man who just rushed by you," Danielle said.

"What man?" the chief asked.

"The guy with the funny hat and beard," Evan told his father.

The chief frowned. "What are you two talking about?"

Danielle paused and looked from the chief to the street. Without saying a word, she rushed past Evan and his father, down the walkway. When she reached the sidewalk, she looked north and then south. The man was nowhere in sight.

"What's going on, Danielle?" the chief asked, following her down the walkway, Evan trailing behind him.

"Was that a ghost?" Evan asked Danielle.

Danielle looked to the chief. "You didn't see him, did you?"

MacDonald shook his head. "If there was a man here when I walked up, I didn't see him."

"I did!" Evan said. "Was he a ghost?"

Danielle looked back down the street again and then to Evan and his father. "I think he was."

"Whose ghost was he?" the chief asked.

"Not a clue. He said he was looking for someone named Alex and Anna. And someone he called the old man. He thought they lived at Marlow House."

"I love coming over here," Evan said. "You always have exciting stuff going on."

Danielle looked at Evan and chuckled, rustling his hair with one hand. She noticed how tall he had grown. Soon he would be taller than her.

"Let's go tell Walt about our visitor. According to the ghost, he plans to return, so hopefully we'll find out who he is then."

"Never boring here," MacDonald muttered.

"Do you have time for a cup of coffee?" Danielle asked the chief.

"Sure, coffee and a ghost story," MacDonald said, following

Danielle back to the house. On his way there, he leaned down and picked up the newspaper, reaching it before Danielle.

"Walt's in the parlor," Danielle said as the three walked in the open doorway. "I'll go get you that coffee, and I have a feeling Evan would like a cinnamon roll."

"Hey, what about me? I like cinnamon rolls too," MacDonald said, still holding the newspaper.

EVAN RUSHED in the parlor door before his father and announced excitedly, "There was a ghost out front!"

Walt glanced up from the sofa. "Morning, Evan, Edward. Ghost, you say?"

MacDonald tossed the newspaper to Walt, who effortlessly caught it. He took a seat on a chair facing the sofa. "Obviously I didn't see it. I believe Danielle was talking to him when we walked up. I don't think she knew he was a ghost until he ran off and realized I hadn't seen him."

"But I did," Evan said. "He had a gray beard and funny jeans. And a faded old flannel shirt. Kinda like the ones my grandpa likes. But it was dirty, like the jeans. And he had a floppy hat."

Walt narrowed his eyes at Evan. "How do you mean, funny jeans?"

Evan shrugged. "I don't know. They didn't look like regular jeans."

"Do you know who it was?" MacDonald asked.

"He does sound familiar. But why would he be here?" Walt asked.

"Who do you think he is?" Evan asked.

"I don't know. I don't even know if it's the same ghost," Walt said.

MacDonald arched his brows. "You have been seeing lots of ghosts lately? Getting more and more like your wife?"

"The ghost I'm thinking about is the one we ran into in the mountains. Evan's description is a match. But how did he get from there to here, and why?"

"Are you talking about the ghost who shot at you?" MacDonald asked.

Evan's brown eyes widened. "A ghost shot at you?"

Walt flashed the boy a smile. "Yes, but fortunately, ghost bullets aren't especially lethal. He was there one minute and then just vanished. Heather saw him too."

"You think he's the same ghost?" MacDonald asked.

Danielle walked into the parlor, carrying a platter with a coffee pot, a clean mug, a glass of milk, a plate of cinnamon rolls, and a stack of paper napkins. "You know who our visitor was?" she asked Walt after hearing MacDonald's question.

"Evan described him. Sounds like the one we ran into in the mountains."

"Did he follow you here?" Danielle asked as she set the platter on the desk.

"If he was the same one, I'd have to assume so. But why?" Walt asked.

Danielle filled the empty mug with coffee. "I don't know if he was the same one, but my ghost was asking for Anna and Alex." She handed the coffee mug to the chief.

"Anna and Alex?" Walt frowned.

Danielle returned to the desk and set a cinnamon roll on a napkin. She handed it and the glass of milk to Evan, who now sat on the sofa with Walt. "Yes. First he asked for Alex. Claimed he lived here." She returned to the desk and placed a second cinnamon roll on a clean napkin and handed it to the chief.

"Did he know where he was?" Walt asked.

Danielle paused a moment and looked at her husband. "What do you mean, did he know where he was?"

"Did he know whose house this was?" Walt asked.

"I suppose. He pointed to the sign out front and said something about this being Marlow House. So yes, if that's what you mean. Why, do you know who he is?"

"No, I don't," Walt muttered.

Danielle shrugged and then picked up a roll, tore it in half, and handed one side to Walt. She took the second half with her to the empty chair next to the chief and sat down. "First, he demands to see this Alex, insisted this was his home. And then he asks for Anna and…" Danielle paused a moment and looked over to Walt. She had just torn off a piece of cinnamon roll and was about to put it in her mouth but stopped and considered her words for a minute while meeting Walt's gaze.

"What is it?" the chief asked.

Danielle glanced briefly to the chief and then looked back to her husband. "Your parents, they were Alexander and Anna."

Walt nodded. "Yes. My father went by Alex."

"Are you suggesting this ghost was looking for Walt's parents?" MacDonald asked.

Danielle shrugged. "All I know, he insisted they lived here. But he was pretty angry. If it was your father he was looking for, I don't think they were friends. He seemed upset."

"And this is the same ghost you encountered in the mountains?" the chief said.

Walt shook his head. "I don't know. The description matches."

"That picture of your parents we found, you look a lot like your father. Is it possible this ghost thought you were your father, and that's why he shot at you?" Danielle asked.

"Why would he shoot at my father?"

Danielle shrugged. "I don't know, but he seemed awful upset with this Alex."

"I can't imagine why," Walt said. "Everyone loved my father."

"I suppose we can always ask him," Danielle said, popping the piece of cinnamon roll in her mouth.

Walt frowned. "Ask him how?"

Danielle looked at Walt. "He said he was coming back."

THREE

He kept his promise and returned to Marlow House. When he arrived, the car that had been parked out front during his prior visit was no longer there. Determined to confront Alex, he marched back up to the front door. What he didn't know, fifteen minutes earlier the occupants had gone to the house across the street. Even the cat who lived at Marlow House was not home.

Standing at the front door, he gave it a vigorous knock, and to his surprise, he found himself no longer standing outside, but in the entry of Marlow House. Confused, he glanced around and wondered how he had gotten inside. He noted the closed front door. But he didn't waste time trying to understand; instead he saw this as divine intervention, his opportunity to confront Alex.

Momentarily tempted to shout out for the man, he resisted and began quietly searching the house, starting with the parlor. One reason not to call out for Alex, it might actually be better to find Anna instead, and if he did, he would tell her everything.

AFTERNOON SUNSHINE REPLACED morning rain clouds. Danielle and Evan had joined Lily and Connor on the beach behind Lily's house. The two women sat in beach chairs, each clad in leggings, with Lily wearing a lightweight hoody over her shirt, and Danielle wearing an extra-long sweater blouse. Evan and Connor sat on a blanket nearby, playing in the sand with trucks, shovels and buckets. Inside the house, Walt visited with Ian.

Danielle's cat, Max, sat in the middle of the blanket with the boys, watching their every move, his black tail swishing back and forth. Sadie crouched nearby on the beach, her eye on a neglected tennis ball at the blanket's edge, waiting for one of the boys to discover it and give it a toss.

Lily watched as Evan helped Connor fill a bucket with sand. With a sigh she said, "I can't believe he's going to be a year next month."

"And before we know it, Evan will be a teenager," Danielle said.

"Or as my mom called it, a stinking teenager." Lily snickered. "I feel so cliche saying how fast they grow up. But it's true."

"That's why it's a cliche," Danielle reminded her.

Lily let out another sigh. "According to all the baby books, Connor should start talking any time now, and I'm just hoping his first word isn't Marie."

Danielle laughed. "If it is, I want to be there when you explain that to Kelly. But I hate to be the one to tell you, it won't be Marie. More likely Grandma Marie."

Lily frowned at Danielle. "Why do you say that?"

"That's what I've heard Marie call herself to Connor."

Lily groaned.

"If you're lucky, it will be just Grandma. That'll be easier to explain. You can always say you taught him that for when he sees his grandparents again," Danielle suggested.

"Perhaps." Lily shrugged.

They sat in silence for a few minutes, watching the boys. Finally, Lily asked, "The ghost this morning, you say he was looking for Walt's parents?"

"That's what it sounded like. Walt's dad was Alexander, and his mother was Anna. The ghost was looking for Alex and Anna and insisted they lived at Marlow House. It has to be who he meant."

"Do you have any idea why the ghost is angry with Walt's dad? And what did he need to tell Walt's mom?" Lily asked.

Danielle shrugged. "I don't know; neither does Walt. He doesn't really talk about his parents, but it's probably because he doesn't remember much about them. From what I understand, his grandparents rarely discussed them. Walt thinks because it was too painful."

"Maybe, but dang, that seems so wrong. But it happens. I had a friend who was about Evan's age when his father died. His mother remarried a few years later. And she never discussed his father. She never talked about what kind of person he was, what he liked to do, nothing. I can't imagine doing that if—God forbid—something happened to Ian." Lily shivered at the thought.

"I suppose everyone handles grief differently."

"How did his parents die?" Lily asked.

"A house fire, Walt was five years old," Danielle told her.

"House fire? So they weren't living at Marlow House at the time? I assumed they all lived at Marlow House."

"You were right, they were living at Marlow House," Danielle said. "That's where Walt was born."

With a frown Lily asked, "Where was the fire? How did it happen?"

"It was at a friend's house. In fact, the friend died too, the wife, anyway. The husband wasn't home. A heater exploded. Sounded horrific," Danielle said.

"That's awful! Walt wasn't there, was he?"

"No. He was at Marlow House when it happened." As Danielle explained, Sadie gave up waiting for someone to throw the ball. She walked over to Lily and Danielle, sitting between them in the sand.

"And this ghost, you said Walt thinks he might be the same one from the mountains?" Lily asked.

Danielle reached out and absently stroked Sadie's back while saying, "When we described him to Walt, he sounded like the same ghost. But after we discussed it a little more, Walt's convinced it's a coincidence and not the same one."

"Why does he think that?" Lily asked.

"The ghost in the mountains had a rifle. The one Evan and I saw wasn't armed. Plus, it seems a little farfetched that the ghost they ran into would show up just days later at Marlow House, looking for Walt's parents."

"The fact your husband used to be a ghost is a little farfetched too." Lily snickered.

BEFORE HEADING OUTSIDE to work in her yard, Pearl Huck-abee traded her favorite cloche hat for a white sailor's cap, its brim turned down. It seemed more sensible considering it had been raining earlier. Unfortunately, she had gotten little work done, distracted by the police car she'd seen driving down the street, slowing in front of her neighbor Heather Donovan's house, and then racing off again.

From what she had read in the newspaper several days earlier, someone had kidnapped Heather and Pearl's other neighbor, Walt Marlow, along with Officer Brian Henderson. They had been left up in the mountains to die. The article made little sense. It said something about witches being responsible. Witches? Pearl couldn't fathom such a thing.

Yet, considering Donovan's appearance, Pearl did not doubt the young woman had gotten involved in some cultish witches' coven and had brought the trouble on herself. Donovan seemed just the type to go exploring in the Devil's playground. Perhaps poor Officer Henderson had been investigating Heather's shenanigans, and it almost got him killed. She hadn't figured out Walt Marlow's involvement, nor had the newspaper article adequately explained what had happened and why.

By the way the police car slowed down in front of Heather's house, she wondered if her neighbor was under surveillance because of the incident. While pondering the possibilities, she glanced to the rear of her yard and spied the same police car moving down the alley, passing Marlow House and then hers.

Pearl dropped the rake she had been holding and scurried toward the back of the yard to have a closer look. When she neared the bushes along the fence separating her property from Donovan's, she heard voices. Taking care not to make a sound, she crept closer to the bushes and looked next door.

The police car parked behind Heather's house, its motor still running. Heather stood by the car, talking to the driver. It looked like Officer Henderson.

"ARE YOU STALKING ME?" Heather asked while leaning against Brian's open car window. She wore gray sweatpants, a red T-shirt and red jogging shoes, with her black hair pulled up in a high ponytail. She hadn't put on any makeup, yet her nails sported fresh black polish.

"I'm just patrolling the neighborhood, keeping the citizens of Frederickport safe," Brian said with a grin. He reached out the window and gave the hem of her shirt a gentle tug. "Going jogging?"

"Yes. I normally go in the morning, but the rain stopped me."

He chuckled. "Was that all that kept you home?"

She grinned. "I can't even imagine what Joe would think if he knew."

"How do you know I haven't told him?" he asked.

She leaned into the window and gave his lips a quick kiss. Pulling back, she said, "Because neither of us needs that kind of BS right now."

"They are eventually going to find out," Brian told her.

"Well, yeah, if you keep cruising by my house," Heather said with a snort.

"You just like the sneaking around," Brian teased.

Heather giggled. "Admit, it is sorta fun."

Brian flashed her a grin and gave her hem another tug. "You go do your jog. But try not to fall over any dead bodies."

"If I find one, I know who I'll call."

HEATHER HUMMED as she sprinted down Beach Drive to the pier. Brian showing up unexpectedly had thrown her off her routine, making her forget her earbuds. So instead of listening to music, she hummed a tune while thinking how everything had changed since those crazy witches had barged into her life.

When she reached the pier, she turned west, and instead of walking onto the pier, she headed down under it, to the beach for her jog north, intending to run by Ian and Lily's, then Chris's house and beyond.

Since she had already warmed up, she broke into a jog once she reached the beach, greeting those along her path as she passed by, her ponytail flopping up and down behind her.

It wasn't a dead body that brought her to a complete stop a few minutes later. But it was close. Directly in front of her, watching her approach, was the ghost of the trigger-happy mountain man she had encountered with Brian and Walt the week before. But unlike the last time, he wasn't toting a rifle. Of course, that didn't mean he couldn't conjure one up at a moment's notice. After all, he was a ghost.

"Are you going to shoot at me again?" Heather asked, slightly out of breath after the quick sprint and jog.

"Do you see a rifle?" he asked.

"Why are you here?" she countered.

"I'm here for Alex. Where is he?" he demanded.

"Who's Alex?" Heather frowned.

"Don't play dumb," he snapped.

"Who are you?" she asked.

"You mean Alex didn't tell you?"

"Why are you here? Why aren't you still in the mountains?"

"You would like that, wouldn't you?"

"I'd rather you move on, like you're supposed to do."

"Move on?" He frowned.

"If you don't intend to move on, at least tell me who you are," Heather said.

"Why don't you just ask Alex," he said before disappearing.

Heather stood alone and glanced around. She noticed a couple of teenagers who had been playing Frisbee on the beach had stopped and now watched her curiously.

Heather groaned inwardly and started jogging again, heading north. A few minutes later she spied Lily and Danielle sitting in beach chairs behind Lily's house, while Connor and Evan played in the sand, with Max lounging on a blanket. She sped up, and a moment later Sadie ran to greet her. The dog trotted alongside Heather as they neared Lily, Danielle, and the two boys, Sadie's tail wagging happily.

When Heather reached Lily and Danielle, she stopped abruptly, slightly out of breath, and said, "Hey, where's Walt? I need to tell him the ghost who shot at us is here. I just saw him."

FOUR

"Let me put Connor down for a nap," Lily said as she carried her son into the house. Danielle, Heather, and Evan trailed behind her, while Sadie and Max remained outside.

A few minutes later, after getting Connor settled, Lily found them sitting at the kitchen table with Ian and Walt. No one suggested Evan wait in the other room while they discussed the ghost. After all, he was a medium.

"So the ghost who shot at us knew your dad?" Heather asked Walt after they finished comparing notes.

"It certainly sounds like it," Walt said. "But I can't even imagine what the connection might be, or what my father could have done to make him so angry."

"Do you look a lot like your dad?" Heather asked. "Because I'm pretty sure that ghost thought you were him."

"We've a wedding picture of Walt's parents, and in the picture, he looked like a younger version of Walt," Danielle said.

"Are you suggesting I am old?" Walt asked with mock indignation.

"Aren't you over a hundred?" Evan asked sincerely. The adults chuckled.

"Technically," Walt said, flashing Evan a wink.

"What does this ghost want with Walt's dad?" Lily asked.

"The easiest way to find out is for us to go home and wait for him to show up. He said he was coming back," Danielle said.

"All right!" Evan stood up.

Danielle looked at Evan and pointed to the chair. "Not so fast, buddy. Sit back down. I think maybe you should stay over here if it's okay with Lily and Ian."

"Certainly," Lily said. "I think that is a good idea."

"Aw, gee," Evan groaned. "I'd like to see the ghost again."

"And you might," Danielle said. "There is always a chance he pops in here, and if he does, Lily and Ian won't see him, but you will. And you don't want him scaring Connor. After all, Connor might see the ghost."

"Oh, you want me to protect Connor?" Evan asked.

"Of course," Danielle said with a smile. "And if that ghost shows up, you tell him Alex is waiting across the street and wants to talk to him. When he leaves, make sure Lily or Ian calls me and lets me know he's on his way."

"Okay, I promise. I'd better go stand guard outside Connor's room." Evan stood up and raced to the hall.

"Do you really think the ghost will come here?" Lily asked when Evan was out of earshot.

"I doubt it. But I think it's best Evan is not there if the ghost shows up again. We don't know what kind of issue he had with Walt's parents, and no telling what he might say," Danielle explained.

"I agree," Walt said. "But I can't imagine what connection he has with my parents, or why he's so angry with my father."

"That ghost probably died up in those mountains," Heather said.

"That's what I figure," Walt agreed. "But what does that have to do with my parents? Who is he?"

"We won't find out sitting around here." Danielle then looked at Heather and asked, "You want to come with us?"

WALT AND HEATHER sat alone in the parlor while waiting for Danielle to return with some sandwiches. Max, who had followed them back to Marlow House, now curled up under the parlor desk, napping. Walt reclined on the sofa, while Heather claimed one of the empty chairs facing him. She had just gotten off the phone after calling Chris, suggesting he come over to Marlow House, when Walt asked, "So how is Brian doing today?"

Setting her cellphone on the side table, she glanced up at Walt and shrugged. "Okay, I guess."

Walt smiled. "We had quite the adventure."

"I'm in no hurry to go camping again," Heather said.

"But it is interesting how traumatic events can bring two people together. Sometimes two people who seem the most unlikely pair."

Heather looked at Walt for a few moments and then groaned. "Seriously, Walt? You know?"

"Max saw Brian's car in your driveway early this morning," Walt explained.

Heather glanced over to Max and frowned. "Nosey cat." She looked back to Walt and asked, "Do you think I'm crazy?"

"Do you really care what anyone thinks about your relationship with Brian?" he asked.

Unable to suppress a grin, she said, "Not really." Her grin quickly faded, and she added, "But his friends, like Joe, will think he's nuts and will let him know. It's one reason I'd rather keep this quiet for now. Not because of what anyone will think, but I'm really enjoying Brian—which honestly surprises the hell out of me—yet I'm not so naïve to think this will last, at least not once his friends find out."

Walt considered Heather's words a moment before saying, "If Brian lets his friends influence his feelings about you, then he doesn't deserve you."

"That's sweet of you to say."

"I also understand the desire to keep it to yourself for now." Leaning back in the sofa, Walt crossed one leg over an opposing knee.

"Like you and Danielle did when you eloped?"

"Exactly. We realized people wouldn't understand—especially those who believed I was Clint. It's not that we felt their opinions would change our feelings or keep us apart, but we just didn't want to deal with it. We simply wanted that time together with no inter-ference and outside drama."

"You understand," Heather said.

Walt nodded. "Danielle knows too. But we won't say anything to anyone. Not until you're ready."

Heather cocked her brow. "You seriously believe Danielle won't tell Lily?"

Walt smiled. "She won't. We had a long talk about it. The only reason I'm saying anything to you, I wanted to tell you we know, in case you needed someone to talk to. We'll respect your privacy, I promise."

WHEN DANIELLE JOINED Walt and Heather in the parlor with the sandwiches and iced tea, she had Chris with her. Instead of coming to the front door, Chris and his pit bull, Hunny, had entered by the side yard. Chris had come into the house through the kitchen door, while leaving Hunny in the yard to play. Chris had been just in time to help Danielle carry the food and beverages to the parlor.

After setting the food tray on the coffee table, Danielle distributed the sandwiches and drinks and then took a seat on the sofa next to Walt, while Chris sat on the empty chair next to Heather. While eating the sandwiches, they filled Chris in on the events of that day regarding the unexpected appearance of the mystery ghost.

"And you're sure this was the same ghost you saw in the mountains?" Chris asked.

"The ghost I saw on the beach today was the same one who shot at us in the mountains," Heather said. "Why did he follow us here?"

"Ghosts in this state rarely stick around long enough to explain why they're doing whatever they are doing," Chris said. "Instead, they keep popping in and out like a flickering lightbulb getting ready to die."

"But in their case, they're already dead," Danielle quipped.

"So when the ghost returns, we shouldn't expect him to sit down and explain why he shot at us, why he was in the mountains, and why he wants to see Walt's dad?" Heather snarked.

Chris shrugged. "Pretty much."

"If he shows up again, let's at least try getting his name," Walt said.

"Knowing when and where he died would help. But it doesn't sound as if he's aware of his death," Chris said.

"At least we're fairly certain where he died," Heather said. "Up in the mountains, considering that's where his spirit was hanging out when we first saw him."

"Was there anything about his apparition that showed cause of death? Like a knife sticking out of his back, a gaping head wound?" Chris asked.

Heather, Danielle, and Walt all shook their heads no.

"He had a rifle when we saw him in the mountains," Heather began. "But he didn't have it when I saw him today."

"He didn't have it when Evan and I saw him, either," Danielle said. "Considering how long he's been dead—I figure a long time if he knew Walt's parents—then it's possible the apparition he shows us may not represent his body when he died. He may have moved beyond that stage. He can summon up a rifle in the same way Walt used to summon up a cigar."

"I hate to say this, Walt, your dad might have had something to do with his death, considering his insistence on seeing your father," Chris said.

"Not necessarily," Danielle said. "He might think Walt's dad had something to do with his death, but it doesn't mean that's what really happened. Look at Stoddard, he haunted me because he thought I killed him."

Chris looked at Walt and smirked.

Danielle frowned at Chris. "What?"

"When I first met Walt, he told me Joe had arrested you for Stoddard's murder." Chris grinned.

"What are you talking about? Joe's the one who got the charges dropped," Danielle said.

"Oh, I know that now, but—" Chris began.

"I have no idea what he's talking about, or how it's relevant to our current situation," Walt said.

"I didn't say it had anything to do with this," Chris argued. "But when Danielle mentioned Stoddard, I remembered what you told me when I asked what the deal with Joe and Danielle was back then. You said they dated briefly, but then he arrested her for her cousin's murder, for Stoddard's murder and for some other murders. Or something like that."

Walt shrugged. "Well, maybe he didn't arrest her for Stoddard's."

Before Danielle commented, the ghost they had been waiting for appeared.

"Where is Anna?" the ghost demanded. "She needs to hear this."

They turned to the ghost, who stood in the open doorway leading to the hallway.

"What is your name?" Heather blurted.

The ghost looked from Walt to Heather. "Ask Alex." He looked back to Walt.

"Alex is never good at introducing us to people he knows." Danielle flashed the spirit a weak smile. "Please, can you tell us your name?"

The ghost glared at Danielle. "Why should I tell you anything? You lied to me. You said you didn't know who Alex was."

"Good one, Danielle," Heather muttered under her breath.

"Why don't you just tell us what you came to say," Walt suggested.

"I want Anna to hear this. Where is she?"

"Tell me the year, please," Danielle blurted.

The ghost looked at her and frowned. "What?"

"What year is it?" Danielle said.

"What kind of question is that?" the ghost asked.

"Please, if you tell me the month and year, I'll tell you where Anna is," Danielle promised.

"It's August 1904, of course. Now tell me, where is she?" the ghost demanded.

"Anna is at the Frederickport Cemetery," Danielle said.

The next moment the ghost vanished.

"There he goes, disappearing again," Heather said with a sigh.

"Well, at least we're fairly certain when he died, summer 1904." Chris looked at Walt and asked, "Does that date mean anything to you?"

Walt looked to Chris, his face expressionless. He nodded. "Yes, it does."

"What does it mean?" Heather asked.

"My parents died in August 1904."

FIVE

R ake in hand, Pearl stopped working for a moment to listen. It sounded like a whimper coming from the north side of her property. Leaning the rake against the house, she left it there and walked toward the fencing separating her yard from the Marlows'. Just as she passed the toolshed, she saw it, a nose sticking through the fence into her yard. She smiled.

"Is that you, Hunny?" she cooed. Hurrying toward the pit bull, she craned her neck to peer into the Marlows' backyard. There didn't seem to be anyone outside with Hunny. When she reached the dog, she fell to her knees, reached through the fence, and took hold of Hunny's head, pulling it to her face and accepting the wet kisses.

"How is my baby?" After a moment of loving up Hunny through the fence, Pearl stood up. "Does Hunny want a cookie?" The dog gave a bark and then sat down, tail wagging, while patiently waiting for the promised treat.

"I'll be right back." Pearl hurried to her house.

"YOUR PARENTS' death had to be somehow connected to the mountain man," Heather insisted.

Chris arched his brows at her. "Mountain man?"

Heather shrugged. "He wouldn't give us his name, and we have to call him something."

"Connected to my parents how?" Walt asked. "My parents died in Frederickport, and like you said, he probably died up in the mountains, considering that's where we first saw him."

"Unless he saw you first in Frederickport, followed you up to the mountains, and then followed you back down again?" Chris said.

They considered Chris's suggestion for a moment, and finally Heather shook her head. "No. I don't think so."

"Why not?" Danielle asked.

"Because I saw him before Walt and Brian. We were walking down a path; I was going first. Brian and Walt were trailing behind me, talking. I sort of barged in on Mountain Man. Totally caught him by surprise. I could tell he didn't expect to see me. He was definitely not a ghost who had been following us. He was holding a rifle, pointed it at me, and I begged him not to shoot. I didn't realize he was a ghost. He asked me what we were doing there, and he accused me of snooping. Oh, and he threatened to shoot me like he had the rest."

"The rest?" Danielle asked.

"Yeah, like he had shot at others up there before me. Also, he asked if I was a woman, which I found insulting. Yet now knowing he was from the early 1900s, I realize my clothes confused him."

"That really doesn't sound like someone who had been following you," Chris said.

"No, it doesn't" Danielle agreed.

"Try to remember what you can about your parents' death or at least that time period," Chris urged.

Walt took a deep breath, exhaled, and then closed his eyes for a moment, considering Chris's question. When he opened his eyes a few moments later, he said, "Actually, there are some things I remember about that time."

Danielle reached out and gently took Walt's left hand in hers. "Go on," she urged.

"I'm not sure if these are memories, or what my grandparents told me and came to feel like memories," Walt said.

"You told me your grandparents rarely discussed your parents," Danielle said.

"They didn't. Not unless I asked them something, and then they would answer and change the subject. I stopped asking, assuming it was a painful topic for them. But when I was about thirteen, I started asking questions about their deaths again. There were things I remembered, but wasn't sure if they were memories, dreams or my imagination," Walt explained.

Danielle gave his hand a reassuring squeeze as she and the others listened.

"I don't have many vivid memories of my parents. But I have one of my mother. It's of me climbing up on her lap, and she'd sing to me. That's one I see clearly. With my father, it's like a series of random snapshots. I remember he had two close friends, Bud and Teddy. I used to call them Uncle Bud and Uncle Teddy. According to my grandmother, they all grew up together. I can close my eyes and see my father with them, like playing horseshoes at the beach or me going with my dad fishing off the pier, and Bud and Teddy were there."

"What happened to them?" Danielle asked.

"Bud moved from Frederickport a couple of months before my parents died. But Teddy, it was his house that burned down. His wife also died in the house fire."

"That's horrible," Heather gasped. "What happened?"

"Maddie, that was Teddy's wife, she was a good friend of my mother's. Actually, they had all grown up together. Maddie got sick about a year before the fire and was confined to her bed. My mother spent a lot of time over at their house, helping Teddy care for her when he was out of town for business. My grandmother resented the time my mother spent over there, feeling Teddy could have made other arrangements."

"What happened that day?" Chris asked.

"My mother was at their house alone with Maddie when my father showed up. The heater exploded not long after he arrived, it started a fire, and none of them got out alive. From what I understand, they were trying to carry Maddie out, but the walls collapsed, trapping them. Teddy had been in Astoria that week on business and didn't get back to Frederickport until after the fire."

"How horrific," Heather muttered.

"What happened to Teddy?" Danielle asked.

"I'm not really sure. I heard he moved down to Astoria, that's where his business was," Walt said.

"He lived in Frederickport and worked all the way in Astoria?"

Chris asked. "Wow, a long commute for those days. I don't imagine many people were driving around in cars."

"My grandfather once told me Teddy had an office in Astoria and another in Frederickport. He would spend part of the month in Astoria, and the rest of the time in Frederickport. My mother would often stay with Maddie when he was in Astoria. After the fire, Teddy closed the Frederickport office and moved to Astoria."

"That seems like a lot to ask of your mother," Chris said.

"There is one thing I remember about the funeral. I asked my grandparents about it once, but they just changed the subject."

"What was that?" Danielle asked.

"At the funeral, my grandmother got upset when Teddy showed up. My grandfather asked him to leave. Which he did. I didn't understand why my grandfather had asked Uncle Teddy to leave and why Grandmother was mad at him. I also asked why Uncle Bud wasn't there. They had been like family, and I felt abandoned. During that time, it seemed as if those closest to me simply vanished —my parents—then Uncle Bud and Uncle Teddy."

"She probably blamed him for their deaths. After all, if he had been home with his wife, your parents wouldn't have been there that day," Danielle suggested.

"When I was older, that's the conclusion I came to," Walt said.

"Is there anything else you remember about that time period?" Chris asked.

Walt let out a weary sigh. "I remember missing my mother before she died, because she had been spending so much time with Maddie. My last memory of her is of me throwing a horrible fit, not wanting her to leave. And then she died… and when I understood she was not coming back… I felt such guilt. I had behaved so ugly."

"Walt," Danielle whispered, "you never told me that."

Walt shrugged. "I suppose it was easier to push the memory aside."

"You were just a little boy," Heather said. "Kids throw fits all the time."

"I suppose. But looking back, for a while I believed one reason she wasn't coming home was because I was a bad boy," Walt said.

"Oh, Walt." Danielle leaned over and gave him a quick hug.

"But none of this helps explain our mountain man," Chris said.

"Sorry," Walt said. "That's about all that I remember about that time."

"What did your father do for a living?" Chris asked.

"He worked for his father," Walt said.

"Did he ever go up in the mountains?" Chris asked.

"The mountains? He would go fishing and camping up there," Walt said. "Why?"

"I'm trying to work out the connection between Mountain Man and your father. If the mountain man died up in the mountains, and he believes your father had something to do with his death, we should figure out when and why your father went up there," Chris said.

"You are assuming Mountain Man blames Walt's dad for his death," Danielle said.

"I know what you are going to say," Chris began. "Just because the mountain man thinks that doesn't mean Walt's father had anything to do with it. Like Stoddard, he could be wrong."

"No, I don't mean that," Danielle said. "It's possible Mountain Man is angry with Walt's father for another reason, something that has nothing to do with intentionally causing his death. Maybe Walt's dad planned to meet Mountain Man up in the mountains to go fishing. And he never showed because he died in the house fire, and Mountain Man got stranded up there and died."

Chris arched his brow at Danielle. "Wow, you really have a knack of coming up with plausible scenarios."

"Only one problem with that one," Walt said.

"Only one?" Chris snickered.

"What?" Heather and Danielle chorused.

"Mountain Man wasn't carrying a fishing pole up in the mountains; he had a rifle. And my father didn't hunt," Walt said.

"My point being, his issue with your dad could be anything," Danielle said.

Heather glanced at the time and stood up. "I would love to stick around and help brainstorm, but Bella has been in the house alone a long time, and I really need to check on her."

"Doesn't she have a litter box?" Chris asked.

"Yes, but that doesn't prevent her from climbing the curtains in retaliation when I'm gone too long," Heather said.

"When you leave, make sure you shut the gate all the way. Hunny's in the side yard," Chris told her.

"I wonder why Hunny hasn't come in the house yet," Danielle muttered, thinking of the pet door.

WHEN HEATHER STEPPED out the kitchen door into the side yard a few minutes later, Hunny didn't greet her. Instead of calling the dog, Heather glanced around, wondering what mischief the pit bull had gotten into. She spied Hunny's wiggly butt at the fence separating Pearl's yard from Walt and Danielle's.

Careful not to make a sound, she made her way toward Hunny to have a closer look. Hunny, so focused on the attention being given her, failed to hear Heather's approach. When Heather reached the fence, she stifled a laugh. There was her grouchy neighbor on her knees, alternating between letting the dog kiss her nose and hand-feeding the dog treats.

"Well, what do we have here?" Heather snarked, sending a startled Pearl to her feet while Hunny turned and greeted her with a wiggling butt. "Imagine my surprise to find you kissing a ferocious pit bull."

Pearl returned Heather's snarky glare and replied, "And imagine my surprise at finding you kissing Officer Brian Henderson earlier today."

Heather's eyes widened in surprise. Speechless, she stared at the older woman.

"I suppose we all have our secrets," Pearl huffed indignantly. She tossed the remaining dog treat to Hunny and then turned, flouncing back to her house without another word.

"Damn," Heather grumbled as she turned toward the gate leading to the alley, Hunny trailing along her side. She glanced down at Hunny and said, "Now I can't very well tell Chris what I saw you and Pearl doing, can I?"

SIX

After pulling into Ian's driveway, Kelly Bartley parked and turned off the ignition, but she didn't immediately get out of her car. Instead, she rested her hands on the steering wheel and studied the diamond on her left ring finger. Wiggling her fingers slightly, she watched as the diamond glittered from the afternoon sunshine streaming in the car windows.

It wasn't that she hated the ring; she found it endearing that Joe had proposed with his grandmother's engagement ring. He had told her she could change the setting if she wanted, but she could tell by his expression he didn't want her to take him up on the offer. Plus, his beloved grandmother—now a widow—was very much alive. She doubted the woman would appreciate the grandson's fiancée remaking the ring given to her by her dead husband.

Unfortunately, it was not her style. Yet strangely, the damn thing fit perfectly. According to Joe, he had not had the ring sized. Apparently, Joe's grandmother and she shared the same ring size.

She had always imagined that when Joe finally proposed, they would pick out the ring together. Letting out a sigh, she looked from the ring to her brother's front door. If honest with herself, Kelly understood that on Joe's salary, he really couldn't afford to be buying engagement rings. Lily didn't have that problem when Ian had proposed to her, considering his annual income. Heck, Lily had her own fortune after her settlement with the Gusarov estate.

With another sigh, Kelly looked back to the ring. She and Joe had been together for over three years now. In the beginning she worried Joe still had feelings for Danielle, but then she moved in with him, and things seemed to get better. But every once in a while, she had that nagging feeling Danielle could have snatched him away from her if she had been so inclined. Recently, she began wondering if Joe was ever going to propose, and even her mother had made cracks about what she called her daughter's "uncertain future with Joe Morelli."

But now that she was officially engaged, she vowed not to let an ugly engagement ring spoil her moment. Kelly cringed when the word "ugly" popped into her head. She had been avoiding that word. She looked down at the ring.

"It's a nice diamond," Kelly muttered.

MARIE SAT in the rocking chair, watching Evan and Connor play on the nursery floor. She smiled at the patience Evan displayed with young Connor as the pair arranged blocks and pushed around toy trucks and cars. Marie had arrived minutes earlier and intended to have Evan tell Lily and Ian she was here, but that could wait. She rather enjoyed watching the boys play and didn't want to interrupt them.

In the living room, Ian and Lily were just about to turn on the television when Sadie jumped up from her place by the sofa and raced to the front door, her tail wagging. Ian got up from the sofa to see who was at the door, and a few minutes later he returned to the living room with his sister, Kelly, by his side.

"Hi, Kelly," Lily greeted her.

"My sister says she has some big news," Ian announced.

Lily looked curiously at Kelly, who stood next to her brother with her hands behind her back while she danced from leg to leg, reminding Lily of one of her students who needed to use the bathroom.

Ian stared at his sister, waiting for her to say something. She flashed him a grin and then abruptly shoved her left hand in his face and said, "Joe and I got engaged!"

"Congratulations," Lily said as she stood up, waiting for her turn to check out the ring.

"When's the big day?" Ian asked, giving the ring a cursory look before Lily took his sister's left hand.

"We haven't set the date yet," Kelly said, snatching back her hand from Lily, allowing her only a quick look.

"When did he ask you?" Lily asked.

"Last night. We had dinner at Pearl Cove; he asked me there. I wanted to tell you in person, and I had so much to do today, so I figured I'd stop by before I have to pick Joe up at work. I didn't want my big brother to hear about my engagement from someone else." Kelly leaned up and kissed her brother's cheek.

"Did you tell your parents yet?" Lily asked.

"Yes, I called Mom this morning. I told her not to say anything to you or Ian yet, that I wanted to tell you myself in person." Kelly grinned.

"Well, congratulations. You guys planning a big wedding?" Lily asked.

"We haven't gotten that far yet. Everything happened so fast," Kelly said.

"Fast? You guys have been together almost four years," Ian grumbled.

Kelly playfully smacked her brother's arm. "Oh, stop. You sound like Mom."

"Let me get a look at the ring again. I barely saw it," Lily said, snatching her sister-in-law's left hand.

Lily stared at the ring for a moment, and before she could comment, Kelly blurted, "It was Joe's grandmother's. It's a family heirloom."

"That's really sweet," Lily said. "So sentimental."

Kelly took back her hand, rubbing her right palm over the ring, and muttered, "Yes, yes, it is."

"Are you having an engagement party?" Lily asked.

"Engagement party? I'm not sure. But I really need to pick up Joe from work. Is Connor awake? I'd love to pop in and see him."

"Yes. He's in his bedroom playing with Evan," Lily said.

"Evan? I heard he was over at Walt and Danielle's?"

"He came over to play with Connor," Ian said.

WHEN KELLY REACHED Connor's open bedroom door, she looked in and smiled at the two boys so engrossed with the trucks and blocks spread along the floor that they didn't notice her standing in the doorway. Before she called out to Connor, motion from behind him caught her eye. The empty rocking chair rocked back and forth in a steady rhythm. Dumbfounded, Kelly stared at the chair as it continued to rock. She didn't notice when Evan looked up a few minutes later and spied her standing in the doorway. But when he called out, "Hi, Kelly," the chair abruptly stopped rocking.

"OH DEAR," Marie muttered after Kelly made a hasty departure after saying hello to Evan and her nephew.

"What's wrong?" Evan asked Marie.

"Nothing, dear. But I think I'll be going now. You boys have fun." Marie vanished.

IAN AND LILY stood on their front porch and waved to Kelly as she pulled out of the driveway.

"What do you think happened in Connor's room?" Ian asked. "She sure left in a hurry. Seemed rather frazzled."

"I can't imagine why. We should ask Evan if something happened." Lily stepped back into the house.

Ian followed Lily inside. "Perhaps she's just in a hurry to pick up Joe. And excited over the engagement. To be honest, considering how long they've been together, I was beginning to wonder if Joe ever intended to ask her to get married."

"Ian, don't hate me for saying this, but that is the most gawd-awful engagement ring I have ever seen."

Ian chuckled. "It wasn't just me?"

Lily turned to Ian and smiled. "You noticed too?"

"Well, yeah. Hard not to. Rather ornate. Not Kelly's style at all."

"She said it belonged to Joe's grandmother. It has a nice diamond, but the setting…" Lily cringed.

WHEN KELLY ENTERED the Frederickport Police Department fifteen minutes later, she found Brian Henderson standing in the front office, talking to Joe.

"I understand congratulations are in order." Brian gave Kelly a quick hug.

"Thanks," Kelly muttered.

"Gee, you don't seem too thrilled about your recent engagement," Brian teased.

"Is something wrong, Kelly?" Joe asked.

"I just stopped by Ian and Lily's to tell them about the engagement," Kelly began.

"Are you saying your brother isn't happy we're getting married?" Joe asked.

"Of course not. It's just that it happened again," Kelly said.

"What happened?" Joe asked.

"The weird stuff that's always happening at their house," Kelly said.

"Like what?" Brian asked.

"You're going to think I'm crazy," Kelly said, lowering her voice at the end of the sentence and glancing around to see if anyone else was around.

"What happened?" Joe asked.

"I walked in Connor's room to see him. Evan was there. The two boys were playing on the floor. And you know the rocking chair in Connor's room?"

"Yes, what about it?" Joe asked.

"It was rocking," Kelly said in a whisper.

"It is a rocking chair. That's what they do," Joe reminded her.

"No one was in it. And it was rocking," Kelly said.

"Isn't that the rocking chair that used to belong to Marie?" Brian asked.

Kelly looked to Brian with a frown.

"Marie Nichols," Brian explained. "Adam's grandmother."

"Yes, I know who you mean. What about it?"

"Maybe Marie's haunting the chair." Brian grinned.

"Not funny, Brian," Joe said.

"He might be right," Kelly muttered. "That would make as much sense as anything."

"I'm sure one of the boys probably sent the chair rocking before you got to the room," Brian suggested.

"You think?" Kelly asked.

"Sure," Brian lied. *I bet it was Marie,* he thought.

Kelly laughed nervously and then said, "I guess I was being silly. But there always seems to be something going on over at that house. Weird stuff that makes little sense. But I'm sure you're right, Evan was probably making the chair rock before I got there."

"Yeah, I'm sure that's it," Brian said.

Kelly smiled at Brian. "I'm surprised to see you working today. I thought the chief told you to take some time off."

"I wanted to get back to work," Brian said.

"Are you working tonight?" Kelly asked.

Brian glanced briefly at his watch and then looked back to Kelly. "I get off in thirty minutes."

"Do you have any big plans tonight?" Kelly asked.

"Just me and my remote," Brian said with a chuckle.

"Oh good! Then you don't have any plans," Kelly began.

"Kelly," Joe said in a warning tone.

"Oh, come on, Joe, Brian doesn't want to stay home alone tonight," Kelly said.

"Actually, I do," Brian said.

"No, you don't. I have this friend who would be perfect for you," Kelly began. "And I've told her about you, and she's dying to meet you. I talked to her earlier today, and she's not doing anything tonight."

"Are you talking about setting me up on a blind date?" Brian asked.

"Think of it more as a double date with me and Joe. She's one of the new docents at the museum. I interviewed her for my podcast."

"Thanks, but no thanks," Brian said. "I'm not really interested."

"But, Brian…"

"Kelly, he's not interested," Joe said.

Kelly let out a sigh. "Come on, Brian, if not tonight, at least consider another night. She really is nice and perfect for you. She's just a couple of years younger than you are."

Brian grinned and patted Kelly's arm. "Thanks for the thought, but I'm not really interested in dating anyone right now."

"WHY DIDN'T you try talking Brian into going out with us tonight," Kelly asked Joe as the two got into Kelly's car.

"He said he wasn't interested." Joe slammed the car door shut and hooked his seatbelt.

"It's sad the way Brian is all alone. He needs a nice woman in his life."

"Considering Brian's track record, he's probably better off this way." Joe snorted.

"Oh, please, that's why he needs someone like me to help him. Ginny would be perfect for him. She's only been married once. She's a widow, not divorced."

"She's a widow? Did she kill her husband?" Joe teased.

"Why would you ask that?" Kelly shoved the key in the ignition.

"The last woman Brian dated killed her husband," he reminded her.

Kelly rolled her eyes and turned on the engine. "Was Beverly Klein the last woman Brian dated? If that's true, we really need to get him out there again. Ginny would be perfect for him, and no, she did not murder her husband."

"Not that you know, anyway." Joe snickered.

SEVEN

"You think he's coming back today?" Chris asked.

"I wish he would, and if he does, I'd like him to stay around long enough to explain his accusations against my father," Walt said.

"It's always a little nerve-racking when they decide to pop in and out, and you don't know why. Ultimately, the goal is to help them move on," Danielle said.

"He can move on after he tells me what I want to know," Walt said.

"He probably headed to the cemetery," Chris said. "After all, that's where Danielle told him your mother was."

"It was kind of the truth. But now that I think about it, I probably should have said something else, especially if we want him to come back," Danielle said.

"Why do you say that?" Walt asked.

"If he goes to the cemetery and starts reading the headstones, he's going to figure out it's no longer 1904," Danielle said.

"And he might decide to move on?" Walt asked.

"Not necessarily," Chris said. "He'll still be confused, and he obviously assumes you're your father."

"I should go to him," Walt suggested.

"To the cemetery?" Danielle asked.

"Yes, if that's where he is. I see no reason to draw this out. If he's looking for my mother, he might be ready to talk to me as opposed to making demands and then disappearing," Walt said.

"He has a point," Chris said. "And like you suggested, reading those headstones will help anchor him in the here and now, which might make him more amendable."

"And I should go alone." Walt stood up.

"Why?" Danielle asked.

"Because he might be less distracted if it's just me," Walt said. "And less likely to disappear before he tells me what I want to know."

AFTER WALT LEFT for the cemetery, Danielle called Lily and told her she could send Evan back over to Marlow House if she wanted. Danielle didn't think the ghost would be returning. Since Connor was ready for a nap, Lily agreed it was probably a good time for Evan to go back to Walt and Danielle's.

"Did he show up?" Evan asked Lily as he prepared to go to Marlow House.

"Yes, only briefly. But they want to talk to him some more, so Walt left for the cemetery," Lily explained.

"Why did he go to the cemetery?" Evan asked.

"I guess after he left Marlow House, he headed down there. Isn't that where ghosts often go?" Lily asked.

"Oh gee, so I probably won't see him again," Evan grumbled.

"You want to see him again?" Lily asked with a grin.

Evan shrugged. "Kinda. Ghosts don't really scare me anymore. Eva said they can't really hurt me. The universe wouldn't let them."

Lily's grin broadened. "Well, that's good to know. I'm going to watch you cross the street, okay?"

"Sheesh, Lily, I'm not a baby anymore," Evan reminded her.

Lily laughed. "Yeah, I know. But humor me."

EVAN STOOD on the sidewalk across the street and waved goodbye to Lily. A moment later he entered the front gate to Marlow House. When he looked back across the street, he saw Lily had gone into her house. He continued to the front door, and just as he was about to ring the doorbell, the mountain man's apparition appeared.

"Are you one of Walt's friends?" the ghost asked.

Evan's eyes widened as he took in the sight.

"I saw you here earlier. You were with that police officer."

"That's my dad," Evan said.

The ghost looked Evan up and down and then asked, "Aren't you a little old to be playing with Walt?"

Evan giggled.

"What's so funny?" the ghost asked.

"I thought you were at the cemetery."

"Why did you think that?" the ghost asked, his voice less friendly.

Evan shrugged. "Lily said Walt went down there to talk to you."

"Why would Walt want to talk to me? I don't want to get him involved in this. It's not his fault. He's just a little boy."

Evan studied the ghost for a moment, remembering how the ghost was supposedly someone who knew Walt's parents.

"Do you know how old Walt is?" Evan asked.

The ghost shrugged. "Five, maybe six. You don't know? I thought you were one of his friends."

"Walt's a friend of mine," Evan said proudly.

"My business is with Walt's dad. Have you seen him?"

"Why do you want to talk to him?" Evan asked.

"I don't really think it's something you need to get involved with. But why did you say Walt went to the cemetery to see me?"

Evan didn't answer immediately. Finally, he said, "I think I meant Walt's dad, not Walt."

The ghost frowned. "That woman in the house said Walt's mom was at the cemetery. Do you know why they would be down there?"

"I don't know. But I bet if you go there, you'll find what you're looking for."

The ghost did not respond. Instead, he stared at Evan and then disappeared.

Startled by the spirit's abrupt departure, Evan glanced around. Pleased with himself for how he had handled the ghost on his own, he grinned and rang the doorbell.

WALT STOOD at the foot of his grave, reading the inscription on his headstone. How many men could look down at the grave holding the remains of their body? *Only a spirit of a man*, he told himself. Yet here he, a living, breathing man, looked down at his own grave. He glanced briefly at the horseshoe scar along his wrist, thinking how Clint's body hadn't had that scar. It had been a scar on his original body—the body buried in the grave he stood before.

Shaking his head at the thought, he looked over to Angela's gravesite and wondered what happened to her after finally moving to the other side. He glanced around, seeing no living people or any spirits in sight. He had already walked through the cemetery once, and if the mountain man had come here, perhaps he had since moved on.

With a sigh, Walt left his graveside and walked to the Marlow crypt. Standing before it a moment later, he reached out and gently brushed his fingertips over the inscription. He remembered when his parents had been laid to rest here.

When his grandmother had passed away, her viewing had been in the library at Marlow House prior to the funeral. There had not been a similar viewing for his parents. Theirs had been closed caskets. At the time he hadn't understood, and he wanted his grandfather to open the caskets so he could say goodbye. After all, he had been with his friend George Hemming at George's aunt's viewing to say goodbye. Yet the real reason Walt wanted his grandfather to open the caskets, he refused to believe his parents were really inside.

For several years Walt held onto that misguided notion, fueled by guilt that the tantrum he had thrown the last time he saw his mother was the reason for his parents leaving him. Yet as he grew older, he came to understand the true reason for the closed caskets —the fire.

"Alex, you're here," a voice said from behind him.

Walt turned around abruptly and came face-to-face with the mountain man. Like the first time Walt had seen him, he held a rifle.

"Are you planning to shoot me?" Walt asked calmly.

"I should," he retorted. "Where is Anna?"

"We need to talk," Walt said calmly. "Please, no matter what I say, don't leave."

"Now you want to talk?" he snapped.

"I'm not Alex," Walt began.

The ghost raised his rifle and pointed it at Walt. "I am tired of your games."

"You want to know where Anna is? She's here. With Alex." Walt turned around and touched the face of the crypt. He then stepped aside so the ghost could see the inscription. "Go ahead, read it. You can read, can't you?"

"Of course I can!" the ghost snapped and then moved closer to the crypt and began reading just the names. His hand holding the rifle fell to his side, but he continued to clutch the weapon. Frowning in confusion, he looked from the names engraved in stone to Walt. "What is this?"

"My name is Walt Marlow. Alex and Anna were my parents. They have been dead a very long time."

"You can't be Walt. Walt is a little boy."

"That little boy grew up," Walt said.

The spirit shook his head. "No. That is impossible. You're Alex. You're just trying to confuse me."

"Then look around at the other graves. When asked what year it is, you said it was 1904. Pay attention to the dates, especially in the newer section of the cemetery. But please, after you look around, don't leave. I need to know why you are looking for my parents. Why you are so angry with my parents."

The ghost scowled at Walt. "I'm not angry with Anna. But she deserves to know the truth."

"What truth?" Walt asked.

Instead of answering the question, the ghost moved to a nearby headstone. He read it and then moved to another and then another. Walt followed him. But when the ghost stopped in front of Walt's grave, he froze. Looking from the headstone to Walt, he said, "I don't understand."

"I didn't consider that," Walt muttered under his breath.

"What's going on?" the ghost demanded.

"I think you know part of it," Walt said.

The ghost shook his head in confusion.

"I know… shoot me," Walt suggested.

"What?"

"Go ahead, shoot me. But after you do, don't leave," Walt said.

Taking Walt up on his offer, the frustrated spirit raised his rifle and pulled the trigger. Bullets flew from the rifle and moved through Walt and then disappeared.

Still staring at Walt, he lowered the rifle and said, "You're a ghost? They're all dead. That's what you are trying to tell me."

"Drop the rifle," Walt said in a calm voice. "And watch it. See what happens."

The ghost let go of the rifle and looked down. It fell to the ground and disappeared.

"Tarnation, I'm dead too," the ghost muttered.

"Be honest with yourself. Part of you always knew, didn't you?" Walt asked. "You're not really that surprised, are you?"

The ghost looked up to Walt. "Are you really Walt Marlow?"

"Yes. Now tell me, why are you so angry with my father?"

"You were such a bright boy. Your father was so proud of you," the ghost said. "It's why I never understood how he could do something like that. Not the way he loved you. And the way I thought he loved Anna."

"What did my father do?" Walt asked.

The ghost stared at Walt for a moment and then laughed.

Startled by the laughter, Walt frowned. "What is so funny?"

"You asked what your father did? Apparently more than I realized. He succeeded. All this time I thought he'd failed, but he didn't, did he?"

"What are you talking about?" Walt asked.

"Your father. He killed me. See, here's the proof!" The ghost gave a slight bow before disappearing.

"No!" Walt cried out. "Come back!"

EIGHT

"S ounds like Evan had an eventful day," the chief said. He had
arrived at Marlow House fifteen minutes earlier to pick up his
son, only to find the boy had fallen asleep in the living room while
watching television. They let Evan sleep while they sat in the parlor.
Danielle had just finished recapping their day for the chief.

"Times like this I really regret that fire downtown," Danielle
said, referring to a fire that had taken place almost eighty years
earlier and had burned down the offices of the local newspaper,
along with its back issues.

"Why do you say that?" the chief asked.

"There's a good chance the ghost has moved on. And if we can't
figure out who he is, I don't think we'll ever know why he believes
Walt's dad is responsible for his death."

"My father isn't responsible," Walt insisted.

"But if we could go through old newspapers during that period,
we might figure out who he is. Or what was going on in 1904. I
suppose we could check out back issues of other Oregon newspapers, but I feel we'd have better luck looking at back copies of the
local paper. And the museum's collection of newspapers prior to
1940 is limited," Danielle said.

"I guess you didn't hear about Ginny Thomas's recent donation
to the museum," the chief said.

"Who?" Danielle frowned.

"Ginny Thomas. I imagine Walt knew her ancestors." The chief paused a moment and flashed Walt a grin.

"Thomas?" Walt frowned.

"Actually, Thomas was Ginny's husband's name. Neither of them ever lived in Frederickport, but her cousin lived in a house she inherited from their grandparents. And Ginny recently inherited it from her cousin. She's a widow, and she moved into the house not long ago," the chief explained.

"What about a donation to the museum?" Danielle asked.

"When going through the attic of the house she inherited, she found stacks and stacks of back issues of the *Frederickport Press*, going back to the very first edition."

"Wow, seriously?" Danielle asked.

"She wanted to clean out the attic, and when she realized how old they were, she donated them to the museum. I guess you don't listen to Kelly's podcast."

"What does Kelly's podcast have to do with her?" Danielle asked.

"She interviewed Ginny. It was an interesting podcast. You should listen to it," the chief suggested.

"Are the newspapers at the museum already?" Walt asked.

"I would assume so. According to the interview, this donation means the museum will finally have a complete collection of all past issues of the *Frederickport Press*," the chief explained.

"I imagine they'll get them bound first," Danielle said. "Like all the other ones they have."

"Oh yes, they said something about that," the chief said.

Danielle looked at Walt. "The museum is open in the afternoon tomorrow; you want to stop by? It's possible the newspapers are there."

HE HADN'T LIED to Kelly. Brian intended to stay home tonight and watch television after picking up some take-out food from Beach Taco. But now, as he sat in his car in front of the restaurant, about to place his order, the idea of eating alone did not sound appealing. Instead of opening his car door, he picked up his cell-phone and placed a call.

"Brian?" came the now familiar voice on the other side of the call.

Leaning back in the car seat with the cellphone to his ear and a new smile on his face, Brian asked, "What are you doing?"

"Gee, I expected you to ask what I'm wearing."

Brian laughed. "Have you had dinner yet?"

"No, I haven't even thought about it. I've been on the computer for the last hour doing some online sleuthing."

"What's up?" Brian asked.

"Remember that ghost who shot at us in the mountains?" Heather asked.

"I remember you telling me about him shooting at us. I couldn't actually see him."

"He's here."

"What do you mean he's here?" Brian asked.

"Seriously? You can't understand a simple two-word sentence: he's here."

"He's in your house?" Brian asked.

"Really, Brian? No, he's here in Frederickport. I ran into him while jogging."

"That *is* your thing," he snarked.

"A ghost is not the same thing as a dead body. But yeah, I see what you mean."

"Why is he here?" Brian asked. "Is that a normal thing for a ghost? Is he following you?"

"It's sort of a long story."

"Do you want tacos?" Brian asked.

"Tacos?"

"I'm parked in front of Beach Taco, about to get something to eat," Brian began.

"And you just decided to call me?"

"I thought maybe you'd want some tacos."

"Were you just planning to drop them off and leave?" she asked.

Brian laughed. "Not exactly."

"Tacos sound kind of good. I'll tell you about the ghost while we eat."

KELLY AND JOE intended to eat at home on Saturday night, since they had gone out to eat at Pearl Cove the night before. But when

Lily called Kelly to tell her they had found her checkbook in the hallway—it had obviously fallen out of her purse when she had been at their house that afternoon—Joe offered to drive Kelly over to pick it up, and since they were going out anyway, they might as well get some takeout.

Kelly thought tacos sounded good, and since they both wanted to beat the Saturday night rush at Beach Taco, they picked up their food before stopping by Lily and Ian's. They drove up to the restaurant just as Brian pulled out of the parking lot.

"I guess Brian had the same idea as us," Joe said.

"I wonder where he's going," Kelly asked, craning her neck to see Brian as Joe pulled into the parking lot. While they had spotted Brian, it didn't look as if he had seen them.

Joe shrugged. "I would assume home."

"But he's going the wrong way," Kelly muttered.

Twenty minutes later, as they drove up Beach Drive on their way to Lily and Ian's, Kelly shouted, "Stop!"

Startled by Kelly's outburst, Joe slammed on the brakes. Now parked in the middle of the street, he glared at Kelly. "Why did you do that?"

"You missed it," Kelly said, staring across the street at Heather's house.

Joe looked across the street. "Missed what?"

"Brian, he's at Heather's. I saw him in the window just before someone closed the blinds."

"I seriously doubt that. Why do you suddenly have Brian on the brain?" Joe asked as he stepped on the gas and headed toward Lily and Ian's driveway.

"No, don't pull in the driveway," Kelly said. "Go down the street."

"What for?" Joe asked, stopping in front of Ian and Lily's house without pulling in the driveway.

"I just want to see if I'm right. Brian's car is not in front of Heather's house, and if he is over there, I bet he parked in the alley behind her house."

"And if you're wrong?" Joe asked.

"If I'm wrong?" Kelly frowned.

"We should make this more interesting. If you want me to drive all around the block, what do I get if you're wrong?" Joe teased.

"I don't know. What do you want?"

Joe considered the question a moment and then flashed Kelly a mischievous grin. "If you are wrong, tomorrow night you make homemade lasagna, my mother's recipe."

Kelly arched her brow and stared at Joe. She had made the recipe before, and while delicious, it was a pain. Before taking the bet, she asked, "And if I'm right?"

"What do you want?"

"If I'm right, we give these tacos to my brother, and you take me to Pearl Cove again."

"Deal." Joe grinned and stepped on the gas.

HEATHER'S LAPTOP COMPUTER, pushed to one side of the kitchen table, made room for the sacks of to-go food from Beach Taco. Brian and Heather sat at the table, each with a plate of food before them, while Heather's calico cat, Bella, corralled a fly in one corner of the kitchen. It had entered the house with Brian.

Ignoring her cat swatting at the fly, Heather filled Brian in on the mountain man ghost while the pair ate tacos, chips and salsa, and each sipped on a cold beer.

"So what's the connection with the ghost and Walt's parents?" Brian asked.

"We don't know. But I talked to Danielle on the phone right before you got here. After Danielle told the ghost Anna was at the cemetery and he disappeared, Walt went down to the cemetery to talk to him, assuming that's where he had gone."

"A cemetery seems like an obvious place for dead people to hang out." Brian snorted.

Heather continued with the story, telling Brian what had occurred at the cemetery.

"So what now? Does this mean the ghost moved on?"

Heather shrugged. "Very possible. But Walt still doesn't know about the connection between this ghost and his parents. And Mountain Man claims Walt's dad killed him. That's what I've been researching on the computer."

"I don't imagine you can Google *who did Walt's dad murder, and why?*"

Heather, about to take a bite of a taco, paused and narrowed her eyes at Brian. "Do I have to hurt you?"

Brian grinned at the threat and wiggled his brows. "You tease."

Heather's frown turned into a smile. "Who are you?"

He picked up a tortilla chip and flipped it in her direction.

She caught the chip and laughed. After eating it, she said, her tone again serious, "I'm just trying to figure out why he would be in the mountains. By the way he was dressed, it looked like he had been there for a while, considering the work boots, denims and flannel shirt, and hat. My first thought, he was a real mountain man. Up there trapping for animal skins, that sort of thing."

"When I think of Oregon mountain men, the pictures I've seen, they make their clothing from animal fur and leather, not denims and flannel. Plus, you believe your ghost died in 1904, that's about two decades after Oregon mountain men faded away."

"Yeah, that's what I found. But then I thought, he could have been up there looking for gold. He accused me of snooping, it was like he was trying to hide something. And I imagine prospectors were protective about their gold mines, especially if they hadn't staked a legal claim yet. It's entirely possible he died up there on that mountain before he could stake his."

"From what I remember about Oregon history, its gold rush ended around the same time as the Civil War began. And when it had its second rush, that took place in Eastern Oregon. In fact, I'm fairly certain there weren't any notable gold mines where we were."

"That doesn't mean there isn't a gold mine up there that no one knows about—except for the ghost," Heather reminded him.

"I suppose," Brian conceded.

"I'd like to find the identity of the ghost. Who was he?"

"I assume he didn't give Walt his name?"

Heather shook her head. "No. And when we saw him over at Marlow House earlier and asked, he just said, '*Ask Alex.*'"

"I wonder if Walt's father really did murder this guy," Brian said.

"I hope not. I know what it feels like to learn you're descended from a murderer," Heather grumbled.

"You can't choose your family."

"Yeah, I get that. But it doesn't really help. For Walt's sake, I'd like to prove the ghost was wrong. But frankly, I'm not sure we can. Especially if the ghost has moved on. Heck, we don't even know who he was."

NINE

"I suppose it'll keep for another day, won't it?" Lily asked as she looked into the refrigerator at the two steaks sitting in the bowl of marinade.

"I was looking forward to having steak tonight," Ian grumbled as he pulled tacos from the to-go sack his sister had left with them. "But I don't think these are going to keep. We should probably eat them."

Lily shut the refrigerator door and turned to face Ian. "What's with your sister lately? First, she practically runs out of here earlier, like she saw a ghost."

"Maybe she did," Ian suggested as he unwrapped a taco.

"Evan said nothing happened in there," Lily reminded him.

Ian shrugged and took a bite.

"And then she randomly gives us tacos when she picks up her checkbook? What is that about?"

"Trying to be nice?" Ian took another bite. "Actually, this is pretty good."

"So why did she really buy us tacos? She said they're going to Pearl Cove for dinner. Was she afraid we were going to invite ourselves along, and she didn't want us coming with Connor, so she figured giving us tacos would keep us from asking?"

"It's possible they ordered tacos for dinner and then decided they would rather eat at Pearl Cove," Ian suggested before taking another bite.

"Ian, they ate at Pearl Cove last night. Remember? Who goes to Pearl Cove two nights in a row?"

"I don't know. Come on, let's eat together." Ian motioned to Connor, who sat in his highchair eating dinner. "Before our son decides he's done."

With a sigh, Lily walked to the breakfast bar and picked up the sack of food. She looked inside. "So what's in here?"

"Tacos, and it looks like some chips and salsa," Ian said.

Lily removed the chips from the sack and set them on the counter. She then pulled the container of salsa from the bag, removed its lid and set it next to the chips. Grabbing a taco, Lily took a seat at the breakfast bar with Ian.

"I wonder where her question about Brian came from," Ian said.

While unwrapping her taco, Lily said, "I'm not sure why she'd ask if we've seen Brian at Heather's, or why she would even care."

Ian shrugged. "Brian and Heather seemed chummy last night— more like friends. Which really isn't surprising considering what they experienced. Brian might have said something to Joe, who said something to my sister, which got that brain of hers spinning."

It does spin sometimes, Lily told herself, yet she didn't share the thought with her husband. Instead, she said, "I have to give Brian credit, he seems to be taking this all in stride."

———

JOE STARED at the prices on the menu and inwardly groaned. Last night he had paid with cash he had saved for the occasion. Tonight would go on his credit card. He looked over his menu at Kelly and found her staring at him.

"What?" he asked.

"We don't have to stay," Kelly said.

"Are you serious?"

She shrugged and set the menu she had been holding on the table. "I got carried away having to be right."

Joe chuckled. "No, I started it. But we could try something instead of the lobster tonight."

"I'll just have a bowl of clam chowder," Kelly suggested.

"That's not enough," he said.

"I'm not that hungry. And I love their clam chowder and bread. Anyway, I know you like their steak. Order that, and you can give me a couple of bites."

"Are you sure?"

"Yes. Actually, clam chowder sounds pretty good to me."

Joe smiled and tossed his menu to the table. "Deal."

Five minutes later, after the server took their order, Kelly asked, "What do you think is going on with Heather and Brian?"

"I don't think anything is going on with them. I just think they're friends now. Which I suppose is understandable, considering their harrowing experience. Although, if it were me and I got lost in the mountains a couple of days with Heather Donovan, I can't imagine myself wanting to keep hanging out with her."

"Agreed. But he would like Ginny. I wish you would talk him into going on a double date with us," Kelly said. "Don't you think it's sad he's all alone?"

"He wasn't all alone tonight," Joe reminded her.

Kelly rolled her eyes. "You know what I mean. Her family moved to this area around the same time as the Marlows. I think it's great she donated all those newspapers to the museum. Finally, they have a complete collection."

"I suspect she just wanted to get rid of them. I wouldn't want to fill up my attic with old newspapers."

"She could have just had them recycled, and that would have been such a loss," Kelly said.

"I wonder if Marie knew her family."

"I assume so. According to Ginny, her family was close to the Marlows, and Marie's father was Walt Marlow's close friend. So I imagine they all knew each other. I never asked Ginny if she knows Adam," Kelly said.

"What did her family do back then? Did they work for the Marlow shipping line?" Joe asked.

"No. When her family moved here, they opened a livery stable," she explained.

"Livery stable?" Joe grinned.

"And one of her great-uncles was close to Walt's father. The original Walt, obviously. Not Danielle's Walt." Kelly giggled and then added, "I guess they grew up together."

"Great-uncle?"

Kelly shrugged. "Well, great-great-not sure how many greats. But one of her ancestors grew up with Frederick Marlow's son. But not a direct ancestor. It was the brother of one of her direct ancestors. The one who owned the livery stable. Actually, he was the brother-in-law of the guy who started the livery stable. Or it was the brother-in-law of the son of the guy who started the livery stable? Or grandson? Not the friend, the other one."

"You totally lost me," Joe said with a laugh.

BRIAN SAT with Heather on her back porch, drinking a beer. Instead of beer, Heather had switched to wine.

"Thanks for the tacos. They were good," Heather said.

"You're welcome." Brian leaned back in the patio chair and took a swig of beer.

"I was thinking about our mystery ghost and how he probably got stranded up in the mountains somehow and died. And how that could have been our fate too." Heather shivered at the thought.

"If Walt's father really was responsible for his death, then him being stranded up there probably didn't get him killed."

"Maybe. But he didn't have any visible wounds. He looks more like someone who got stuck up there and died, considering his beard."

"Visible wounds? Ghosts have wounds?" Brian asked.

"Sometimes. A disoriented spirit often takes on the same appearance he had right before dying. Which is why you might see a ghost with a meat cleaver imbedded in his bloody head if that's how someone killed him."

"Lovely imagery," he said dryly.

"I thought you would appreciate it."

"Have you seen a ghost like that?" he asked.

Heather shrugged. "No. But it's possible. Although I did see one with a piece of broken glass sticking out of his back. Scared the crap out of me."

Brian cringed. "I can imagine. Maybe our ghost got bit by a snake and died. Since he didn't have Walt to save him. A snake bite you probably wouldn't see."

"We were lucky to have Walt with us. Made fishing easier."

"Amen to that," Brian agreed and took another swig of beer.

"You know what I read when researching Oregon mountain men?" Heather asked.

"What?"

"During the gold rush, the prospectors often carried sourdough starter with them so they could make their own bread. According to some articles, they would sleep with the starter to keep it warm and alive."

"I'm sorry, what is sourdough starter?" Brian asked.

Heather frowned at Brian. "Don't you like sourdough bread?"

"Sure. But what does that have to do with sourdough starter?"

"It's what you need to make sourdough bread. Bread needs some sort of leavening agent, like yeast or baking powder, or sourdough starter. You can make sourdough starter by mixing flour and water, and somehow it collects the yeast from the air," Heather explained.

"Wouldn't they need some sort of oven to bake this bread?" he asked.

Heather shrugged. "I don't know what they baked it in. I didn't read that far. But I think I should try making some."

"Why?"

"To be more self-sufficient. And the next time we get stranded in the mountains, I can make homemade sourdough bread to eat with our fish," Heather said.

Brian cocked a brow at Heather. "So the next time some crazy witches kidnap us, you're going to make sure you have sourdough starter with you?"

"It only takes flour and water," Heather reminded him.

"Oh, so you're going to make sure you have a bag of flour with you?" he teased.

"A glass jar too."

Brian laughed.

TOGETHER WALT and Danielle sat on the front porch swing, a blanket draped over their laps to ward off the chill of the evening. Walt sipped brandy while Danielle enjoyed a glass of wine. Looking up to the moonless sky, Danielle said, "We're lucky it's not raining. According to the radio, it's raining in Astoria tonight."

"It feels like we may get some later." While holding his brandy with his right hand, Walt wrapped his left arm around Danielle and pulled her closer.

"You think he moved on?" Danielle asked.

"Very possible," Walt said. "You know, I've been thinking of those mountains since talking to our mystery ghost."

"In what way?"

"I remember my father used to go fishing with Teddy and Bud up in the mountains. They would ride horses up there and camp. I'm not saying it was the same place they took us. But it could have been. I remember wanting to go, but Mom said I was too young, and Dad would tell me he would take me with them when I got a little older. Of course, that time never came."

"I'm sorry," Danielle whispered.

Walt shrugged. "That was a very long time ago. Maybe I never made it up to the mountains with them, but I remember going fishing on the pier, and Teddy and Bud were there. It must have been that last year. I have this memory of us standing on the end of the pier and Dad fixing my fishing pole. Uncle Teddy and Uncle Bud were arguing."

"Arguing? About what?"

Walt considered the question for a moment and then shrugged. "I don't know. I just remember my father telling them to knock it off. And they stopped."

"What were your uncle Bud and uncle Teddy like?"

"First, they weren't my real uncles."

"Yes, I understand that."

"I remember Uncle Teddy would sneak me candy, and Mom would get annoyed. But aside from that, I don't recall anything specific, just that they were around a lot when I was little. I assumed they really were family. But after my parents died, and my grandfather asked Teddy to leave the funeral and Bud didn't even show up, I felt abandoned. Looking back, they were flashes from my early childhood memories, before my parents died."

A meow interrupted their conversation. Both Danielle and Walt looked down to see Max sauntering toward the swing.

"Max, what are you doing out this late?" Danielle asked as the cat jumped up on the swing with them.

Walt looked at Max and arched his brows. "Really?"

Max made himself at home on Danielle's lap and stared up into Walt's eyes.

"What is he saying?" Danielle asked.

"He was just over visiting Bella. Seems Heather had another visitor tonight."

"Really?" Danielle looked down at Max and stroked his back. "Gee, Max, you and Walt are becoming a pair of gossips."

TEN

In her last years of life, Marie Hemming Nichols grew reliant on her grandson, Adam, for transportation. She understood Adam had his own life and a business to run, so she had tried not to be a burden, and when possible, she found alternate forms of transportation, such as procuring rides with friends. Yet as the years moved on, more and more of her friends found themselves in the same situation as her, no longer driving. Or they had moved to the other side, where they no longer needed an automobile.

Almost three years had gone by since Marie had moved from the living world to the spirit realm. She had delayed her ultimate move to the other side and instead remained to observe and occasionally interact with the living—as a ghost. When Walt had been a ghost, he'd found offense at that word. Marie rather liked it. "I'm a ghost," she would sometimes tell herself before breaking into a giggle.

One perk about being a ghost, she did not need to rely on others for transportation. When in a hurry, she could simply focus on her destination and within moments be transported to the spot. When not in a hurry, she could take her time and enjoy the journey, sending her spirit sailing along the rooftops, a ghostly version of the Flying Nun.

She especially enjoyed this experience during the early evening, when people gathered in their homes, warm lights brightening their windows. Not being in a hurry Saturday evening, this was how she traveled to Marlow House, leisurely drinking in the sights and sounds of Frederickport.

Just as she flew over the rooftop of Pearl Huckabee's house, she spied a curious sight. Pausing mid-flight, Marie looked down and watched as Pearl—Marie assumed it was Pearl—crouched along the bushes lining her fence on the south side of her property, the fence separating Pearl's yard from Heather's.

Curious to see what the woman was up to, Marie floated down to the ground, the illusion of her blue and green floral sundress's hem fluttering gently. Just as she was about to land next to Pearl, Marie reached up and straightened her straw garden hat. A moment later, her shoes settled on the ground next to Pearl. In reality, the shoes, along with the feet inside the shoes, were nothing but an illusion. An illusion Pearl could not see.

"What are you doing?" Marie asked the woman.

Pearl wiggled closer to the fence, bending at the waist, her backside protruding while her nose pushed its way through two flowering bushes, their buds closed for the evening.

Curious to see what had Pearl's attention, Marie stuck her head through one bush. She looked to the lit area of Heather's back patio and spied Heather and Brian sitting on Adirondack chairs, each with a beverage in hand, chatting. Considering the lack of lighting along the fence, Marie doubted Heather would see her if she glanced over. But because of the patio light, both she and Pearl could see them.

Pulling herself out of the bush, Marie looked over at Pearl, who continued to crouch by the fencing, spying on her neighbor.

"You really should not be such a snoop!" Marie said, impulsively giving Pearl's backside a reprimanding swat.

Pearl let out a yelp and stood up abruptly, her face no longer smashed between two bushes. Both of her hands grabbed hold of her injured backside. She looked around warily and then scurried toward her house.

Next door, Brian and Heather heard Pearl's yelp, and both glanced toward the bushes while Heather asked, "What was that?"

MARIE WATCHED as Pearl quickly retreated inside her house, slamming the back door closed behind her, followed by the sound of the deadbolt snapping into place.

"That lock will not keep me out." Marie snickered. A wave of guilt washed over her. Marie looked upward and said, "Okay, I guess I shouldn't have done that. Sorry."

With a sigh, Marie floated back up, off the ground, again by the rooftops. She continued to her destination, gliding over the fence separating Pearl's yard from the Marlows'. She spied Walt and Danielle on the front swing and continued toward them. A moment later she floated down from above, landing in front of the swing.

"Your neighbor Pearl is a busybody," Marie announced once her shoes made touchdown.

"Evening, Marie," Danielle greeted her.

"Were you flying by and just dropped in to say hi?" Walt teased.

"It's one of the many advantages of being a ghost," Marie beamed.

Walt shrugged. "I wouldn't know. When I was a—spirit—I didn't get out much."

"What about Pearl?" Danielle asked.

"I caught her spying on Heather and Brian. Those two seem to have gotten rather chummy since their little adventure in the mountains. Brian's over at Heather's right now. The two are sitting on her back porch, visiting. Unlikely pair, if you ask me. But he seemed smitten with her when they were up on the mountains. Of course, he's too old for Heather."

Danielle looked to Walt and said, "I don't think Heather's secret is going to stay one for long."

"What secret?" Marie asked.

Walt and Danielle exchanged glances, and Danielle said, "Obviously, they've become good friends since their misadventure in the mountains."

Marie arched her brow. "How good of friends?"

"You'll have to ask Heather," Danielle said.

"You haven't seen a strange ghost hanging around, have you?" Walt asked.

Marie frowned. "Strange ghost?"

Danielle shivered. "Can we take this conversation in the house? It's getting cold out here."

Twenty minutes later, Walt sat in the parlor with Marie, telling her about the mountain man ghost, and what the ghost had told him in the cemetery, while Danielle was in the kitchen, throwing together a quick dinner. Walt had just finished the telling when Danielle walked into the parlor, carrying a tray with two roast beef sandwiches, some potato chips, chocolate chip cookies, and two glasses of iced water.

Marie, who had been sitting on the sofa next to Walt, moved to a chair facing the sofa, allowing Danielle to take her place after setting the tray on the coffee table in front of Walt.

"You have no idea who he is?" Marie now faced Walt and Danielle.

"None," Walt said, picking up one sandwich.

"And you think he might still be around?" Marie asked.

"It wouldn't surprise me if he has moved on now that he understands he's dead," Walt said. "But if he hasn't moved on, I really would like to talk to him again. Who is he, and why does he think my father is a murderer?"

"On a positive note, a ghost does not necessarily know who killed them. I certainly didn't know who killed me. Walt, you didn't even realize Roger had murdered you, and Stoddard believed Danielle had killed him. So his claim may have no substance. But when I see Eva, I'll see if she knows anything. She always seems to know more than the rest of us," Marie said.

"Tomorrow we're going to the museum," Danielle said. "According to one of Kelly's podcasts, someone donated what appears to be a complete collection of the *Frederickport Press*. All the way back to the first edition. We want to look through the 1904 ones and see what happened back then that might give us a clue to what the ghost is talking about. Or tell us who he is."

"Interesting. I wonder who donated the papers," Marie said.

"Kelly interviewed the woman on her podcast," Danielle explained. "I didn't hear it, but the chief did, and he told me about it. The woman recently moved to Frederickport after inheriting a house from her cousin. Her family are longtime residents of Frederickport, dating back to when Walt's grandfather first settled here. She found newspapers stacked in the attic of the house she inherited, and she wanted to clean it out. After realizing how old they were, she checked with the museum, and of course they said they wanted them. I never heard about it until the chief told me. I missed the last Historical Society meeting, and the last time I spoke to Millie, she never mentioned it."

"You say her cousin died and left her the house?" Marie asked.

"That's what the chief told me," Danielle said.

"I wonder if that's Emily Pavlovich," Marie said.

"Who's that?" Danielle asked.

"She died a while back; I attended her funeral," Marie said. "We had a pleasant chat before she moved on. I have to say she was surprised to see me." Marie chuckled.

"Why do you think it's her?" Walt asked.

"Emily's family has been in Frederickport for as long as mine," Marie explained. "We never really socialized; she was much younger than me. But I'd known her for years, which is why I felt obligated to make a showing at her funeral. Her cousin was there, a nice-looking young woman, a little younger than Joanne. Widow, according to Emily. She told me that's who the house was going to, and she was rather excited the cousin decided to settle in Frederickport. Emily hated the idea of the house being sold to strangers."

"I take it Emily didn't have any children to leave her house to?" Danielle said.

"No. Sadly, her only daughter died when she was still in high school. Quite tragic. She got into drugs, overdosed. Although, some suspected it was suicide," Marie explained. "And her husband died about ten years ago."

"That's so sad," Danielle muttered.

"And from what I recall, Emily and her mother were hoarders. It wouldn't surprise me to find stacks of newspapers in her attic. I'm sure that's not the only thing her poor cousin will have to haul off," Marie said.

"Do you know what their name was? Pavlovich certainly doesn't sound familiar," Walt said.

"No, it wouldn't. That was her husband's last name, and he moved to the area from somewhere back east," Marie explained. "I doubt you would recognize her maiden name, because as I recall, she inherited the house from her mother's side of the family. I don't know her mother's maiden name, but I remember my father saying her family started the livery stable in Frederickport."

Walt perked up. "Really?"

"You remember who that was?" Danielle asked.

"Certainly. When I was younger, I enjoyed going down there to see the horses," Walt said.

"Where was the livery stable in Frederickport?" Danielle asked.

"You know where you normally get your gas?" Walt asked.

"Yes."

"It was along there. The Uncle Bud I mentioned, his family owned it," Walt said.

"So this Emily is related to your uncle Bud?" Danielle asked.

"Distantly. As I recall, his sister married the man who owned the livery," Walt said.

"I'll be curious to see if you find anything of interest in those old newspapers," Marie said. "In the meantime, I'll track down Eva, see if she's heard anything about your mystery ghost." The next moment Marie vanished.

ELEVEN

The morning sun peeked over the treetops, casting an eerie shadow over the cemetery. He had returned to the mountains after talking to Walt Marlow the day before, and there he had found it—his grave. If honest with himself, he always knew. But he didn't want to acknowledge the painful fact, so he had lied to himself. Yet the burden of what he had known weighed heavily on his soul, making him unable to move on, unable to accept the rest of it. After seeing Walt Marlow, he understood it was time to step out of his confusion and face his eternity.

Standing alone in the Frederickport Cemetery, he thought this was where he should be, not up alone in the mountains in a shallow grave, far from his family. He stared at the headstone and read the inscription. He hadn't noticed it on yesterday's visit, but he found it not long after arriving this morning. Destiny had brought him to the spot. Yesterday he had not been ready to see it, nor would he have understood. Yet now he did.

"This is where I should be," he told himself. The next moment he vanished.

POLICE CHIEF MACDONALD had Sunday off, but both Joe and Brian were on the schedule. When Joe showed up for work, he found Brian sitting in the lunchroom, having a cup of coffee.

"Morning," Brian greeted him when Joe entered the room.

Joe glanced at his watch and said, "You're here early. Did I read the schedule wrong?"

"No. I didn't feel like making coffee at home, so I came in early."

"Is it feeling a little lonely at your place now?" Joe asked.

Brian frowned. "What do you mean?"

"Your cousin, didn't she go home Friday morning?"

"Oh… yeah." Brian sipped his coffee.

Joe walked over to the coffeepot and grabbed his mug from the overhead cabinet. As he poured himself a cup of coffee, he asked, "So what did you do last night?"

"Nothing."

Joe glanced over at Brian, a filled coffee mug in hand, and said, "Kelly and I had dinner out last night."

"Yeah, I figured that," Brian said.

"Oh, so you saw us at Beach Taco?" Joe asked.

"Beach Taco? No, were you there? I was talking about Kelly wanting me to join you last night for dinner with that friend of hers."

"Oh…" Joe sat down at the table with Brian.

"So you guys went to Beach Taco too? I picked some food up for dinner. Is Kelly mad at me for not going out with you last night?"

"No. Of course not. I understand not wanting to find yourself on a blind date with someone you may not even be interested in," Joe said. "I told Kelly it's better to introduce two people on neutral territory, with no prior commitment, and then let them decide if they want to take it farther."

"Like speed dating?" Brian laughed.

"Have you tried speed dating?" Joe asked.

Brian laughed again. "No. And I'm not into internet dating either. But the fact is, my little time in the mountains helped me see things differently."

"What do you mean? What things?" Joe asked.

"How we see people, how we want them to be—or judge them by preconceived notions. Take Walt, for example, you've never really liked him. But I suspect your feelings for Danielle had something to do with that."

"I have no feelings for Danielle," Joe insisted. "At least not those feelings."

"I'm talking about the feelings you had for her back then. And I misjudged him, so it wasn't just you."

"You like Walt?" Joe asked.

"Yes, surprisingly, I do. He's been through things you could never imagine. But I also learned something about myself."

"What was that?" Joe asked.

"The women I've gotten involved with over the years. The type of women I found attractive. They were women who went out of their way to please me. They wanted me to find them attractive."

Joe laughed. "And that is a bad thing?"

"I didn't think so. But they weren't doing it because they really cared about me. They were doing it to get something from me," Brian said.

"You're talking about manipulation?" Joe asked.

Brian let out a sigh. "Yeah, I guess I am. Looking back, I was pretty good at finding the manipulative ones."

"WELL, WHAT DID HE SAY?" Kelly asked. She sat at her desk in her home office, talking on the phone to Joe.

"He isn't interested in going on a date with a stranger. And I totally get that," Joe said.

"But they really would be perfect for each other," Kelly insisted.

Joe recounted Brian's observation regarding his past poor choices.

"Then I know she would be just what he's looking for," Kelly said.

"I don't think he's currently looking. That's sort of the point."

"Come on, Joe. You know what I mean."

"Like I suggested last night, it would be better if he met her without being obligated to spend a few hours with her, and then leave it up to him if he wants to ask her out," Joe said. "And who knows, maybe Ginny wouldn't be interested in him once she meets him."

"Does that mean you'll bring him by the museum today?" Kelly asked.

"Okay. But I'm doing this because it's the only way you'll stop bugging me. You know, Kelly, you can be damn persistent," Joe said.

"But it is one of my endearing qualities," she cooed.

"Not sure about that. But okay, when we go to lunch today, I'll tell him I need to stop at the museum. But after he meets her, then you need to back off. Agreed?"

"I promise, Joe."

WHEN DANIELLE and Walt entered the museum on Sunday afternoon, Kelly and a woman neither of them recognized greeted them.

"Hi, Kelly, surprised to see you here. Doing some research?" Danielle asked.

"Hi, Danielle, Walt," Kelly returned, the woman at her side silently observing the new arrivals. "I just stopped by to talk with Ginny. Have you guys met?" She glanced at the woman at her side.

"You aren't Ginny Thomas, are you?" Danielle asked. "The one who donated the newspapers?"

"You listened to my podcast!" Kelly beamed.

"Yes, I am." Ginny smiled. "Kelly said Walt and Danielle? Would that be Walt and Danielle Marlow?"

"Yes, and it's nice to meet you. In fact, we were hoping the newspapers might be here," Danielle said.

"I'm afraid not," Ginny said. "The museum sent them out to the bindery. I don't think they'll be back for a couple of weeks."

"I mentioned that in the podcast," Kelly said.

Danielle looked at Kelly and smiled. "I confess, I haven't listened to your podcast—but I intend to. The chief told me about it —and about the donation to the museum."

Ginny looked at Walt and said, "Apparently, our families were friends."

"The chief mentioned Thomas is your married name. What was your family's name who lived in Frederickport?" While Walt remembered the family who owned the livery stable, he wondered which branch of the family Ginny came from.

Kelly chuckled. "I doubt you'll recognize it." She looked at Ginny and said, "Walt is actually a very distant cousin of the

Marlows, who were friends with your family. He's been in Frederick-port for just a couple of years."

"I'm not sure how distant," Ginny noted, "considering he looks like the spitting image of the Walt Marlow who knew my ancestors. That is, of course, if the portrait the museum has is an accurate depiction."

"It is," Danielle said. "I credit the uncanny resemblance to the fact they are both descended from double cousins of twins."

"What do you mean?" Ginny asked.

"It's when a pair of identical twins marry another set of iden-tical twins, and their children are biological siblings," Danielle explained.

"Interesting." Ginny looked from Danielle to Walt and said, "I find it terribly romantic Walt Marlow's portrait is here with Eva Thorndike, although I imagine it gets a little crowded since his wife is in there too."

"Romantic?" Danielle frowned.

Ginny turned to Danielle. "Yes, considering how madly in love he was with the woman."

"I think they were just good friends," Danielle said. "They knew each other since they were children."

Ginny reached out and briefly touched Danielle's wrist and said, "I seriously doubt that. The man named his yacht after the woman. No, he was passionately in love with Eva, everyone knew that, which might have been the downfall of his marriage, if his wife really did plot with her brother to murder him, which you seem to think, by some online articles I've read. Yet now, I like to imagine they are finally together."

Walt reached out and discreetly took one of Danielle's hands in his, giving it a reassuring squeeze.

"So why are you guys here?" Kelly interrupted.

"We heard about the newspapers and were curious to see them," Danielle said.

"And I'm still curious. What was your family's name who settled in Frederickport?" Walt asked Ginny.

"My maternal grandmother was Franny Becker Sawyer. Her paternal grandfather, Wesley Becker, started the livery stable in Frederickport. The house I inherited from my cousin belonged to our Sawyer grandparents."

"Really?" Walt said. "Yes, the Beckers."

"You sound like you remember them," Kelly teased.

Walt smiled at Kelly. "You forget, I've done my own research on the area."

Ginny reached out and touched Walt's arm. "I loved your book, by the way. I heard you have a second one coming out?"

"My brother helped him get his agent," Kelly told Ginny.

"Yes, I'm very grateful for all Ian's help," Walt said.

The next moment the front door of the museum opened, and in walked Joe and Brian.

"Hey, guys," Danielle greeted them.

Kelly rushed to Joe's side, kissed his cheek, and then took his arm, turning to face Ginny. "I want you to meet my fiancé, Joe Morelli. Joe, this is my friend I have been telling you about, Ginny Thomas. And Ginny, this is Brian Henderson, he's one of Joe's friends, and they work together."

Ginny stepped forward and shook Joe's hand and then Brian's. To Brian she said, "Kelly told me about your harrowing adventure."

"It was some adventure." Brian chuckled, looking warily from Ginny to Kelly.

"Of course, I heard what they said over the news, but I would love to hear more about it," Ginny said.

"Walt here was on the adventure too. You think you might put it in one of your future books, Walt?" Brian teased.

Walt started to say something, but Kelly immediately cut him off. She began rambling about Brian and Ginny, noting all the things she thought they had in common. Brian abruptly interrupted her and said, "I hope you will excuse me for a minute, but I've been trying to get ahold of Walt since yesterday, and now that he's here, I really need to talk to him about something." Brian reached out and took hold of Walt's arm, ushering him outside.

"Why do I think you made that all up?" Walt said when the two men got outside.

"What makes you say that?" Brian asked in faux innocence.

Walt chuckled.

"I had to get out of there," Brian grumbled. "Kelly is trying to play matchmaker, and damn Joe is an accomplice. I expect more from him."

"Yes, but Joe doesn't know about you and Heather, does he?" Walt asked.

Brian looked at Walt a moment and then said, "Heather told me, you know. I can't believe your cat has been spying on us."

Walt laughed. "Since Max only talks to ghosts and me, don't worry about him spreading it around. I told Heather that Danielle and I promise not to say anything. It's your business to keep it to yourself or share."

"Thanks. I appreciate that. Heather also mentioned the trigger-happy ghost is in Frederickport and knew your father."

"Apparently. That's why Danielle and I stopped by the museum today. The woman Kelly is trying to hook you up with recently donated back issues of the *Frederickport Press* to the museum, going back to the first issue. We were hoping to find some clues in the old papers to help us figure out who the ghost is, or what my father might have been involved in back then."

"The ghost won't just tell you who he is?" Brian asked.

Walt shrugged. "He hasn't so far. And it's possible he's moved on now that he's finally realized he's dead."

Brian laughed.

Walt frowned. "What's so funny?"

"I was trying to imagine myself having this conversation with Joe."

TWELVE

B rian and Walt were still standing out front of the museum, talking, when a couple walked up to them and asked if the museum was open. After Brian told them it was, they thanked him and then entered the building. A few minutes later Joe stepped outside.

"You ready to leave?" Brian asked Joe.

Joe glanced back to the museum and then looked at Brian. "I guess. Are you finished talking to Walt?"

"Yeah, I think we're done." Brian flashed Walt a smile, said goodbye, and then started toward the car.

"Later, Walt," Joe muttered, reluctantly trailing behind Brian.

When they reached the vehicle, Brian said, "I need to trust the people I work with."

Joe frowned. "What is that supposed to mean?"

"I'll humor your girlfriend when she tries to play matchmaker, but I expect more from you," Brian said as he unlocked the car.

"I just—" Joe started.

"Save it. Just please, give me the heads-up next time, would you? I'm too old for this nonsense."

"Kelly only wants to help," Joe said as he got into the car.

"Who said I needed help in my personal life?"

INSIDE THE MUSEUM, Danielle stood alone in the front lobby with Kelly while Ginny took the couple who had entered minutes before on a tour of the exhibits. Kelly walked to the front door and opened it a few inches, peeking outside. A moment later, she closed the door and returned to Danielle.

"Terrific, Joe and Brian are leaving," Kelly grumbled.

"I assume they have to go back to work," Danielle said.

"What I wanted was to introduce Brian to Ginny. They would be perfect together."

"Well, you did introduce them," Danielle reminded her.

Kelly rolled her eyes. "They barely talked before Walt dragged Brian outside."

"Um, it was Brian who asked Walt to go outside," Danielle reminded her.

"Whatever…" Kelly shrugged. "No offense, but I wish you guys had come to the museum on another day."

Before Danielle could respond, Walt walked back into the museum.

"Did Brian say anything about Ginny?" Kelly asked Walt.

"Aside from the fact he wasn't in the mood for matchmaking?" Walt asked.

Kelly groaned. "So he knew?"

"He's not stupid," Walt said.

"I just wanted them to meet, she's so nice, and Brian's had such rotten luck with women. He's totally given up on dating."

"Why do you say that?" Danielle asked.

"Spending Saturday night with Heather? What does that tell you?" Kelly asked.

Danielle and Walt exchanged quick glances. "Excuse me?" Danielle said.

Kelly waved a hand dismissively. "I don't mean anything like that." She laughed at the idea and then said, "But Joe and I drove by Heather's yesterday on the way to my brother's, and I saw Brian in the front window."

"You're certain it was Brian?" Walt asked.

"Sure, we saw his car. Anyway, my point being, he's obviously given up on dating. After all, when I asked him to double date with us last night, he insisted he wasn't interested. Instead, he would rather hang out with Heather. I know it's because you all had that bonding moment up in the mountains, and he sees her as his new pal. But really, there's no future in that, and I can't imagine it thrills Heather, him hanging around," Kelly said.

"You accomplished what you set out to do," Walt said.

"What do you mean?" Kelly asked.

"You introduced Brian to your friend," he explained.

"Yeah, right. That's what your wife said," Kelly grumbled.

"They have met each other, and if Brian is interested, then it is up to him to make the next move. If you think about it, with match-making, all you can really do is introduce the couple. There is nothing you can do beyond that," Walt said.

"I suppose you're right. If it's meant to be, it will work out," Kelly said. She glanced at her watch. "Well, I need to get going. Tell Ginny I'll talk to her later."

After Kelly left the museum, Danielle asked Walt, "Do you really believe that? That Brian might be interested and consider pursuing Ginny?"

Walt shook his head. "Not at all."

"I'm just wondering, when did she see Brian's car parked at Heather's?" Danielle asked.

"Brian has been parking in the alley behind her house."

"Which means Kelly must have seen Brian in her window and then had Joe drive down the alley," Danielle suggested.

"Which means Joe saw Brian's car parked there too. I wonder what he thinks about it."

"I doubt Joe has a clue what's really going on," Danielle said.

"I agree."

Danielle glanced toward the exhibit area and said, "While you were outside, Ginny told me she donated some old photographs to the museum that you might be interested in. The exhibit isn't finished, but they have some photos up. Since we're already here, want to check them out?"

ENLARGEMENTS of vintage black-and-white photographs covered one side of a portable wall in the center walkway of the original exhibit section of the museum. According to the exhibit's small placard, Ginny Thomas had donated the photographs from her family's Frederickport collection.

Ginny stood on the far side of the museum with the couple who had entered while Walt had been outside with Brian. Walt and Danielle stood by the new exhibit, looking over the photographs.

"I don't believe it," Walt muttered, stepping closer to the largest photograph. Danielle moved closer; her attention focused on the people in the picture.

"That's your father," Danielle whispered when she recognized one man in the photograph. Had she not read the dates posted with the display, she might have assumed Walt was the man in the picture. But when taken, Walt had only been three years old, assuming they had the correct date.

"Yes. That was in front of the livery stable," Walt said. He pointed to the two men with his father. "The one on the right is Bud. The other one is Teddy."

Danielle pulled out her cellphone.

"What are you doing?" Walt asked.

"I'm taking a picture of it, of course. That photo of your dad is going in our album." She snapped several shots. Just as she was putting the phone back in her purse, Ginny walked up to them, while the couple she had been showing around remained at another exhibit on the other side of the room.

"I was going to suggest you check out that photograph," Ginny said. "I imagine you noticed the resemblance between one of the men in the picture and your husband."

"Yes. By the date, I assume the picture is of Alexander Marlow, Frederick's son, and Walt Marlow's father," Danielle said.

"It is." Ginny now stood next to Walt and Danielle, looking up at the photograph. "When I first saw Walt Marlow's portrait in the museum, it struck me how much he looked like his father in this picture. In fact, I double-checked the dates. At first, I wondered if they had been mislabeled, and it was Walt Marlow." Ginny paused a moment and smiled at Walt. "The other Walt Marlow."

Walt flashed her a grin.

"But since I knew that was Bud in the photograph, and considering he disappeared a few years later, then I knew he couldn't have had his photograph taken with an adult Walt Marlow. And I have to say, I still can't believe how much you look like them. That family resemblance is certainly strong with the Marlows," Ginny said.

"What do you mean, he disappeared?" Walt asked.

Ginny turned from the photograph to face Walt. "The man to the right of Alexander Marlow was Bud Benson, my great-grandmother's brother. According to the stories passed down in the family, he disappeared back in 1904. Just fell off the face of the earth."

"That was the year Alex and Anna Marlow died," Danielle noted.

"Yes. Ever since I moved back to Frederickport and started going through my cousin's things, I've been sucked into family history and the history of Frederickport. In fact, that's why I joined the Historical Society and volunteered to be a docent. I've visited Frederickport since I was a little girl. Recently, I read about how Alex Marlow and his wife, Anna, died in a house fire, along with the wife of one of Bud's other friends. He's also in that picture." Ginny turned back to the photograph and pointed to Teddy's picture.

"His name was Ted Newsome. Actually, I suppose he's sort of a shirttail relative. It was his house that burned down. So tragic, poor little Walt Marlow was just five when it happened. Left orphaned," Ginny said.

"What do you mean, a shirttail relative?" Walt asked.

"I learned all this when working on our family tree and going through these old photos. My great-great-grandfather founded the livery stable in Frederickport back in 1871," Ginny explained.

"A year after Frederick Marlow founded the town," Danielle noted. "And the same year he built Marlow House."

"Yes." Ginny nodded. "I'm still working on the Becker family line, but I'm fairly certain August Becker Senior and his wife, that's my great-great-grandfather's parents, had ten children. Only two of them settled in Frederickport. One was my ancestor who started the livery here, Wesley Senior, and another was his brother, August Becker Junior."

"August Becker?" Walt muttered.

"You've heard that name?" Ginny asked.

"It sounds familiar," Walt said.

"From what I've learned, he was, like, twenty years older than his brother, Wesley. When August was a young man, he was the first in his family to head west, landed in California during the gold rush. In fact, that's what brought him there. It's where he made his fortune, and eventually he left California and settled in Frederickport. He and his wife had no children. His wife's sister settled in Frederickport with her husband. He worked for the Marlow Shipping line, and they had one son. That's the other man in the photograph, Ted Newsome."

"I see what you mean by shirttail relative," Danielle muttered as she looked at the photograph.

"Oh, and something interesting about August Becker's wife," Ginny said. "From what I learned, she was into the temperance movement. In fact, she might have been involved in what's known as the Temperance War of 1874. But I'm still researching that."

"Temperance War?" Danielle frowned.

"Really more of a riot, in Portland, from what I understand," Ginny said.

"You also mentioned the other man in the photo disappeared," Walt said. "Do you know when?"

Ginny smiled at Walt. "I'm surprised you're so curious about him. I would think you'd be more interested in learning about Alex Marlow."

"It just sounded intriguing," Walt said.

"It's that writer in you. Always looking for a new story, I bet." Ginny said. She looked back at the photograph. "He went missing in 1904. According to family lore, he was an adventurer. A dreamer. He couldn't seem to settle down in a job. His sister tried to get him to work at the livery, but of course, that was not exciting enough— according to the stories told." Ginny nodded at the photograph. "Those three were close friends. Alex Marlow worked for his father, and Ted worked for the Marlow line too, like his father. That was until he married into money. And according to the stories, he quit and tried one failed business venture after another—even after his wife became ill and disabled."

When Ginny noticed the couple she had been helping look her way, she excused herself and left Walt and Danielle alone at the exhibit.

"Did you hear what she said?" Walt asked Danielle when Ginny was out of earshot. "Bud went missing in 1904."

"The same year your parents died."

THIRTEEN

S till standing next to Walt, looking at the photograph, Danielle
said, "I wonder what happened to Bud. Going missing sounds
so ominous."

"And the same year my parents died," Walt added.

"Although it doesn't mean it was ominous. It's possible he moved
and was lousy at keeping in touch with family."

"That's true; they didn't have your Facebook," Walt teased.

Danielle turned to Walt. "When Ginny mentioned that August
guy, the one whose wife was involved with the temperance movement, you sounded like you recognized him."

"I did. But I never knew he was Ted's uncle," Walt said.

"Did you know him well?" Danielle asked.

"No. But I knew who he was," Walt said. "And that he had
money, but I wasn't aware of where it came from. And I will
confess, I'm having a problem imagining it's true."

"Why?"

Walt shrugged. "I can't envision him as someone who left the
convenience of the city to prospect for gold. That was a rugged way
of life. But I suppose he was much younger then. When I knew him
—although I never actually knew him—he didn't seem like someone
who would be comfortable camping. Plus, his wife was not the only
one in the temperance movement; they both were. My grandfather
couldn't stand the man."

"Why? Because they supported the movement? I remember you weren't too keen on it yourself."

Walt chuckled. "True. Yet that wasn't the only reason my grand-father disliked the man. Zealous piety irritated Grandfather."

Danielle arched her brows. "Piety? And zealous at that?"

"Yes. August Becker considered himself quite the man of God. The rest of us were going straight to hell. As I recall, Becker even had issues with the minister of his church. Supposedly, he once called the man a heathen." Walt chuckled.

"How did he get along with his brother, the one who started the livery stable?" Danielle asked.

"Supposedly, he loaned his brother the money to start the business. I'm not sure if that's true, and frankly I find it hard to believe."

"Why is that?" Danielle asked.

"Growing up, I understood they had some sort of falling-out and had nothing to do with each other."

"Maybe it was over the business loan," Danielle suggested. "Loaning money can ruin relationships."

"Perhaps. One thing I recall, it seemed the man was always about to die any minute. Supposedly he was sickly; the doctor was constantly at his house."

"That's kind of sad," Danielle said.

"The old coot outlived me," Walt said with a snort. "He was well into his nineties when I—well, you know. I have no idea when he finally passed."

"Do you remember his wife, the temperance lady?" Danielle asked.

Walt shook his head. "No, she died years earlier. I was just a little boy. I've no memory of her ever being alive. He never remar-ried. Never had children."

They moved down the wall, now turning their attention to the other photographs in the display. Walt stopped at the third one and pointed to it. "That's August Becker's house."

Danielle leaned closer to the photograph of a two-story house with a horse and buggy out front. "Is that in Frederickport?"

"Yes."

"Where? I've never seen it before."

"It's not there anymore," Walt said. "It's where Beach Taco is now."

"Really?" Danielle looked from the photo to Walt. "They used to have residential houses along there?"

"No one knows that. How come you do?" a male voice asked them.

Walt and Danielle turned around to find a twenty-something man with dull gray eyes and scraggly dishwater blond hair standing behind him. He wore faded denims and a white T-shirt. Danielle thought he looked out of place at the museum.

"Excuse me?" Danielle asked.

The young man pointed to the picture they had just been looking at. "I heard what you said about that being where Beach Taco is now. No one knows that."

"But you did?" Danielle asked.

"Cory, are you done?" Ginny asked as she walked up to the three. The couple she had been talking to had left the museum.

"Yes, I was coming to tell you, but you were with those people," he told her.

"Thanks for all your help," Ginny said. She then turned to Walt and Danielle. "Do you know Cory Jones?"

"I know who they are," Cory said, looking at Walt and Danielle.

"I'm afraid we haven't met," Danielle said.

"Cory's my neighbor," Ginny explained. "He's been helping me bring some things that I've donated to the museum."

"They recognized August Becker's house and where it's at," Cory blurted. "I didn't think anyone remembered that house."

Ginny glanced at the photograph and frowned. "I don't understand. I haven't labeled that picture yet."

"I think Cory misunderstood," Danielle said quickly. She glanced at Cory and then back to Ginny. "That's what often happens when you overhear just part of a conversation. We naturally assumed that photo was taken in Frederickport, and since the house wasn't familiar, I wondered where it had been. Walt's done extensive research on the area and guessed it was where Beach Taco is now. Considering Cory's reaction, I assume Walt was correct?"

"Yes, he was." Ginny said.

"It didn't sound that way to me," Cory muttered under his breath.

"Did you say you were leaving now?" Ginny asked Cory.

"Yeah," he grumbled.

"Okay. Thanks again for all your help." Ginny flashed him a smile.

When he walked away, Ginny said, "I'm surprised you've never met Cory. He's a little different, but he loves to be helpful. He grew up in the house next door to mine."

"I was wondering, when did August Becker die?" Walt asked. "Do you know?"

"Right after the stock market crash of 1929. He lost everything. My grandmother used to say that's what killed him, but I suspect his death had something to do with the fact he was a few months shy of his hundredth birthday," Ginny said with a chuckle.

"When did they tear his house down?" Danielle asked, looking back at its picture.

"A few years later, I think. I still can't believe you actually guessed where that house had been located. I really don't see how you could look at that picture and come to that conclusion," Ginny said while examining the photograph.

"I remember that house," a voice called out at the same time glitter began falling from the ceiling. Oblivious to the voice and glitter, Ginny continued to chatter on, talking about the other photographs she intended to include in the exhibit.

Both Walt and Danielle glanced over Ginny's shoulder and spied Eva hovering in midair so she could see over Ginny and get a better view of the exhibit.

"Remember that house, Walt?" Eva asked. "Old Man Becker lived there. We used to dare each other to go knock on his door and then run like the devil before he answered it." Eva laughed gaily at the idea.

New visitors silenced Ginny, not Eva's laughter. She excused herself so she could see to them, leaving Walt and Danielle alone with Eva. When Ginny left them, Eva's apparition moved downward until her feet touched the floor.

"You used to do a knock and dash?" Danielle asked with a giggle.

"I believe it was Eva's idea," Walt said.

"True," Eva said with a sigh. "And I appreciate the fact you didn't blame me when Old Man Becker caught you running away that one time and told your grandfather on you." Eva looked at Danielle and said, "Your husband is a true gentleman."

Danielle chuckled. "Yes, he is."

Eva turned to Walt and said, "I met Old Man Becker right before he moved on. It was at the church service for his funeral."

"Was he surprised to see you?" Walt asked.

"He asked me why I hadn't gone to hell for my sinful life," Eva said with a snort. "He obviously had a low regard for motion pictures, not to mention the theater."

"That was rude," Danielle said.

Tilting her head ever so slightly, Eva absently tapped her right index fingertip along her chin before saying, "Actually, he seemed rather relieved."

"Relieved?" Danielle asked.

"Yes. Coming to the end of his road, so to speak, and worried about being held accountable for his own sins."

"I wonder what type of sins Becker worried about, sitting alone in that house all those years," Walt scoffed.

"I suspect it had something to do with inappropriate feelings for a young married woman. I believe it might have been his sister-in-law, from what he said back then," Eva explained.

"Would that be Ginny's great-great-grandmother?" Danielle asked.

Eva shrugged. "He didn't go into specifics."

"I seem to recall Ginny mentioning there were about ten siblings in his family, so depending on how many of them were brothers, there could be quite a few sisters-in-law to choose from," Walt noted.

"Maybe that's why he moved here," Danielle said in a wistful tone. "When he left to find his fortune, one of his brothers stole the love of his life, so he moved away from the rest of his family and settled in Oregon and eventually married his kindred spirit, fellow temperance devotee," Danielle said.

Walt cocked a brow at Danielle. "Nice to know I have someone to go to when I need help working out a plotline."

Danielle grinned at her husband. "Always happy to help."

"In Old Man Becker's case, I think it was more about an already married sister-in-law, from what he said. Of course, he didn't get into specifics. He was rambling mostly, trying to work it all out, wondering if he should move on or stick around. I think seeing me convinced him he could avoid punishment by remaining here. After all, he truly believed actors were doomed to hell," Eva explained.

"But he moved on?" Danielle asked.

"Yes, I believe so. Although I suppose he might have followed his body to the cemetery and stuck around for a while. As you know, back in those days I avoided Frederickport Cemetery because Angela was there. She was simply too annoying. But since I've been going back there, I've never seen him. So I have to assume he eventually moved on," Eva said. "But I don't suppose you wanted to see me to talk about Old Man Becker. What's this Marie told me about the ghost from the mountains following you down here?"

Walt and Danielle took turns filling Eva in on the recent events involving their mystery ghost. When they finished, Eva let out a sigh. "There are no rumblings on my end. But I will certainly keep an eye out."

FOURTEEN

D anielle was taking the lid off her slow cooker to check its simmering contents when a knock came at her kitchen door. She re-covered the cooker and glanced toward the knock. A moment later the door opened, and Heather stepped inside.

"I didn't hear you say come in, but I saw you standing there," Heather said as she closed the door behind her.

"Ahh, a peeping Tom!" Danielle teased.

Heather shrugged. "I figure it's payback for your cat snooping on me."

"Fair enough," Danielle said. "Want a glass of iced tea?"

"Sure." Heather watched as Danielle reached into one of the overhead cabinets and retrieved two tall glasses. "What's in the Crock-Pot? Smells good."

"Chicken. I'm making chicken tacos for dinner," Danielle explained as she set the glasses on the counter next to the refrigerator. She opened the freezer and began filling the glasses with ice.

"Sounds good. I came over to see if you've found out anything new about our mountain man, and I have a baking question." Heather took a seat at the kitchen table.

"Baking?" Danielle closed the freezer and opened the refrigerator. She removed the pitcher of tea and filled both glasses.

Heather continued to watch Danielle. "Have you ever made sourdough bread?"

"No. But Lily used to make it." Danielle carried the glasses over to the kitchen table. After setting them down, she removed the lid of the cake plate sitting on the center of the table, revealing a stack of moist brownies. She nodded to the plate. "I'm more of a dessert baker. Help yourself."

Heather snatched a brownie, and Danielle re-covered the platter.

"Although, I have toyed with the idea of giving sourdough bread a try. But I buy it from Old Salts, and they make great sourdough, so I haven't bothered," Danielle said.

"I want to try. I like the idea I can make bread without relying on store-bought yeast and baking powder." Heather took a bite of the brownie.

"You still have to buy flour," Danielle reminded her.

"Now you're sounding like Brian."

Danielle grinned in response.

"By the way, I talked to Brian before I came over here. He said he saw you and Walt at the museum."

"Yes. In our quest to uncover the identity of our mystery ghost, we were hoping to go through some newspapers that were recently donated. But they aren't there yet."

"He told me about the woman who donated those newspapers. And how Kelly is trying to set him up with her." Heather glanced down at her brownie and pulled off a piece.

"Ahh, he told you. Well, he didn't seem very interested. He made an excuse that he had to talk to Walt about something so he could wait outside for Joe," Danielle explained.

Heather nodded. "Yeah, Brian told me that too. So, tell me, you think this woman would be perfect for Brian?"

"Obviously Brian didn't think so."

"Yeah, I suppose. But I don't really get why he wants to hang out with me." Heather took another bite of her brownie.

"Can I ask you something?" Danielle asked.

Heather swallowed her bite of brownie and looked up to Danielle. "What?"

"Why do you want to hang out with Brian?"

Heather shrugged. "He's funny. When I first met him, I didn't think he was funny. I thought he was kinda a jerk. But he's got a silly side, and he's more open-minded than most people. I remember how Ian totally flipped over the entire ghost thing, but Brian, well, he takes it all in stride."

"Life is short. Spend time with people who make you happy. Don't overthink it."

Now finished with her brownie, Heather absently fiddled with her glass of tea. "Brian also told me Joe proposed to Kelly."

"Yeah, Lily mentioned it before I ran into them today. I congratulated Joe and Kelly when I saw them at the museum," Danielle said.

"Did you see Kelly's ring?" Heather asked.

"Um… yeah." Danielle took a sip of her tea.

When Danielle did not elaborate, Heather asked, "Well, what does it look like?"

Danielle shrugged. "It's a ring."

Narrowing her eyes, Heather studied Danielle for a moment. "Okay, spill it. What aren't you saying?"

Danielle looked at Heather and cringed. "It's the most gawd-awful ring I've ever seen."

Heather's eyes widened. "Really?"

"I guess it's a family heirloom. Lily told me about the ring when she told me about Kelly being engaged."

"And what did Lily think about the ring?" Heather asked.

Danielle shrugged and cringed again. "She thought the same thing—but you have to promise not to say anything."

"Considering Kelly is trying to hook Brian up with her friend, does finding pleasure in knowing she has an ugly engagement ring make me a bad person?" Heather smirked.

"Only if we tell Kelly what we think."

"Just imagine, that ring could have been yours," Heather teased.

"That was never happening."

Heather grinned at Danielle and then asked, "So, about Mountain Man, I guess you didn't find out anything at the museum?"

Danielle told Heather about Ginny and the new exhibit and that they had talked to Eva while there.

"I'll have to go down and check it out," Heather said.

"Walt and I are going over to Ginny's tomorrow. She has more photos at her house, and she told Walt and me we could go through them. It was kind of cool to see that photo of Walt's father."

"YOU WANT me to teach you about sourdough bread?" Lily repeated Heather's request. The two sat in Lily's living room, Lily on the sofa while Heather sat on the floor with Connor, pushing around toy trucks.

"Danielle said you used to make it," Heather said.

"Yeah, that was before Mom killed Matilda," Lily grumbled.

"Your mother did what?"

Lily let out a sigh and leaned back on the sofa. "Poor Matilda was always so faithful, reliable. I could count on her. When Dani inherited Marlow House, and I came up to Oregon with her for the summer, I really couldn't bring Matilda with me, so I stuck her in the freezer."

"Ahh... I assume you're talking about your sourdough starter. I read people often name theirs."

Lily nodded. "When Mom thought I'd died, and she cleaned out my place, she went through the freezer and had no idea what that stuff was in the jar, so she tossed it."

"Can't you make new starter?" Heather asked.

"I could. And I considered it. But Ian is not a big fan of sour-dough bread," Lily explained.

"He doesn't like sourdough?"

Lily shrugged. "He says the crust is too hard. I could make it for myself and then cut it in half and freeze for later, like I used to, so it doesn't go to waste. But I figure Old Salts makes pretty good sour-dough, so I just buy it."

"That's what Danielle says."

"But if you want to try, I'm more than happy to help you. But first, you need to make your starter. That takes about a week. In the meantime, I'll find my bread recipe for you. Do you have a digital kitchen scale?"

"Yes."

"How about an instant-read thermometer?"

"Yes."

"A Danish whisk?" Lily asked.

Heather frowned. "A what?"

"Don't worry, I have an extra one I'll give you. How about a cast-iron Dutch oven?"

Heather nodded. "Yes."

"Great. So you need to get a glass jar. You can use a canning jar. I kind of like the little jars with the clamp glass lids. But it doesn't matter. Do you have any all-purpose flour and wheat flour at home?"

"I have both, and I also have a glass jar."

"Terrific. You'll want to write this down," Lily said.

Heather grabbed her cellphone from her purse she had set on the floor by the sofa and prepared to enter Lily's instructions in her cellphone's Notes app.

"Ready?" Lily asked.

"Yes."

"There are lots of different starter recipes out there. This is just the one that worked for me," Lily said.

"Gotcha. So what do I do?" Heather asked.

"In your clean jar, mix together a hundred grams of whole wheat flour and a hundred grams of lukewarm filtered water. Stir well."

Heather frowned. "Filtered water?"

"I read chlorine the city puts in the water can interfere with the process. If you don't have filtered water, just leave the water on the counter for a couple of hours first, and the chlorine should evaporate."

"Then what?" Heather asked.

"Mix it well, then loosely cover and set it on the kitchen counter somewhere warm. If you cover it tightly, the jar can explode when the mixture expands."

"I don't want that. Then what?"

"Do nothing the next day. But on the third day, remove half of your starter, and then add a hundred grams of all-purpose flour to the jar and a hundred grams of warm water. What you're doing is feeding the starter. Mix well. And then cover again, loosely, like you did before, and put it in a warm place. Then do the same thing every day for the next week. Your starter will start getting all bubbly when it comes to life. When you get to that point, I'll help you with your first loaf of bread."

"What do I do with the stuff I take out of the jar?" Heather asked.

"That's called sourdough discard. This week, just toss it. Later, I'll give you some recipes you can use it in. But for now, just get rid of it."

"Why do we do that?" Heather asked.

"You need to make room in the jar," Lily explained.

"I was wondering who was here," Ian said when he stepped into the living room. Both women looked up at him.

"Lily said you were in your office working. What are you doing working on a Sunday?" Heather asked.

Ian sat down in his recliner and said, "I was just getting a letter off to my editor. Any news on the mystery ghost? Have you seen him again?"

"No, but Danielle and Walt went over to the museum this afternoon to read some recently donated past issues of the *Frederickport Press*," Heather explained. "Hoping to find something that might help them figure out who our mountain man ghost is, and why he thinks Walt's dad killed him."

"Yes, I talked to Walt about it. I understand they met Ginny and Cory," Ian said. "My sister has become friends with Ginny. She interviewed her on her podcast. She's the one who donated the newspapers. Kelly was there when Walt and Danielle stopped by. Apparently, Joe and Brian stopped by when they were there. It seems my sister is playing matchmaker."

"I can't believe she's trying to set up Brian," Lily said with a snort. "Who's Cory?"

"He lives next door to Ginny. I met him when I helped Kelly set up for the podcast at Ginny's house. Quirky guy. Ginny says he's been helpful, but Kelly finds him a little creepy. Personally, I don't think he means any harm. He's just obsessed with local history."

"Obsessed? How?" Heather asked.

Ian shrugged. "I suppose I expect that type of interest from people like Millie, someone older who is active in the local historical society, or someone like Walt, who writes about it. And in his case, lived it." Ian chuckled and then continued. "But Cory's in his twenties, doesn't have a job. I think he lives on an inheritance from his mother. From what I understand, he dropped out of high school, and he doesn't seem to have any friends. According to Ginny, he goes nowhere, never has anyone over. He's been helping her clean out the house she inherited, but he pores over everything they've removed. Ginny said since she isn't paying him much, she indulges him. But he makes Kelly uncomfortable."

FIFTEEN

"What are you doing?" Walt asked Danielle on Monday morning as he set one of the two cups of coffee he carried on the desk next to her. She sat at the computer in the library, her cellphone in hand.

"Sending those pictures I took yesterday to the computer," Danielle explained. "Thanks for the coffee."

"Doesn't it do that automatically?" Walt stood over Danielle, watching while sipping his coffee.

"It's supposed to. I think I have some settings wrong. Either that, or my computer hates me."

Walt chuckled and took another sip while watching Danielle bring up one photograph she had just downloaded to the computer. It filled the monitor. She enlarged the picture, bringing the faces in closer.

Danielle leaned toward the monitor and said, "I can't get over how much you look like your father."

"I suppose it should be no surprise, considering how much I look like Clint."

"True," Danielle agreed.

"It's amazing your phone could take such an excellent picture. At one time I never imagined such things." Walt watched as Danielle continued to enlarge the photograph, the men's faces filling the monitor.

"Holy crap!" Danielle yelped.

"What?"

"Don't you see it?" Danielle asked.

"See what?" Walt asked, taking a closer look at the monitor.

In response, Danielle enlarged the picture again, but this time zooming in on one face.

"Look. It's our mountain man," Danielle said.

Walt shook his head. "No. That's Uncle Bud."

"Look at the eyes, Walt. The beard hides most of the mountain man's face. But look at the eyes, the nose. That's our ghost."

Walt set his coffee mug on the desk and then leaned closer to the computer. He studied the image on the screen.

After a prolonged silence, Danielle asked, "Well, what do you think?"

"I think you may be right. But it makes little sense."

"It gives me another reason to take Ginny up on her offer and go to her house today. But instead of just looking through her photographs, I wonder what she knows about your uncle Bud," Danielle said.

"It didn't sound like she knew much aside from the fact he disappeared. Which is news to me."

Danielle turned from the computer and looked up at Walt. "What exactly do you remember about Bud? I know you said he didn't go to your parents' funeral because he'd moved from Frederickport a few months before your parents' death."

"Back then, no one said anything about him disappearing. I'm not sure when it was, but I remember asking my grandmother why Uncle Bud hadn't been at the funeral, and she said something about him moving a few months earlier."

THE PACKARD DRIVING down the street was younger than most of the houses in the neighborhood, one of the older residential areas in Frederickport. Danielle paid attention to the addresses, and when she saw Ginny's, she pointed to it, and a few moments later Walt parked in front of the house. Danielle glanced at her watch, and as Walt turned off the ignition, she said, "Wow, we timed this perfectly. We told Ginny we'd be here at noon, and it's 11:59."

"Does that mean you want to wait in the car for a minute?"

Walt teased.

"Funny." Danielle opened her car door.

A few minutes later, the pair stood on the front porch. They soon discovered someone had taped a small piece of paper over the doorbell's button. On the paper someone had written 'out of order.' After reading the makeshift sign, Danielle knocked on the door. When she did, it opened several inches. Not only was it unlocked, but it hadn't been closed all the way.

Startled at the unexpected door opening, Danielle called out, "Hello?" Hesitant to just walk in, she called out again, "Hello? Ginny? It's Danielle Marlow." She knocked on the door again, and when she did, it pushed open wider. Still no answer.

"Maybe she left the door open on purpose, for us to come in?" Danielle suggested.

Walt glanced at his watch. "She was expecting us at noon. It's now several minutes past."

"I hope everything is okay," Danielle said nervously. "Ginny, hello! It's Walt and Danielle Marlow!"

Still no answer.

Danielle hesitantly stepped into the house and looked around. "She might have fallen and hurt herself."

Walt followed Danielle into the unlit entry hall. It led first to a living room area. By the looks of the vintage and worn furniture, Danielle assumed it had belonged to Ginny's cousin. They continued down the hallway and found what looked like a study, if one judged by the oak desk covered in boxes and two bookshelves pushed against one wall, and a card table in the center of the room.

Stepping back into the hallway, Danielle called out, "Ginny? It's Danielle Marlow."

Still no response.

"I should check the house, and you stay here," Walt suggested.

"Why?" Danielle asked.

"Just stay here, Danielle, please. You know I can take care of myself, and I would rather not worry about you."

"You think something is wrong, don't you?" Danielle whispered.

"Not necessarily. But the house is open, and she was expecting us. Just let me check the rest of the house and see if I can find Ginny. Like you said, maybe she fell. Which is possible if she's moving things around, and if she hit her head, she could be unconscious."

"Then I should go with you."

Walt let out a sigh and said, "Please just stay here in case it's something else. Humor me."

"Okay," Danielle reluctantly agreed. She pulled her phone from her purse. "I'm going to call for help if we need it."

Walt gave her a nod and continued down the hallway. Danielle remained standing in the entry hall, not far from the open doorway.

"Ginny?" Walt called out. "It's Walt Marlow. Is everything okay?"

Danielle didn't hear a response to Walt's question, and she could no longer see him. She glanced back to the open door, the afternoon sunshine streaming in. To her right was the archway leading to the living room, to her left the open doorway leading to the study. Next to it was another door, which Danielle assumed was the coat closet.

Danielle anxiously waited for Walt. A loud crashing sound coming from the back of the house startled her. Before she had time to respond, the door she assumed led to the coat closet flew open, and standing in its doorway stood Cory, an ax dangling from his right hand.

He grinned at her. "Hello." He stood in what looked like the entrance to the basement. Danielle had been wrong. The door led to the basement, not a coat closet.

Her eyes fixed on the ax. Something red covered its blade. Blood?

"Are you alone?" Cory asked.

Danielle inched away, her back hitting the wall. She froze, her eyes still on the ax.

"She said your husband was coming," Cory said.

Danielle licked her lips nervously and then looked from the ax to the front door. A part of her wanted to run for it, while another part did not want to abandon Walt and have him stumble into Cory without warning. She looked back at the ax. But where was Walt? she wondered. And what was that crashing sound?

Cory laughed, and Danielle's eyes flashed up to his face. He waved the ax and said, "The way you keep staring at this, I have to wonder if you think I'm going to use it on you." He laughed again. "But don't worry, it's duller than dull." He tossed the ax aside and said, "But I guess I could still use it to smash open your noggin." He laughed again.

Danielle stared at Cory, uncertain what to say, when Walt came walking down the hallway. He didn't immediately see Cory, who continued to stand in the doorway leading to the basement, out of Walt's view.

"I couldn't find her," Walt said.

"Oh, your husband came with you," Cory said, stepping into the hallway. His sudden appearance brought Walt to an abrupt halt.

"Where did you come from?" Walt demanded.

"I was in the basement," Cory said. "Ginny told me to leave the front door open for you, said you might get here before she returned."

"Where is Ginny?" Danielle asked, her heart no longer racing.

"She's at the store, buying drain cleaner. If you have to use the bathroom, don't use the first one down the hall. The sink is backed up," Cory explained. He turned around and picked up the ax.

"What are you doing with that?" Walt asked.

Cory looked at the ax in his hand and smiled. "I was looking for a plunger; I saw its handle and thought that's what this was. I'd just picked it up when I heard something upstairs. Ginny said you were coming over. Forgot I was holding it when I saw your wife. I'm afraid it might have scared her." He giggled.

"What's that red on the blade?" Walt asked.

Cory touched the blade with one finger and wrinkled his nose. "Looks like paint. At first I thought it was blood." He laughed again.

"I'm afraid I knocked over some boxes when I walked into the kitchen. I don't think I broke anything," Walt said.

Cory shrugged. "No problem. I put those boxes there. Those are some things Ginny thought you might be interested in. Come on, I'll show you."

Ax in hand, Cory started down the hallway, walking past Walt. Walt and Danielle exchanged glances. Halfway down the hallway, Cory stopped and opened a door, which, unlike the first door he had stepped from, did lead to a closet. He set the ax in the closet and then closed the door. "I'll take that back to the basement later," he mumbled and then continued down the hall. Walt and Danielle again exchanged glances before silently following.

DANIELLE STOOD by the refrigerator and watched as Cory and Walt straightened the boxes, returning some items that had fallen onto the floor.

She silently watched, studying Cory's face and asking herself why he looked familiar. It was possible she had run into him around town, or perhaps he had shown up at one of the events she had hosted at Marlow House. She was about to ask him if he had attended any when she remembered Ginny had introduced him as Cory Jones at the museum. Recognition dawned.

"Are you related to Bill Jones?" Danielle asked. Bill Jones was the handyman who worked for Adam Nichols. When she had first moved to Frederickport, Bill and Adam had broken into Marlow House, searching for the Missing Thorndike. But they had put all that behind them, and she now considered Adam a close friend. While she didn't think of Bill as a friend, she trusted him enough to hire him for work around Marlow House. Cory looked like a younger version of Bill.

Cory looked up to Danielle and asked, "You know my uncle?"

"Yes. So you are related to Bill," Danielle said. "I definitely see the family resemblance."

Walt, who had not been paying attention to the conversation, had instead been picking through some photographs in one box. He pulled out a photo and said, "Here's a picture of Bud."

Cory looked curiously at Walt. "You know who Bud was?"

"I know he was a good friend of Alex Marlow, one of my distant cousins," Walt said.

"They say he disappeared. Some say the treasure got him killed," Cory whispered.

"Treasure?" Danielle asked.

"They were all looking for it," Cory said in a conspiratorial voice.

"Oh, you're here," a new voice said from the doorway leading from the kitchen to the hallway. They all turned to the voice and found Ginny standing there.

"Cory, did you ever find that plunger?" Ginny asked.

"No, but I found an ax."

Ginny laughed and said, "I'm afraid an ax won't work, not unless I want to rip out the plumbing. Why don't you go back down to the basement and see if you can find it, please?"

Cory gave her a nod and abruptly left the room.

SIXTEEN

"I'm sorry I wasn't here when you arrived," Ginny said. "But we had a little plumbing problem."

"That's fine. Cory explained," Danielle said.

"Cory mentioned something about your great-grandmother's brother, Bud, searching for a treasure?" Walt asked.

Ginny arched her brows. "Did he?"

"Yes. It sounded like an interesting story," Walt said.

"Walt's always looking for story fodder to give him inspiration," Danielle interjected.

"I suspect he got the story from Caitlin, my cousin's daughter. Cory and Caitlin were friends, and as I recall, Caitlin was quite the imaginative storyteller. Unfortunately, she got into drugs and after that had a problem telling fact from fantasy. It was quite tragic. She died of an overdose."

"Cory seemed to think Bud's disappearance involved a treasure," Danielle said.

"Yes, I suppose that's as good an explanation as any. I guess he could have come up with alien abduction," Ginny said with a snort.

"Do you have any idea what happened to Bud?" Walt asked.

Ginny shrugged. "No, not really. But back then, someone could move away and easily lose contact. He was my grandmother's uncle, and she told me he wasn't close to his sister. From what I know, there was a falling-out between him and his brother-in-law, my great-

94

grandfather. But I never heard what it was about. I don't think my grandmother knew."

"So there was a falling-out, and that's why he left?" Danielle asked.

Ginny shrugged. "It's what I always assumed. But that's only a guess. I just know he left sometime in 1904, and the family never heard from him again."

"Cory's version was more interesting," Walt teased.

"Yes, it is." Ginny grinned. "And Cory really has been helpful." Ginny glanced around the kitchen, taking in its vintage pink and gray linoleum flooring, the worn cabinets, its white paint chipping off and stained. "This house just needs a lot of work. I'm afraid my cousin didn't keep up on things after her husband died. And for all Cory's quirks, he's rather handy."

"Older houses require a lot of work," Danielle said.

Ginny flashed Danielle a smile. "You would know. I imagine you had your hands full when you inherited Marlow House."

"I was fortunate. My great-aunt never lived in Marlow House, but she kept it well maintained. We had to replace the appliances, and there was some plumbing required before installing the washer and dryer, but I was lucky, it was in pretty good shape."

"I read Marlow House was haunted," Ginny said with a grin.

"Oh, that. The ghost wasn't much trouble," Danielle joked. "And I eventually got rid of him."

Ginny laughed. "An exorcism?"

Danielle shrugged. "Something like that."

"Fortunately, no ghosts here," Ginny said.

Danielle started to respond but froze when the space behind Ginny swirled and changed colors, giving way to a bright light. Mesmerized by the sight, both Danielle and Walt stared while Ginny remained unaware of the apparition taking form behind her. She continued to prattle on, now talking of the improvements she planned for the property.

Danielle blinked her eyes several times and stared at the image of a young woman now standing behind Ginny, her long blond hair straight and falling past her shoulders. She glared unhappily at Walt and Danielle. "You stay away from my treasure. Do you under-stand?" she said before disappearing.

By the time Ginny stopped prattling on, Danielle and Walt had regained their composure and directed their attention to the boxes as Ginny began showing their contents.

As it turned out, there was nothing of special interest inside for Walt and Danielle, no more photographs of Walt's father or clues as to why Bud had disappeared.

"Did your grandmother ever talk about the relationship between her uncle Bud and Alexander Marlow?" Danielle asked after they finished going through the last box.

"Just that they were good friends. She seemed rather proud that her uncle was so close to the son of Frederick Marlow. They had grown up together. After all, Frederick Marlow was the founder of Frederickport and an extremely wealthy businessman. So naturally, my grandmother enjoyed name-dropping."

They chatted for another fifteen minutes before Danielle and Walt said their goodbyes and thanked Ginny for letting them look through the old photographs. Ginny walked them to the front door, watched them walk out, and then shut the door.

When Walt and Danielle reached the Packard, Cory seemed to appear out of nowhere.

"Wow, I like your car," Cory said.

"Thank you," Walt said as he opened the passenger door for Danielle.

"I wasn't making up stories about the treasure," Cory whispered as he glanced back to the house, its front door now closed and Ginny nowhere in sight. He looked back to Walt and Danielle and said, "I heard what Ginny told you. But I probably shouldn't have said anything about it. It's Caitlin's treasure anyway, and she wouldn't be happy if someone else started looking for it and found it."

Cory glanced up to the house and saw Ginny standing at a window, looking outside. "I gotta go," he snapped and then dashed away, heading to his house next door.

After Walt and Danielle got into the car and shut the doors, they sat there a moment.

"First question, who is our ghost?" Danielle asked. "It's obviously not the cousin, this ghost looks too young."

"The daughter who died?" Walt suggested.

"That's the obvious conclusion. Caitlin's manner of death makes her a prime candidate for a spirit unable to move on without help. Yet Caitlin was in high school, and our ghost looks a little old for high school."

"Are you suggesting this spirit needs some help to move on?" Walt asked.

"It appears that way."

"Are you volunteering?"

"Helping spirits move on seems to be the reason for this gift," Danielle said. "But first, I'd rather learn more about Cory."

"He is an interesting fellow. I rather wish he hadn't run off. I wanted to ask him what was this treasure." Walt started the ignition.

"Let's go to Adam's office."

"Why?" Walt asked as he pulled the car out from the sidewalk, into the street.

"He might be able to tell us a little about Cory," Danielle suggested.

"AW, YES, CORY. WEIRD LITTLE DUDE," Adam said, leaning back in his desk chair. "He used to work with Bill, and he was actually pretty good, caught on quick, but no people skills. And after a few customers complained, Bill let him go. Now he occasionally hires him, but only if the customers are out of town and they don't need to interact with Cory."

"What did they complain about?" Danielle asked.

Adam shrugged. "I'm not really sure. I suspect he just creeped them out. He's Bill's sister's kid, and he's pretty much messed up. Too many drugs, if you ask me. I'm talking about the sister. Not sure if Cory uses, but wouldn't surprise me, considering some past company he kept. But Bill insists he's clean."

"I assumed Bill's brother was his father. They have the same last name," Danielle said.

"She never married. I don't know who the father is. It's not that Cory is a bad kid. Hell, Bill and I got in more trouble. He's just sort of a misfit," Adam said.

"He mentioned a Caitlin," Danielle said.

"She was the neighbor, died of an overdose. Caitlin was, like, his only friend. I remember he was pretty broken up over her death. Bill worried about him at the time. Even though Bill had to let him go, he cares about his nephew."

97

"How does Cory support himself?" Walt asked.

"Bill's parents left the house to his sister. I guess they figured she needed it more than Bill, what with her having a kid, being unmarried and not being able to hold down a job. They set up a trust before they died, so each month Cory gets a small check, pays the utilities, food and what he needs. The way they set it up, it went to the daughter, and when she died, it went to Cory. If something happens to Cory, then Bill gets the house and whatever money is left."

"How does Bill feel about that?" Walt asked.

"Honestly, Bill was pretty cool about it. He never seemed upset with his parents for taking care of his sister—even though she was always a loser—or his weird little nephew. If anything, it always pissed off Bill about Cory's father, who, in Bill's opinion, ruined his sister and never stepped up to the plate with his son."

"So Bill knows the father?" Danielle asked.

Adam shook his head. "No. If he had, I imagine Bill would be in prison now, serving time for killing the jerk. But the fact is—something I won't tell Bill—his sister was messed up when this guy found her. Drugs will do that to a person."

"Cory also mentioned something about a treasure—a treasure Caitlin told him about," Danielle said.

Adam laughed. "So Cory told you about that?" He laughed again.

"You've heard about this treasure?" Danielle asked.

"Sure. Bill told me about it, back when Cory was working for him. Cory was pretty obsessed with finding it. This was back when Caitlin was still alive, and the two had these big dreams to find it and then run away together. I didn't know Caitlin, but Grandma knew her mother. From what I heard about her, sounded like she wasn't much different from Cory's mom. Messed up with drugs."

"Was Cory's mother still doing drugs after she had Cory?" Danielle asked.

"No. I have to give her credit for that; she got clean, and she tried to be a good mom. Her parents were there for her. But she always struggled and had mental problems."

"So what was the story of the treasure?" Danielle asked.

Adam stared at Danielle for a moment and then laughed. "Seriously? Are you looking for another treasure? I think you've exceeded your limit."

Danielle rolled her eyes. "I'm just curious."

Adam shrugged. "According to Cory, someone in Caitlin's family found a treasure somewhere in Oregon. I have no clue where, or even what type of treasure. Cory was secretive about that—claimed he promised Caitlin he wouldn't tell anyone; it was just their secret. And he claimed he saw part of the treasure."

"So what are we talking here, gold, diamonds, stock certificates?" Danielle asked.

"Your guess is as good as mine," Adam said. "If there was a treasure and Caitlin really knew where it was, I don't think she ever told Cory, because he's still living alone at the house Bill grew up in."

SEVENTEEN

When Walt and Danielle returned to Marlow House on Monday, they found Marie waiting for them in the living room. She sat on the sofa, reading a magazine, and Danielle couldn't help but think how the sight of the magazine hovering over the couch, its pages turning, might look to some poor unexpected visitor to Marlow House, who might peek in the front window when no one answered the door. She grinned at the thought and saw no reason to reprimand Marie. After all, if someone was peeking in their windows, it served them right to get a little shook up, considering it wasn't nice to look in someone's window. One never knew what one might see.

"Finally, I have been waiting forever," Marie said as she closed the magazine and tossed it to the coffee table. "I'm dying to find out if you discovered the identity of the mystery ghost."

Before they could say anything, Marie held up one hand and said, "No smart aleck crack about me already being dead."

"Yes, we've identified our ghost," Danielle said as she sat down on a chair across from Marie. Walt sat next to her.

Marie perked up. "You did?"

Danielle explained who he was, and how they came to that determination.

"He's Emily's great-uncle?" Marie asked.

"Technically, it's Emily's great-great-uncle," Danielle explained. "Brother to her great-grandmother. If I'm following that correctly."

Marie looked at Walt and asked, "This is the one you called Uncle Bud?"

Walt nodded. "Yes. And this makes even less sense than it did before."

Marie leaned back in the sofa and said, "I know you've already talked to Eva about this. After she left you at the museum, we discussed the possibility he'd followed you up to the mountains and followed you back here."

"We considered that, but we're fairly certain he didn't follow us up there," Walt said.

Marie nodded. "Yes, and you're right."

"He is?" Danielle asked.

"Eva and I took a little trip up to the mountains, talked with some folks up there."

"Folks?" Danielle frowned.

"Actually, a black bear, who was not happy when Eva disturbed his sleep. And a mountain lion who was rather friendly," Marie explained.

"Um… and why did you go up there?" Danielle asked.

"Eva wanted to see if your ghost had been in the area for a long time. The easiest way to find out is to talk to some locals. According to the bear, your uncle Bud has been in that area since before he was a cub. His mother warned him about Bud. Occasionally your uncle Bud takes to shooting at the wildlife, but most understand he's rather harmless, so they generally ignore him. But according to the mountain lion, she hasn't seen him in the last few days."

"That confirms what we thought," Danielle said. "But why was he up there? How did he die?"

"We didn't stick around to find any graves, but I imagine if we found his grave, we might find a clue on how he died," Marie suggested.

"Since he didn't seem to grasp the fact he was dead—at least not until Walt talked to him at the cemetery, I have to believe his apparition is an accurate depiction of what he looked like when he died."

"It doesn't look like a wild animal mauled him," Walt said.

"No. And it's possible that if whatever killed him killed him quickly, he didn't realize he was dead, so his apparition won't show any signs of his death," Danielle said.

"Why do you say that?" Marie asked.

Danielle looked over at Walt. "I imagine Walt's corpse showed ugly red marks around his neck from the rope."

Walt frowned at Danielle. "Please, do we need to bring that up?"

"Sorry, but it is relevant. When you were a ghost and thought you were alive, I would never have guessed how you died," Danielle said.

"I suppose she has a point." Marie looked at Walt. "Unless this Bud returns, you may never find out what happened—until you move over to the other side."

"Something I'm not eager to do," Walt grumbled.

"I wonder when he died," Marie said.

"When Danielle asked him the date, he said August 1904. The same month and year my parents were killed. I have to assume his last memory in reference to a date would be around his time of death."

Danielle looked to Walt. "Did you ever see Bud wearing a beard?" Danielle asked.

"No. That's why I didn't recognize him."

"Can you remember the last time you saw him?" Danielle asked.

Walt considered the question a moment and then said, "I'm fairly certain it was that last Easter with my parents. My grand-mother had everyone over for Easter dinner."

Danielle grabbed her cellphone off the nearby table and did a quick search. A moment later she looked up and said, "Easter fell on April 3 in 1904. He obviously grew that beard sometime after you saw him at Easter. Like you, I assume he died up in those mountains —the same month your parents died."

Danielle then told Marie about their time over at Ginny's house and Cory's talk of a treasure.

"Interesting," Marie said. "When you mentioned Bud, I didn't give it much thought. But the treasure—I've heard about it before."

"Adam had too. We talked to him about it." Danielle then recounted to Marie their visit with her grandson.

"As I recollect," Marie began, "Adam never met Caitlin. She was much younger than him. But I remember her, a troubled girl."

"We saw a spirit at Ginny's," Danielle said.

Marie arched her brow. "You did? You didn't mention it. I don't imagine it was Emily. I'm certain she moved on."

"This was a much younger woman. We wonder if it was Caitlin, especially considering how she died. But you mentioned your friend's daughter was in high school, and this was a young woman, not a teenager," Danielle said.

"What did she look like?" Marie asked.

"Somber—but she was a ghost. Long blond, straight hair, no bangs. She looked to be about twenty. Pretty, but a little plain. Thin. She mentioned a treasure. Told us to leave it alone."

"Sounds like Caitlin. She was seventeen when she died, a senior in high school. But she always looked older than her age," Marie said. "I imagine that's Caitlin you saw. Poor Emily, she was looking forward to seeing her daughter when she passed over, and she's not there."

"I'm surprised she didn't see her before she left," Walt said.

"That happens," Danielle reminded him. "Back when you were still haunting Marlow House, there were a few times some ghost showed up that you never saw."

"True," Walt agreed.

"But it is such a shame." Marie sighed.

"What do you know about this treasure Cory and Caitlin talked about?" Danielle asked.

"I seriously doubt there really is a treasure," Marie said. "More a family legend with the hint of a treasure to spice things up."

"I'd like to learn more, because the person at the heart of this legend has accused my father of murder," Walt said.

Marie let out a sigh and settled back on the sofa. "As Walt knows, Bud's sister married the man whose family started the livery stable in Frederickport. They had two sons and one daughter. The daughter was Emily's grandmother."

"And I assume Ginny's?" Danielle said.

"Correct," Marie said with a nod. "She had two daughters, one was Emily's mother, and the other was Ginny's mother. From what I understand, Ginny's mother left the area when she married, and her sister stayed in Frederickport. Emily had one sibling, a brother. He died years ago. When I spoke to Emily at her funeral, she told me her cousin Ginny was an only child. Growing up, Ginny spent summers in Frederickport, visiting her grandmother and cousin. When the grandmother died, Emily and her husband purchased the grandmother's house from the estate."

"I just assumed the house passed down in the family," Danielle said.

"No. Emily's parents had a house in Frederickport, but they both died before Emily's grandmother. Emily was just a young bride at the time. From what I recall, they still owed a great deal on the house, had bills, and there really wasn't much for Emily to inherit. Emily's husband did well, and when the grandmother passed, they bought out the cousin's share—since the house went to both Emily and her cousin. But frankly, I doubt the cousin was happy about it. But she has the house now, so I suppose it all worked out."

"I don't understand?" Danielle frowned. "If the grandmother left the house to both of them, why did Ginny let her cousin buy her out of her share if she didn't want to sell?"

"It was a stipulation in the grandmother's will. She wanted to be fair, I suppose. But she couldn't divide the house. Of course, they could sell it and divide the profits. But she understood Emily was sentimental about the property, so she left a stipulation in the will that the house went to both granddaughters, but Emily had the option to buy out her cousin's share at full market value. And if Emily didn't want to buy the house, her cousin then had that option."

"You said Ginny wasn't happy about it. Did she want to buy out Emily's share?" Danielle asked.

Marie shrugged. "I assume so. At least, from what Emily said. Which was why she left the house to her cousin. I think she felt a little guilty about it."

"So what about this family legend?" Walt asked.

Marie laughed. "Oh that! My, I wandered off topic, didn't I? It's just something a friend once told me. Her daughter had been friends with Emily, and once Emily confided in her daughter that her great-uncle had been an explorer who brought home treasures but had disappeared after being kidnapped by pirates."

Walt arched a brow. "Pirates kidnapped Bud?"

Marie chuckled. "I seriously doubt it. But my friend overheard the girls and felt Emily's mother needed to know about her daughter's outrageous story telling. The very next day, her mother marched Emily back over to her house, and the poor girl had to apologize and confess that she had made the entire thing up. My friend regretted telling the mother."

"How embarrassing, for everyone," Danielle said.

"But it didn't end there. Years later, when Emily had a teenage daughter, Adam told me a story about Bill's nephew—who lived next door to Emily. It was practically identical to what Emily had told her friend, but this time, it was Caitlin telling the story to Bill's nephew."

"Did they ever say what kind of treasure?" Danielle asked.

Marie shook her head. "No. But I got a little curious, did a little more investigating, and discovered Emily's grandmother did in fact have an uncle who went missing."

EIGHTEEN

T ears streamed down the young boy's face while hiccup sobs replaced the rebellious tantrum cries that had filled the foyer just minutes earlier. His grandmother's right hand clutched one of his hands tightly as she led him up the staircase, giving him no opportunity to further protest.

Begrudgingly, he followed her to the second floor. Glancing back over his shoulder, he looked down to the now closed front door where his mother had departed just minutes earlier, leaving him even after he had begged her to stay.

"Don't drag your feet, Walt," his grandmother scolded when they reached the second-floor landing. He sniffled and used his free hand to dry his nose on his shirt's cuff. Exhausted from the rigorous fit of tears, he entered his bedroom, his hand still gripped firmly by his grandmother. Once again, he had lost the battle. All he could do now was retreat, take a nap, and maybe his mother would come home earlier today, and they could start fresh.

His grandmother released his hand, abruptly grabbed him around the waist, and lifted his feet off the floor, setting him on the edge of his bed. She placed one hand on his right shoulder while the other hand tipped his chin upwards until his eyes looked into hers.

With her right hand, she removed the cotton handkerchief she always kept in her apron pocket and wiped away the remaining tears.

"Love, you are making yourself sick. And you are breaking your poor mother's heart," his grandmother said in a kind voice.

"I just wanted her to stay with me," he whimpered. "She's always gone."

"And she wanted to stay with you. But sometimes we have obligations, and we don't get to do what we want." She shoved the handkerchief back in her pocket and then rustled his mop of dark babyish boy curls with one hand.

He looked up into his grandmother's face, his big blue eyes filled with unshed tears. "Then why did she go again?"

Leaning over him, she let out a weary sigh, swept the boy up into her arms, and hugged him while resting one cheek against the top of his head. "You are not a baby anymore, Walt," she said in a whisper. "You need to start acting like a big boy and stop with these tantrums. I don't even want to think what your papa or grandfather would say if they had been here and witnessed your tantrum."

"Are you going to tell them?" Walt whispered back.

After letting out another sigh, she said, "No, it will be our secret. And I'm sure your mama won't be saying anything to them either. But honestly, Walt, you need to stop doing this to your poor mother. Don't you know how difficult it is for her to leave you each day?"

Before his grandmother left the room, she tucked him into his bed for a nap. He didn't bother arguing that if he was a big boy, why did he have to take a nap? The tantrum had been exhausting. He had no energy for arguing. Just minutes after his grandmother left the room, he fell asleep.

When Walt woke up, he sat up in bed, rubbed his eyes, and looked to the window. Sunshine streamed into the room. Hungry, he climbed out of bed.

"YOU SLEPT A GOOD HOUR," his grandmother said when Walt walked into the kitchen. "You ready for some lunch?"

"Yes, please," he said as he climbed into a chair at the kitchen table.

A few minutes later his grandmother set a plate of food before him, and just as he took his first bite, the kitchen door opened, and his father walked into the house.

"Papa!" Walt greeted him excitedly.

"Alex, did you come home for lunch?" Walt's grandmother asked as Alex rustled his son's hair in greeting. Walt remained at the table, eating his lunch.

Alex glanced at his son and then looked back at his mother. "I'm going over to Teddy and Maddie's. But I wanted to talk to you first."

"Can I go with you, Papa?" Walt asked, wanting a chance to apologize to his mother.

"Not today, son. But I'm hoping I won't be long, and your mama may come back with me."

"She is?" Walt brightened.

"What's going on?" Walt's grandmother asked.

"We can talk about it in the hall," Alex said, flashing a glance from his son to his mother. She nodded and headed to the doorway. When Walt got out of his chair to follow his father and grandmother, his father told him to stay put.

Remaining at the kitchen table, Walt looked from his lunch to the doorway his grandmother and father had gone through. He wondered what was going on and why adults always had secrets. Tempted, he considered sneaking from the table to eavesdrop at the doorway, but he feared if his father caught him, especially after being expressly told to stay put, he would get a good whipping. It wasn't that his father's whippings hurt his backside much, but they injured his pride, and to Walt that was more painful.

Walt's father and grandmother returned to the kitchen a few minutes later. Alex rustled Walt's hair again and told him to finish his lunch and to be a good boy.

"I'll walk you out," Walt's grandmother said. She looked at Walt. "Finish your lunch. I have to run to the Hamiltons' to pick up some eggs, and I want you to stay inside. I might be gone a while, and you need to stay in the house. Do you understand?"

Walt looked up to his grandmother while his father stood by the back door, waiting. When Walt did not respond, Alex said, "Walt, what do you say to your grandmother?"

"Yes, ma'am." Walt watched his grandmother and father leave out the back door.

WALT DIDN'T UNDERSTAND why his grandmother always made him stay inside when she ran errands. Why couldn't he just play outside while she was gone? It was more interesting outside, especially this time of year. This afternoon the sun shone brightly, the perfect day to climb one of the trees in their yard.

He stood at the parlor window, looking outside, when he spied something of interest in his front yard, a kitten. One of the neighbor's cats recently had kittens, and Walt wondered if one of theirs had somehow wandered over into his yard. Concerned over the kitten's safety, especially considering the large dogs who wandered the neighborhood, Walt decided to break his grandmother's rule and rescue the young animal. Plus, there was no reason she had to find out. He could simply catch it and then sneak it back into the neighbor's yard where it belonged.

Confident in what he should do, Walt left the parlor and stepped out the front door. Once outside, he spied the kitten playing by a bush near the front walkway. Before going to it, Walt glanced around, wanting to make certain his grandmother was not already on her way home. Seeing she was nowhere in sight, he started for the animal.

Just as he reached the kitten, it darted under one of the large bushes along the front of the house. Without thought, Walt followed it into the bushes. Once there, hidden in the foliage, he sat on the ground, and instead of grabbing the skittish animal, he lured it to him by breaking off a small twig and twitching it in front of the feline. Cats had scratched Walt before, and he was hesitant to grab at the wild ball of fur and tiny claws.

The kitten, now engrossed in Walt's play, swatted playfully at the leaves on the small twigs. They played for several minutes when Walt heard footsteps on the front walk. He froze. Had his grandmother returned?

Walt peeked out from the bushes and spied his father's horse tied up to the fence. Walt frowned, confused, as his father had left in the buggy. But then he saw the man standing at the front door, Uncle Teddy. Suddenly it made sense. Uncle Teddy's horse looked just like his father's. His father used to laugh and call them a matching set.

Not wanting to reveal himself, Walt remained hidden in the bushes. He watched as Teddy rang the doorbell and waited. After a few minutes, when no one answered the door, he watched as Teddy grumbled something and then turned from the door and headed down the walk. Teddy got onto the horse and rode away.

Turning his attention back to the kitten, Walt discovered it had escaped. Getting out from the bushes, Walt brushed the dirt off his clothes and looked around. The kitten was nowhere in sight. Worried his grandmother would come home soon and catch him outside, Walt hurried back to the house.

———

WALT WOKE ABRUPTLY and sat up straight in bed. His breathing labored, he felt as if he had just finished running a marathon. He glanced at Danielle, who had been sleeping beside him. She stirred and then sat up groggily, rubbing her eyes. Walt looked to the window. Early morning sunlight streamed into the room.

"Are you okay?" Danielle asked.

When he didn't answer and continued to stare blankly across the room, she gently turned toward him and touched his shoulder. "Walt?"

"I remember," Walt stammered.

Danielle frowned. "You remember what?" Reaching over to her nightstand, she turned on the light, brightening the dimly lit room.

"Uncle Teddy was there that day, in Frederickport."

"What are you talking about?" Danielle asked.

Walt repeated his dream to Danielle in every detail.

"You're saying it wasn't just a dream?" Danielle asked.

"I'm not saying it was a dream hop, exactly. But it's exactly how I remember that last day with my parents—the day my parents died. I'd forgotten some of it, but I remember now. I'd forgotten Teddy was there. He told them he had been in Astoria. That he had returned after the fire. But he was in Frederickport that day."

"If he was, why didn't you tell your grandparents?"

"At the time, I never thought it was important. My grandmother told me to stay in the house, and if I told her about Uncle Teddy coming to the house, she'd ask me why I hadn't answered the door for him. I couldn't very well tell her I was outside hiding in the bushes. Plus, at the time I didn't know it mattered. And years later, when I understood more about that day, I didn't remember it all. But why didn't I remember?" Walt frowned at his own question.

Danielle took one of Walt's hands in hers and gave it a squeeze. "Not only were you very young, losing your parents after that would be traumatic for any child, and you were only five. Plus, you already felt guilty for throwing a tantrum the last time you saw your mother. Suppressing memories is not uncommon. What I'm wondering, why are you remembering this now?"

"Because obviously, none of this is a coincidence," Walt said.

"How do you mean?"

"Bud's death so close to my parents'. Teddy lying about where he was. Bud disappearing and blaming my father for his death. Those three were close; they grew up together. And if we want to figure this out, we need to find out what my father, Teddy, and Bud were doing back then. And why did they all die except for Ted? What ever happened to Ted? And what did my father tell my grandmother that day? What did she know that she never told me?"

"I'm wondering if one of them is trying to tell you now," Danielle said.

Walt looked at Danielle. "What are you saying?"

"We both know that when someone moves on, one of the few ways they can communicate with the living is by a dream hop. Dream hops come in various forms. We've both been in dream hops where the past replays before us—like your dream last night."

NINETEEN

Ian and Lily sat with the Beach Drive mediums at a large booth at Pier Café, about to have breakfast. Young Connor, considered a medium since he could see both Marie and Eva, sat on Heather's lap while she absently kept him entertained with a makeshift napkin puppet. Walt had just finished telling the group about his dream after Danielle had updated them on their visit to Ginny's house.

Heather sat next to Lily, who sat next to an empty highchair, with Ian on the other side. Across the table, Danielle sat between Chris and Walt. The window behind Chris, Danielle and Walt looked out to the ocean.

"And you think this was a dream hop?" Chris asked.

"Not exactly," Walt said.

"It was a dream hop," Danielle argued. "Like when Harvey showed me in a dream what happened to him. And Walt did it a few times too, and so did Emma."

"Does that mean someone else was there, showing Walt these things?" Chris asked.

"No," Walt said. "But I know what Danielle is saying. It felt like one of those dreams. But I'm not sure if someone wants me to remember what happened—or if it was my subconscious wanting me to remember."

"Are you sure it was exactly what happened back then?" Lily asked.

"Obviously, that was a long time ago. But it was as I remember that day," Walt said.

"But you didn't remember seeing Teddy before the dream?" Lily reminded him.

Walt looked to Lily. "No. But have you ever forgotten something, and then when someone reminds you, it all comes back?"

"Yes," Lily said.

"So does this mean you think this Teddy dude killed your parents?" Heather asked as she tweaked Connor's nose with the puppet, making him giggle.

"I believe he lied about where he was that day," Walt said. "According to what I remember my grandparents saying back then, Teddy had been in Astoria for a few days and didn't return until that evening."

"I wonder if the local police station would have any records on the case, like they did with Walt's death," Lily said.

"It doesn't sound like they investigated the fire as arson, so I would think you'd have to look at what records the fire department had," Chris said.

"There was no fire department in Frederickport back then," Walt said. "It was all volunteer."

"Even if there were any old reports on the fire to review, I doubt they would tell us much. It was a good forty years or more after Walt's parents' death that fire science was even a thing," Ian said.

"So basically, we can just speculate," Danielle said. "Even if Bud's spirit makes another appearance, it's unlikely he knows anything about the fire, considering he seemed to believe Walt's parents were still alive."

"And if this Bud has moved on, we probably won't learn what role Walt's father had in his death," Heather said.

"I don't believe my father killed him," Walt insisted.

"But there seems to be a connection between the deaths," Ian said. "It looks like Bud, your parents and Teddy's wife all died the same year—possibly the same month, and all under questionable circumstances. Walt said the three had been best friends. I'm not a huge believer in coincidences. If I were, I wouldn't have researched some topics I have over the years."

Lily turned to her husband and asked, "Okay, let's say this is a story you want to research. Where would you look?"

Ian considered the question for a moment. Finally, he said, "It seems the one person who survived that year was this Teddy. What happened to him?"

"I know he closed his office in Frederickport and moved down to Astoria, where his other office was located," Walt said. "My grandmother once mentioned he later remarried, but that's about all I know."

"Considering he lied about being in Frederickport the day of the fire, I would see what you can find out about Teddy, his life after your parents' and his wife's deaths," Ian suggested. "It's also possible you misunderstood the timeline of when Teddy arrived back in Frederickport. He could have stopped by Marlow House but didn't return to his home until after the fire."

"I think you'll find something if you look," Heather said.

Chris looked at Heather and asked, "Why do you say that?"

"Because Walt had that dream for some reason. It was telling him to look into it," Heather said.

Danielle nodded. "I agree."

"But I also want to know about that treasure of Bud's," Heather said.

"Any idea what kind of treasure it's supposed to be?" Ian asked.

"When we mentioned the treasure to Ginny, she claimed not to know anything about it, not until Cory mentioned it," Walt said.

"But Marie did say something," Danielle interjected.

Before Danielle could finish her thought, Carla arrived with their breakfast. Lily took Connor from Heather and put him in the empty highchair by her seat while they passed plates of food around the table.

After Carla served the food and left the table, Chris asked Danielle, "What did Marie say about the treasure?"

Danielle retold Marie's anecdote of a young Emily and then her daughter telling stories of Uncle Bud's treasure and pirates.

"Pirates?" Heather smirked after Danielle repeated Marie's story.

"So are we talking about a pirate treasure?" Lily asked.

"When I was growing up, there used to be a story about a pirate treasure buried up in one of the local mountains," Walt said.

They all turned to him. "You never told me that before," Danielle said.

Picking up a piece of toast from his plate, he gave a shrug. He said, "It's just a story my grandfather told me." Walt took a bite of the toast and then noticed his friends continued to watch him.

"We want to hear the story," Heather said impatiently.

"I don't think it has anything to do with Bud's treasure," Walt said, setting what remained of his toast back on his plate.

"Tell us anyway. I love a good treasure story," Danielle said.

"That's because you are always stumbling over treasures," Chris teased.

"Now you sound like Adam," Danielle said before taking a bite of bacon.

"According to my grandfather, about two years after he settled here, a ghost ship washed up on shore," Walt began.

"Ghost ship?" Heather frowned.

"A ship without a crew," Ian explained.

"Oh, you mean like the *Eva Aphrodite*," Heather said.

"Yes. Apparently, the ship washed up during a severe storm," Walt explained. "They discovered it the next morning, and no one was on board, and they didn't know where it came from. That morning the local livery stable discovered someone had taken a carriage and horses during the night. Later, people started specu-lating that whoever had been on the ship had stolen the carriage and horses."

"Is this the same livery that Bud's sister owned?" Danielle asked.

"Yes, but this was before Bud was born. And probably before his sister was born. I imagine the stable was then owned by her future in-laws," Walt said.

"So what does this have to do with pirates?" Heather asked.

"When they first inspected the wreckage, they found what looked like marks where someone had dragged something from the ship, like a large chest. There were some matching grooves left in the road, along with evidence of a carriage—which they believed was the missing one. Yet before they could search the wreckage for more evidence, or discover where it came from, another storm hit and washed the ship back out to sea, where it disappeared."

"And they never learned where it came from?" Heather asked.

"No. The stories grew, and people were convinced the ship was one pirates had commandeered, and that when they washed up on shore, they had to move their treasure. It made for a good story." Walt grinned.

"And they never found out what happened to the carriage and horses?" Lily asked.

"Not the horses, but months later they found what was left of the carriage up on one of the local mountains. Which mountain, I don't know," Walt said. "But that's where that story evolved."

"I assume treasure hunters searched for this elusive pirate treasure?" Danielle asked.

"If so, that was before my time. I heard the story years later, when I was about eleven. By then most people didn't believe there was a treasure. Oh, there were those who speculated pirates buried it up in the mountains, but it was always said more in jest. Even if there had been a treasure, I think most people felt it was long gone. While they found the carriage, they never found the horses. The pirates—or whoever was responsible—obviously got away with whatever they took with them," Walt said. "And whatever they took may not have been worth anything."

"I don't think Marie knows about this story," Danielle said. "She mentioned pirates, but nothing about this story."

"She may never have heard it," Walt said. "It's something I heard when I was a child, but I don't recall anyone talking about it in later years."

"But could this be the treasure Bud was supposedly looking for?" Heather suggested.

Walt shrugged. "I was told he moved a few months before my parents died. I heard nothing about him off treasure hunting until Cory."

"What happened to the carriage they found up in the mountains?" Ian asked. "Were they sure it was the same one stolen from the Frederickport livery?"

"The owner of the livery stable took a trip up to the mountains after someone reported finding the carriage. I assume they brought it back with them, but I don't know for sure," Walt said.

"Maybe," Heather said with a conspiratorial whisper, "they brought the carriage back, and the pirates had accidentally dropped some treasure, leaving it behind in the carriage. They found it, didn't tell anyone, but the story of the found treasure was passed down in their family, and then Bud heard about it from his sister, and he took off looking for it because his sister told him where they found the carriage."

They all stared at Heather.

116

Finally, Chris said, "You shouldn't have given up writing."

"What do you mean?" Heather frowned.

"You should consider fiction," Chris teased.

Heather laughed. "Yeah, well, my writing career was brief and not especially productive. I'd better stay where I am."

Chris glanced at his watch. "If you're going to do that, we need to finish breakfast and get to work. We have those people coming in, in about thirty minutes, remember?"

AFTER CHRIS and Heather finished breakfast and said their good-byes, Danielle said, "You know, Heather's theory was not a bad one."

"I thought that too," Ian said.

"So what are you guys going to do now?" Lily asked.

Walt considered the question and then looked at Danielle. "I have some things I need to do today, but why don't we take a drive to Astoria tomorrow and see if we can find out what happened to Teddy?"

"I'm game," Danielle said. "And while you finish what you have to do today, I'll see what I can find online."

TWENTY

Later Tuesday afternoon, Danielle came knocking on Lily's front door. She had a question for Ian. Lily answered the door and then led Danielle towards Ian's office, explaining Connor was in his room taking a nap.

"You haven't seen Marie, have you?" Danielle asked while following Lily down the hallway. Lily flashed Danielle an eye roll, to which Danielle responded, "You know what I mean."

"I'm fairly certain she hasn't been here today," Lily said as she opened the door to Ian's office. He looked up from his desk and greeted Danielle as the two women walked into the room.

"I was wondering if you could ask your sister something," Danielle said.

"What's that?" Ian asked.

"I'm not sure if this is going to help us figure this thing out, but Walt and I started talking more about this treasure Bud was supposed to be after, and we wondered if it was linked to the ship that washed up on shore. According to Ginny, when Cory mentioned it, she claimed not to know anything about a treasure Bud was looking for."

Ian arched his brow. "And?"

"But that doesn't mean she doesn't know something about the ship washing up on shore and the stolen carriage. Some story passed down in her family. Maybe she just didn't connect the two. Walt didn't at first," Danielle explained.

"What would you like me to do?" Ian asked.

"I know Kelly did an extensive interview with Ginny, and not everything made it to the podcast. I was wondering if you could ask if Ginny ever discussed the stolen carriage they found up in the mountains or the ghost ship. That all happened long before Bud's time, so I understand why she didn't connect the two," Danielle explained.

"Sure, I would be happy to," Ian said.

"Kelly's coming over in a little while," Lily said. "Ian can ask her then."

"Thanks, I really appreciate it," Danielle said.

"Did you do any online sleuthing?" Lily asked.

"Yes, I did. I was going to tell you about it." Danielle paused a moment and looked at Ian. "If you have time. I know I interrupted your work."

Ian laughed and pointed to the loveseat in his office. "Yeah, right, you imply you found something, and you think I'll have you tell me later? Sit down."

Danielle flashed Ian a grin and then took a seat on the small sofa with Lily. Ian pushed his chair away from the desk and, while still sitting in it, rolled himself closer to the sofa.

"I searched old newspapers online. While they don't have back copies of the *Frederickport Press*, they have other Oregon papers. I found a wedding announcement for a Theodore Newsome and Josephine Piller of Astoria, in November 1904. Teddy's last name was Newsome," Danielle explained.

"Wow, his wife dies in August, and he remarries a couple of months later?" Lily scoffed.

"Consider the time. Marriage was typically a practical arrangement, not necessarily about romance. It wasn't uncommon back then for someone to remarry fairly quickly," Ian reminded her.

"Anything else?" Lily asked.

"There was an obituary for a Josephine Piller Newsome, in June of 1905."

"They didn't have a very long marriage, did they?" Lily said. "Any idea what happened to her?"

"It didn't say in the obituary. I haven't found any articles on her death." Danielle glanced at her watch. "I need to get going. I want to do some more research before Walt and I go to Astoria."

"Are you still going tomorrow?" Lily asked.

"That's the plan," Danielle said.

"I'll call you tonight and tell you what Kelly says," Ian promised.

———

KELLY ARRIVED about a half an hour after Danielle returned to Marlow House. Lily opened the door for her sister-in-law but didn't bother showing her to the office. She had just gotten Connor up from his nap, and he was in the living room, playing with blocks. Lily didn't want to leave him alone.

When Kelly walked into her brother's office, she found him sitting at his desk, typing on the computer. He looked up from his keyboard, stopped typing, and smiled.

"Working hard?" Kelly asked, meandering over to the desk.

Ian pointed to a stack of papers sitting on the corner of a nearby shelf. "I got the papers you wanted together. They're right there."

Kelly picked up the stack and began shuffling through them.

"Why don't you sit down. I wanted to ask you about something," he said.

Clutching the stack of papers to her chest, she looked at her brother. "Why don't we go to Pier Café and talk there? Like we used to do, just the two of us. Get something to eat," Kelly suggested.

"I had breakfast there this morning," Ian told her.

Kelly frowned and asked, "Who with?"

"Just all the neighbors," Ian said.

"You mean like Walt and Danielle?" Kelly asked.

"Yes, and Chris and Heather," Ian added.

"We don't really do anything together anymore," Kelly grumbled.

"That's not true," Ian argued.

"Yes, it is. You have all your new friends, and I'm not included," Kelly said.

"They are your friends too," Ian argued.

"Not really," Kelly grumbled. "It would just be nice if you and I could sometime go out to lunch, just the two of us. Talk like we used to."

"I told you, I already ate at Pier Café today."

"Ian," Lily said from the open doorway. Both Kelly and Ian looked her way. "I think it would be nice if you accepted your sister's invitation. Sorry, but I overheard your conversation. You two are kinda loud. But I totally understand what she's saying. If my brother and sister lived closer, I'd like to spend some one-on-one time with each of them and not have to deal with their significant other—if they had one." Lily grinned. "Go get some pie, spend some quality time with your sister, and be grateful you have a sister who wants to spend time with you."

Kelly stared at Lily, her eyes wide. Finally, she muttered, "Thank you, Lily."

Ian let out a sigh and stood up. "I guess I shouldn't argue with the two most important women in my life."

"That's probably a good idea," Lily said. "Oh, and bring me home a slice of apple pie if they have any.

AFTER IAN and Kelly sat in the small booth at Pier Café, Kelly asked, "Am I really one of the most important people in your life?"

"Why do you even ask that?" Ian said.

Kelly shrugged. "It's just that I don't feel as if we are as close as we used to be."

"Naturally, things are going to change. I'm married now; you're about to get married. Lily and I have a child. You're still important to me, but we each have our own separate lives."

"I suppose." Kelly sighed. A moment later, a server came to their table and took their orders.

After the server left, Ian said, "I wanted to ask you something. About when you interviewed Ginny Thomas."

"What about it?" Kelly picked up the cup of coffee the server had poured before leaving their table.

"Did she ever mention anything about a stolen carriage from her family's livery stable that ended up in the mountains?" Ian then recounted what Walt had told him about the incident, leaving out references to Walt's former life or mention of a ghost. Ian embellished some facts, unavoidable unless he wanted to reveal to Kelly the truth about Walt.

Ian didn't believe telling his sister the truth about Walt would ever be a good idea. He wanted his sister to be happy, and she was in love with Joe Morelli. Ian understood Joe was even more a skeptic than he had been, and he feared that if he told Kelly about Walt, she could never keep that secret from the man she loved. It could destroy Kelly and Joe's relationship, because Joe would be unable to believe what Kelly told him. The secret had almost destroyed him and Lily.

"No, but it sounds interesting. I'm meeting Ginny in about an hour over at her house; I'll ask her then. Makes me want to look through those old newspapers."

"Any idea when they will be at the museum?" he asked.

"A week or so. I'm not really sure."

AFTER KELLY DROPPED her brother off at his house on Tuesday afternoon, she drove over to Ginny's. Ginny had discovered a box of vintage magazines she thought Kelly might be interested in seeing.

The two women sat in Ginny's kitchen, the magazines spread out on the table, but they were not alone. Cory sat quietly in one corner of the room, assembling cardboard file boxes Ginny had purchased.

As Kelly thumbed through one magazine, she said, "Oh, Ian wanted me to ask you about something. Are you familiar with a ghost ship that washed up at Frederickport back when the town was first founded? Sort of like the *Eva Aphrodite* did a few years back. Remember, that yacht Walt Marlow once owned?"

"I remember reading about the *Eva Aphrodite* washing up on shore," Ginny said. "It was the yacht Walt Marlow name after Eva Thorndike."

Cory looked up from what he was doing and listened to the conversation.

"But there was another one, years ago. Do you remember hearing about it?" Kelly asked.

Ginny shrugged. "I guess. I believe there's an article on it in one of the old newspapers. You can read about it when they get back from the bindery."

"There was also something about horses and a carriage taken from your family's livery stable. Someone stole them the same night the ship washed up on shore. I guess they discovered them missing the same morning they found the shipwreck."

Ginny frowned at Kelly. "How would you know about that?"

"I imagine there's an article about it in one of the old newspapers," Kelly suggested.

"Yes, but how did you read it?" Ginny asked. "I was told there aren't any copies of those editions aside from mine."

"Oh, I didn't," Kelly said. "Walt told my brother about it, and they were curious if you knew anything about the story. Maybe something passed down in your family. But I'm sure they'll be excited to read that newspaper when the museum gets them."

"I still don't understand. How did Walt hear about that story? You told me he's a relative newcomer to Frederickport."

"According to my brother, it's a story that Marie Nichols told Danielle. I guess it's something Marie's father told her."

"Marie Nichols?" Ginny frowned.

"Marie's family has been here forever. I imagine she knew your cousin. Marie passed away a few years back."

"What exactly did she tell Danielle Marlow?" Ginny asked.

"I assume just the story about a ship washing up, and the stolen carriage and horses. And something about people speculating pirates had taken a treasure off the ship and hauled it up to the mountains. They never recovered the horses, but they found the carriage in the mountains. They were curious what you might have heard about it," Kelly said.

"Not really much more than what you're telling me," Ginny said. "Why exactly are they asking about this now?"

"I asked my brother that question too. He wasn't really clear. But I got the impression they seem to think the carriage was found up in the mountains where the kidnappers took Walt. They were up there for a couple of days. I don't know exactly what happened up there that got them thinking about this. You might ask Brian Henderson if you run into him."

I really think they would be perfect for each other, Kelly thought to herself. *I wish Brian had given her a chance.*

TWENTY-ONE

Heather stood at her open closet and wondered what she should wear tonight. She had arrived home from work fifteen minutes earlier. Brian had called her that afternoon and invited her on a beach picnic. The weather reporter predicted clear skies for the August evening. Heather liked the idea of going to a remote beach where they didn't have to worry about running into someone they knew who would ask a zillion unwelcome questions. Plus, it would be a pleasant change from hanging out at home. After Brian told her he planned to pick up food from Old Salts, she offered to bring a blanket to sit on. Glancing at the clock in her bedroom, she told herself to hurry; Brian would arrive in an hour.

BRIAN HENDERSON SAT at a table at Old Salts Bakery, waiting for his order. He picked up the newspaper someone had left on the table and flipped through its pages. He started to read an article and then glanced up for a moment and noted how crowded it was tonight. *It should slow down in a few weeks when summer visitors return home*, he thought. Looking back at the article, he continued to read.

"Well, hello. Brian Henderson, right?" a woman's voice said a few minutes later. Brian looked up to find Ginny Thomas standing over the table, grinning down at him.

Brian folded his newspaper and set it on the table. "You're Kelly's friend. Right? We met at the museum."

Her grin broadened. "Yes. I'm Ginny. Are you here alone?"

"I'm just waiting for my take-out order," he explained.

"Do you mind if I join you?" she asked, sitting down before he could respond. "I ordered takeout too." She looked around the restaurant and said, "They're pretty busy tonight, aren't they?"

Brian glanced around and noted there were no empty tables. He silently chided himself for momentarily assuming she was hitting on him. She just wanted to sit down, Brian thought.

"It's always like this in August. Last rush of the summer," Brian said.

"Cory, that's my neighbor, he told me about their cinnamon rolls. They are absolutely to die for," she said.

Brian smiled. "Yes, their cinnamon rolls are famous. Is that what you're having for dinner?"

She laughed. "No, although I added a few to my order. I'm trying the pastrami. Cory told me they had pretty good sandwiches too."

Brian nodded. "They do."

"If you're planning to take your food back home, we could always eat ours here, together."

"I appreciate the offer, but actually, I'm taking the food to a friend. I imagine the friend would be a little annoyed if I ate it before I arrived," Brian said.

Ginny grinned. "Oh, I understand. I figured if you were planning to eat at home alone, anyway." She shrugged. "I'll be honest, I haven't met that many people in Frederickport yet. Kelly has been really nice, and the people at the museum. But frankly, Kelly is a little young, and the others at the museum..."

"A little old?" he finished with a chuckle.

"Yes!" She laughed. "I find local history so fascinating, but it seems all the docents are my parents' age."

"I have a friend who used to docent, and she's closer to Kelly's age."

"Really? If she's still there, I've never met her," she said. "What's her name."

Brian didn't answer immediately. Finally, he said, "Heather Donovan."

Ginny considered the name for a moment, and then her eyes

widened. "Ahh, she's the other one kidnapped with you and Walt Marlow. I read about it in the newspaper, and of course, Kelly mentioned it. I admit the article left me curious. So much it didn't say."

"Such as?" he asked.

"Well… where exactly did they take you? The newspaper didn't say specifically."

Brian told her, and she asked, "Did you discover anything interesting up there?"

Brian frowned. "I'm not sure what you mean."

She shrugged. "Were there any old cabins up there you could take refuge in? Maybe some caves? It all sounds so frightening."

"No. There were no cabins where we were. At least, none that we came across."

Someone from behind the counter called out Brian's name.

"My order's up. It's been nice talking to you," Brian said as he stood.

BRIAN PARKED in the alley behind Heather's house. Leaving the food in his car, he walked up to the back door and knocked.

A moment later Heather answered the door and said, "Hi. I'm almost ready, but I need to feed Harvey first. Come on in."

Brian followed Heather into her kitchen and asked, "Isn't your cat's name Bella?"

"I was talking about my sourdough starter," Heather said, grabbing a glass jar that had been sitting on her kitchen counter. "Almost forgot all about it. I started it on Sunday, and today's the first day I need to feed it." She unscrewed the jar's lid.

"You named your starter Harvey?" he asked.

"Yeah." She looked at Brian; the ponytail she'd fastened on the top of her head bounced. After work, she had changed into stretch denims and a long sweater blouse. It fell below her hips. "People name their starters. I decided to name mine after the ghost of Presley House. After all, if it weren't for poor Harvey, I probably wouldn't have moved to Frederickport."

"So what does Harvey eat?" Brian asked.

"Flour and water," she said.

"Sounds like a prison diet," Brian quipped. He stood in the

kitchen and watched as Heather set the jar on a small kitchen scale. After weighing it, she frowned and reached up into a cabinet and grabbed an empty jar. She set it next to the jar of sourdough starter.

"What are you doing now?" he asked.

"I'm supposed to throw out half of the starter to make room for what I need to add. But that seems so wasteful. So I'm going to just move half to another jar and then feed both of them. That way I'll have two jars of starter. Sound like a good idea?"

He shrugged.

NOT TRUSTING Brian to spread out the blanket without kicking sand on it, Heather insisted on doing it herself while he stood nearby with the food. Instead of getting annoyed, he laughed at her and laughed again when she stuck her tongue out at him.

When they finally sat down in the middle of the blanket, the sound of the surf behind them, Brian told Heather about his encounter with Ginny at Old Salts, as he pulled the food from the to-go sack.

"I need to check her out." Heather glanced up from the sandwich Brian had just handed her and smiled. "I want to see what your type is, according to Kelly."

"I suspect Kelly sees my type as someone much older," Brian said while opening a bag of potato chips.

"I'm an old soul," Heather said.

Brian grinned. "I suspect you are."

They continued to eat their sandwiches when Heather stopped eating and blurted, "Oh, I forgot to tell you, your Ginny is living with a ghost."

"She is not my Ginny, and what ghost?" Brian frowned.

Heather told Brian what Danielle had told her about their visit to Ginny's house and the ghost they had seen.

After she described the ghost, according to Danielle's depiction, Brian said, "It sounds like Caitlin Pavlovich."

"That's Ginny's cousin's daughter, right?" Heather asked.

Brian nodded. "Yes. I was on that call. It's one time I would have preferred to have that day off. She was so young, just a senior in high school. I remember her poor mother, and Cory."

"The neighbor?" Heather asked.

"Yes. Cory Jones. Bill Jones's nephew," Brian explained. "He's the one who found her. I'm not sure who was more hysterical, Cory or Caitlin's mother."

"Danielle said it was an overdose, but some suspect it was a suicide," Heather said.

"True. The final ruling was an accidental overdose, but frankly, I wondered. Considering what was in her system, I can't understand how she took that much, not expecting it would kill her. But as I recall, the coroner at the time was a friend of Caitlin's father, and I suspect he felt accidental death would be easier for her mother to handle than suicide."

Heather frowned. "Is that ethical?"

Brian shrugged. "I suppose everyone has his own idea of ethics."

"Danielle is worried about Caitlin. She wants to help her move on. But she has her hands full right now, trying to figure out this other thing. Maybe I should do it?" Heather suggested.

"You?" Brian frowned.

"Sure. According to Eva, that's one reason there are people like me and Danielle. Our purpose is to help guide spirits to the other side. Sometimes they need help. They get stuck, like this Caitlin."

"Danielle didn't do a very good job guiding Walt to the other side," Brian teased.

Heather shrugged. "That's because they had some unfulfilled destiny."

"Ahh… yeah, soul mates. We discussed this."

"I have an idea. You can take me over to Ginny's house."

"What?" Brian frowned.

"Surely you can come up with some excuse to take me over there. And when there, I can try to contact Caitlin and help her move to the other side."

"And what am I supposed to say to her when we show up?" he asked.

"We don't have to just show up. You can call ahead of time. Tell her we're coming over."

"And what am I going to tell her?" Brian asked.

"I don't know. But you can think of something."

Brian arched his brows at Heather and asked, "Don't you think that would be just a little awkward?"

Heather considered his concerns for a moment and then smiled.

"Yeah, I guess you're right. I suspect if you know Kelly is trying to hook you up with Ginny, Ginny knows it too."

"That's what I assume since Kelly mentioned she told Ginny about me," Brian said.

Heather let out a sigh. "Okay, I'll figure out something else."

"No, you forget about Caitlin's ghost. I'm sure Danielle and Walt will figure something out without dragging you over there."

"You aren't the boss of me." Heather smirked.

Brian studied Heather, noting her defiant and stubborn expression. After a moment he said, "I have a feeling no one is the boss of you."

Heather's smirk turned into a grin. "You know, there is an upside to that."

"How so?" Brian asked.

"I don't want to be the boss of you, either." Heather smiled confidently. "So you can be you, and I can be me."

"You were a little bossy over that beach towel," he teased.

TWENTY-TWO

"I've been thinking about when we have a baby," Danielle announced while she refilled Walt's cup with coffee on Wednesday morning. He sat at the kitchen table while Danielle stood over him.

Walt smiled up at Danielle, silently noting how attractive she looked in the sundress, with her hair pulled back in a fishtail braid. "Do you have something to tell me?"

She refilled her cup that sat across the table from Walt's. "Not yet. But it's only a matter of time considering how committed you are to this project."

Walt chuckled and asked, "So what were you thinking about?"

Danielle walked over to the counter, set the coffeepot down, and then returned to the table and sat across from Walt.

"We should move into my old bedroom," Danielle told him.

"You mean my old bedroom?" Walt teased.

"Yeah, it was your bedroom before it was mine. It should be ours now."

"Why?" he asked.

"I don't like the idea of being on a different floor from the baby. Even if we keep the bassinet in our bedroom for a while, that's only temporary. We should turn the attic room into your office. You use it as an office anyway."

Walt considered Danielle's suggestion and then nodded. "I like your idea."

"Unless you'd rather use another room as your office and turn the attic room into a guest suite," Danielle said.

Walt shook his head. "As it is, I never felt that comfortable with the hidden staircase from the attic bedroom to the original master when it was a guest room. This is better, and convenient, if I want to work at night."

"Great, then that's what we'll do." Danielle grinned.

A knock came at the kitchen door, and the next moment Heather peeked her head in before anyone yelled for her to come in.

"Have any coffee?" Heather asked.

"Morning, Heather," Walt and Danielle chimed.

Danielle added, "Coffee's on the counter."

"Thank you. I ran out and forgot to pick some up." Heather walked to the counter. "But that's not why I came over. Well, it's one reason I came over, just not the only one." She opened an overhead cabinet and removed a coffee mug. After filling it with coffee, she took it to the kitchen table and sat down.

"What do you need?" Danielle asked.

"First thing, do you have any empty jars?" Heather asked.

Danielle frowned. "Um, what kind of empty jars?"

Heather shrugged. "Like old peanut butter jars, mayonnaise jars, whatever."

"I usually keep a few on the top shelf of the pantry. Help your-self," Danielle said.

"Thanks." Heather took a drink of her coffee.

"What do you need jars for?" Walt asked.

"Someplace to store my sourdough starter. I used the two jars I already had, but I'm going to need some more," Heather said.

"Ahh, so you're going to try baking sourdough bread? I'll be curious to see how it turns out," Danielle said.

"I'm just in the starter stage," Heather said.

"Starter stage?" Walt asked.

"I'm making the starter. Lily says it takes about a week before it comes alive," Heather said.

"Comes alive?" Walt frowned. "Are you Dr. Frankenstein?"

"I guess. Something like that. Lily says it'll get all bubbly and double in size. When it does that, it's ready to bake with. But I have a few days before I get there," Heather said.

131

"Good luck, and I want to see your first loaf," Danielle said.

"You don't want to taste it?" Heather asked.

"Let me see it first."

"I guess I don't blame you," Heather said with a shrug. "The other thing I wanted to talk to you about, Caitlin's ghost."

"What about her?" Danielle asked.

Heather recounted her conversation with Brian about the ghost haunting Ginny's house.

"And you want to help her move on?" Danielle asked.

"I figure you and Walt are so busy dealing with the mountain man, you really don't have the time. I asked Brian to take me over to her house, but it made him uncomfortable, so I won't push him. But I realized, I can do it without his help. All I have to do is go to the museum, start up a conversation with the new docent—after all, I used to docent—and then find some excuse to get her to take me to her house."

"You could show an interest in vintage magazines. She has quite a collection," Danielle suggested.

"So you think it would be alright if I did this?" Heather asked.

"Sure. It's a great idea," Danielle said. "Someone has to help that poor girl move on. And like Marie mentioned, her mother was looking forward to seeing her when she passed over. How sad to think she wasn't there."

"Kinda like Walt's folks," Heather said.

"They died before me," Walt reminded her.

"Yeah, but I bet they didn't expect you to stick around this long," Heather said.

"I have things to do," Walt said stubbornly.

"Hey, I'm glad you stuck around," Heather added.

"When do you plan to see Caitlin?" Danielle asked.

Heather glanced at the kitchen clock. "Well, I need to get to work. Not sure what days she docents. I should probably find out her schedule first. I'll call down to the museum at lunch today and take it from there."

"I'll be curious to find out how it works out," Danielle said.

"What are you doing with your ghost problem?" Heather asked. "Still going to Astoria today?"

"Yes. We're starting at the cemetery," Walt said. "Yesterday, Danielle discovered Teddy's second wife died just months after their marriage."

Heather cringed. "He sounds like the male version of the black widow. How did she die?"

"The obituary didn't say, but it listed the cemetery. We figure we'd start there. It's always possible there's some gossipy ghost who hasn't moved on, yet knows all the scandals of those interned," Danielle said.

BECAUSE OF THE OVERCAST WEATHER, they took Danielle's Ford Flex to Astoria instead of Walt's Packard. Walt drove, something he did when they were together. Danielle didn't miss driving and rather enjoyed having her own chauffeur. Walt, being a man born in the late 1800s, never felt completely comfortable with a woman behind the wheel. He wasn't proud of this and intellectually understood there was no merit to his feelings, but he chose not to share it with Danielle and was grateful she seemed to prefer him behind the wheel. Had driving been important to her, he told himself he would deal with his irrational discomfort, but he was grateful he didn't have to deal with that emotion now.

Danielle sat in the passenger seat, looking at her smartphone, using it to find the location of the cemetery mentioned in Josephine Newsome's obituary. Walt drove right to it, with Danielle's help, and parked out front.

When he turned off the ignition, he looked toward the cemetery and asked, "Did that obituary say where her grave is located?"

"No." Danielle unfastened her seatbelt.

Minutes later Danielle and Walt wandered through the cemetery, looking for Josephine's grave.

"There was a time this was the last place I'd want to be," Danielle said, taking in her surroundings.

"Yes, I remember. What happened?" Walt asked.

Danielle shrugged. "Since moving to Frederickport, meeting you, I've become more comfortable with my gift and with encountering spirits."

"I wonder if we'll find a spirit today who can help us."

"We should probably go to the office, see if it's open. I assume there's an office here," Danielle said as she walked alongside Walt.

"Why?" he asked with a frown.

"They might tell us where the grave is located. I imagine there's some sort of directory to help us find it."

"We don't need to do that. We'll find it," Walt insisted.

Danielle stopped walking and laughed.

Walt stopped, turned, looked at his wife and asked, "What is funny?"

"That is such a guy thing, not wanting to ask for directions," she teased.

"That's rather a sexist thing to say," Walt said indignantly.

"Sexist? That coming from the guy who has to do all the driving?" Danielle snickered.

"I do all the driving because you don't like to," Walt insisted.

"So you are just being a nice guy?" Danielle asked.

"I'm not a nice guy?"

Danielle gave Walt a grin, stepped closer to him, and then reached up and gave him a quick kiss. "You are an amazing guy. But I suspect my driving makes you nervous. And I'm pretty sure it's because I'm a woman."

Walt stared into Danielle's eyes a few moments and then asked, "You knew?"

Danielle shrugged. "I was pretty certain. No one likes to drive as much as you say you do. Well, maybe some do, but I just don't get it. And you seem pretty comfortable when Ian drives. You haven't driven with me enough to know if I'm a crappy driver or not. So I have to assume it's because I'm a woman."

"Are you annoyed at me?" Walt asked.

"Don't be silly. After all, I'm not without sin," she chirped, taking his hand and leading him down the path.

"How so?" Walt asked.

"I've exploited your sexism for my own selfish purpose." She snickered. "I have my own chauffeur!"

Walt tightened his hold on Danielle's hand and pulled her closer as they continued to walk through the cemetery. Several minutes later they encountered a cemetery groundskeeper. Danielle asked him which part of the cemetery they might find graves from the early 1900s. He pointed out the direction; they thanked him and walked that way.

"Aside from the groundskeeper, I haven't seen anyone," Walt whispered as they read the headstones.

"I assume you're referring to someone from the spirit realm," Danielle said.

"I thought that's why we came. Not sure how finding her grave is going to help us much. Isn't the point to find a spirit who might have been around during her burial, who knows something? But it looks rather dead around here."

Danielle giggled.

Walt rolled his eyes. "You know what I mean."

Still walking with Walt, Danielle glanced to the right and then froze. Her abrupt stop brought Walt to a halt. "Bingo. I found one."

Walt looked over to where Danielle stared. At first glance, one might mistake the spirit for a living woman. What gave her away, she stood in the middle of an upright headstone, her upper body protruding from its top while her feet stuck out of its face.

"Shall we go introduce ourselves?" Walt asked in a whisper.

"I hope she doesn't disappear on us," Danielle whispered back.

Plastering a smile on her face, Danielle took a deep breath and, with Walt, turned to the ghost staring at them and began walking in her direction.

"Hello, please don't disappear," Danielle called out.

The ghost frowned and glanced around for a moment and then looked back to Walt and Danielle. "Surely you aren't talking to me?"

"Yes, I am. I have a question I need to ask you," Danielle said cheerfully.

"You can see me?" The spirit frowned.

"Yes, we both can."

"Interesting," the ghost muttered. "I don't think you're ghosts. You arrived in a car. I never saw a ghost arrive in a car before. Only in a hearse."

"No, we're not ghosts," Danielle said, now standing about six feet from the spirit. She would have walked closer but didn't want to walk on the grave.

"I've met a few like you before," the ghost said.

"My name is Danielle, and this is my husband, Walt." Danielle felt it best not to share her last name, for fear the ghost might recognize Walt's full name, and it would just confuse matters.

"We're looking for the grave of Josephine Piller Newsome," Walt explained. "Would you know where it is?"

"Josephine? Why in the world would you want to talk to her?" the ghost asked.

"She's here?" Danielle asked.

"I assumed you already knew that since you asked where her grave was," the ghost said.

"Yes, but we were looking for her grave. Are you saying her ghost is here?" Danielle asked.

"Yes, and I wish it weren't!" the ghost ranted.

TWENTY-THREE

"You are..." Danielle began, glancing at the inscription on the headstone; she read off the name.

"Oh, this isn't mine," the ghost scoffed, stepping out of the headstone and onto the grave, fully revealing herself.

If the apparition's appearance reflected her body when last alive, Danielle guessed the woman had been in her thirties when she had died. Considering her style of clothing, the death had occurred in the 1960s. She wore a hot pink miniskirt paired with an orange and pink blouse. Her short pixy haircut sported an orange beanie sitting at a cocky angle. Taller than Danielle by a good three inches, Danielle briefly wondered if the woman had died of starvation considering skinny might be a more accurate description than thin. Yet Danielle determined that wasn't likely considering the fitted clothes.

"Although, I rather wish it were mine," the ghost said, glancing back briefly at the headstone. "That cheapskate husband of mine picked out one of those boring flat things. I guess it makes it easier to mow."

"Can I ask who you are?" Danielle inquired. "Your name?"

"Darcy Browning," the ghost said with a grin. "I can't believe you can actually see and hear me!"

"Nice to meet you, Darcy. You said Josephine was here, not just her grave. Her ghost?" Danielle asked.

"Oh, she's been here forever," Darcy explained. "I can't imagine why you're looking for her."

"Can you tell us where we might find her, please?" Danielle asked.

Darcy pointed in the same direction the groundskeeper had pointed earlier, the same direction Walt and Danielle had been walking before they saw Darcy. "You'll find her over there, under some big trees, next to her grave. Unless she's in one of her snits and doesn't want to talk to anyone, then I'm not sure where she goes. When not pouting, she stays by her grave most of the time, waiting for someone to visit. Of course, no one ever does. But if you are planning to visit her, I imagine you'll make her day."

"Thank you," Walt and Danielle chorused.

"She's so annoying and has been here forever. Long before I ever arrived."

"Do you know why she's here?" Danielle asked.

"Of course I do. She won't stop blabbering about it. That's why I avoid her side of the cemetery," Darcy said. "She's being punished."

"Punished?" Danielle asked, remembering Angela.

Darcy nodded vigorously. "She doesn't feel it's fair, of course, since her husband shoved her down the stairs, and it was all his fault, or so she claims."

Danielle frowned. "What was his fault?"

"That whole thing with his first wife."

Walt and Danielle exchanged quick glances before Danielle asked, "What about his first wife?"

"She claims she knew nothing about it. But she lied for him, told everyone he had been in Astoria that day. She was just happy to get rid of the wife so they could get married. Of course, once married, I guess he decided it wasn't such a bargain. Frankly, had I been married to Josephine, I would probably have shoved her down some stairs too. Maybe she's right, and he didn't mean to kill her. They were in an argument, I guess they did that a lot, when it got a little heated, and he gave her a shove to shut her up."

"Her husband killed her?" Walt asked.

"According to her, he didn't mean to do it because he cried like a baby when he realized she was dead. I thought, I bet he cried like a baby because he figured he wasn't going to get away with bumping off wife number two like he had his first wife," Darcy said.

"He murdered his first wife?" Danielle asked.

Darcy frowned at Danielle. "Didn't I just say that?"

"What do you know about the first wife's murder?" Walt asked.

Darcy shrugged. "Nothing, really."

"Do you know what happened to Josephine's husband?" Walt asked.

"No clue. According to Josephine, she hasn't seen him since she followed her body back to the morgue and then ended up here. Which makes me think he missed her funeral. But you'll have to ask her about that."

"Um, can I ask… why are you here? You obviously know you're dead," Danielle said.

Darcy laughed. "Of course I'm dead. You'd have to be dead to hang out at a cemetery as much as I do."

"Don't you want to move on?" Walt asked.

"Not especially. And it's not because I'm being punished like Josephine, if that's what you're wondering."

"Then why?" Walt asked.

"It's because of that cheapskate husband of mine. He certainly didn't seem like a cheapskate before I married him, with all his money and how he loved to spend it on me. But once we walked down the aisle, he goes tighter than Fort Knox. But then he had to up and die just as I was just getting ready to move on. My death came as a surprise; that's why I stuck around so long, getting used to the idea. I never saw that truck coming."

"A truck hit you?" Danielle asked.

"And in a crosswalk too!" Darcy shook her head in disgust.

"Well, you look pretty good for being hit by a truck," Danielle noted.

"I didn't always," Darcy said. The next moment her vision morphed into a bloodier version of her former self, this one of her body after being hit by a truck. It remained that way for just a few moments before changing back. "It took me a while to figure out how to put myself back together again."

"You said your husband showed up. Is he here now?" Danielle asked, glancing around.

"No way! If he were, I certainly wouldn't be. But the moment he saw me at his funeral, he gets all sentimental and assumes I stuck around for him. I told him to go first, and when he did, I stayed."

"You didn't want to spend eternity with your husband?" Walt

asked.

Darcy turned her attention to Walt, looking him up and down. "Maybe if he had looked like you. But I didn't marry someone old enough to be my grandpa because I wanted to spend eternity with him. He was supposed to go first, not me."

"If you don't want to spend eternity with your husband, you don't have to," Danielle said.

Hand on hip, Darcy glared at Danielle. "You know that for sure?"

"Well... no... but..." Danielle stammered.

"Not this ghost. I'm giving him time to forget about me before I move on. I figure a century or two should do it." The next moment Darcy vanished.

Danielle looked at Walt and said, "She was charming. And I think she liked you."

"What she said about Josephine lying for Teddy has me wondering," Walt began.

"Was Teddy being unfaithful with Josephine while Maddie was still alive, or did Josephine have a thing for her boss, which was why she lied for him, and then she ended up with the object of her affection?" Danielle suggested.

"Which didn't turn out for her. But yes, that was what I was wondering," Walt said.

"Let's go find Josephine and see what she says."

Together Walt and Danielle walked toward the trees Darcy had pointed to. Before they reached the spot, they spied a woman standing under the branches, her pale blue gingham skirt fluttering around her bare ankles, with her white-blond hair falling in soft curls around the shoulders of her fitted blouse.

Danielle was fairly certain they weren't looking at a living woman. It wasn't just the fact the woman stood barefoot in the cemetery, but her head appeared to be sitting lopsided on her neck.

"Is that Josephine?" Walt whispered when they both came to a stop.

"If so, my guess, she broke her neck in the fall," Danielle whispered back. "And she hasn't figured out how to put herself back together again." They resumed walking toward the apparition.

"You can see me," the woman said when Walt and Danielle were about ten feet from her.

"Are you Josephine Newsome?" Danielle asked.

The ghost ignored Danielle's question and stared at Walt. "You're Alex Marlow, aren't you? You're a ghost, too. I thought you were alive for a minute there. But you can't be alive. I know you're dead," the ghost said.

"He's not Alex Marlow; he's a distant relative," Danielle explained. "And he's not a ghost, neither am I. We're very much alive."

The spirit turned her attention from Walt to Danielle "Is that what I am, a ghost?"

"What do you think?" Danielle asked.

The ghost shrugged. "A spirit."

Danielle flashed Walt a look and mumbled under her breath, "Another one like you."

Ignoring Danielle's comment, Walt looked at the ghost and asked, "Are you Josephine Newsome?"

The ghost shrugged and said, "Yes. I was hoping you were Alex Marlow, thinking they had sent you to tell me it was okay for me to move on now, and I didn't have to go to that other place. It wasn't my fault, you know. I didn't know he was going to do it."

"Do what?" Danielle asked.

Josephine looked at Danielle. "He told me he had to do it. Alex was going to ruin everything."

"Teddy killed them, didn't he?" Walt asked.

She looked at Walt and smiled softly. "He didn't want to. Bud told Ted what Alex intended to do, and Ted went right to Marlow House to confront Alex. He figured he could talk him out of it. But Alex wasn't there, and by the time Ted got home, Alex had already told Maddie, and she had agreed to go back to Marlow House with him and Anna. Maddie was going to leave her husband and live with the Marlows. They really should not have interfered with a husband and wife."

"Why did Teddy have to kill them?" Walt asked. "If you were seeing him then, why didn't he just let Maddie go back to Marlow House?"

She stared at Walt a moment and then said, "You don't understand. No one understands!" The next moment she vanished.

Walt and Danielle had more questions, so they waited around Josephine's grave, hoping she would return. But after a few hours, they realized the spirit of Josephine Newsome did not want to talk to them anymore.

"She's avoiding us," Walt said.

"Yeah, I get that feeling too. But we've learned a lot. Let's go home. I'm hungry. And I don't want to hang around here until dark. Now that we know where she is, we can always ask Marie or Eva to come talk to her. They can get here quicker than we can."

"Agreed," Walt said, taking Danielle's hand as they headed toward the parking lot.

Once back on the highway and comfortable in the passenger seat, Danielle asked Walt, who had been relatively quiet since Josephine's abrupt departure, "Are you okay?"

Hands firmly on the steering wheel, his eyes down the highway, Walt said, "What did my father tell Maddie to get her to leave Teddy? Was it about his infidelity? Assuming he and Josephine got together when Maddie was still alive. If so, I just don't understand why he felt he had to kill them. Why? It makes little sense. They were friends for years."

"Money can do that to people. You told me Maddie brought significant money into the marriage."

"Yes, money that would have stayed with Teddy," Walt said.

"What do you mean?" Danielle asked.

"You forget how different laws were back then. Even if my parents took Maddie to Marlow House to live, Maddie still couldn't touch the money she brought into the marriage, at least not without Teddy's approval."

"Couldn't she have sued him?" Danielle asked.

"Danielle, most men back then would not have a problem with Teddy having a girlfriend, considering his wife was bedridden. And knowing how sickly Maddie was, I find it hard to imagine she would consider suing him for divorce. There has to be more to this."

Danielle did not respond. Instead, she considered Bud's spirit and how he had insisted Alex had killed him. But then another thought popped into her head. Abruptly she turned in the seat to Walt and said, "Wait a minute. She said Bud told Teddy something, which was why Teddy wanted to confront your father. Was that right before Teddy went to find your father, when you saw him at Marlow House? Before he went to his house, before the fire? If so, that means that Bud was still alive when your father died."

"Which means my father had nothing to do with Bud's death," Walt said.

TWENTY-FOUR

W hile Walt and Danielle visited the cemetery in Astoria, Heather sat at work, thinking about Caitlin's lingering spirit and how the girl's mother had moved on to the next realm, expecting to find her daughter waiting for her. Heather understood some spirits, like Marie and Eva, chose to stick around. But Caitlin, a spirit of a teenager who had died tragically, still haunting her family home, worried Heather. She wanted to help the girl come to terms with her reality and move on in her journey.

When lunch hour rolled around, instead of getting something to eat, Heather drove to the museum to see if the new docent was on duty. She decided her visit would not appear spontaneous if she called first, inquiring about docents.

To Heather's delight, the docent who greeted her when she walked into the museum was an unfamiliar face, and one who appeared to be the right gender and age of Ginny Thomas. A quick glance at the docent's name tag confirmed her suspicion.

So this is who Kelly thinks would be perfect for Brian, Heather thought. *I don't see it.* Ginny, unaware of Heather's scrutiny, explained the museum's admission price and the benefit of membership to the Frederickport Historical Society.

"I'm already a member of the historical society," Heather said, interrupting Ginny in the middle of her spiel. One perk of membership of the historical society was free admission to the museum. "My name's Heather Donovan."

"The Heather Donovan?" Ginny asked.

"No one ever called me a *the* before," Heather muttered.

Ginny grinned. "I meant the one I read about in the paper last week."

Heather let out a sigh. "Yes, that one."

"I'm so happy to hear you all made it safely home," Ginny said.

"Me too."

"My name's Ginny Thomas," Ginny said, pointing to her name tag. "I'm a new docent at the museum. I heard you used to be a docent here."

"Yes, I did."

"You don't docent anymore?" Ginny asked.

Heather shrugged. "I don't have as much time as I used to, with my job and all."

Ginny nodded. "I understand. I'm retired, so I have lots of free time."

You look awful young to be retired, Heather thought. But then she remembered the woman was a widow and assumed the husband must have left his wife with enough money so she didn't have to work.

"I met your fellow—not sure what to call them—captives? Walt Marlow and Brian Henderson."

"You can just call them my friends," Heather suggested.

"Such a harrowing experience!" Ginny gushed. "What brings you to the museum today?"

"Um… I was wondering if the museum had a collection of vintage magazines. I heard they've gotten some new things in."

"No, but I have a collection at my house you are more than welcome to look through. They belonged to my cousin. She was a bit of a hoarder, I'm afraid."

"I heard about the collection of newspapers you donated to the museum. I'm eager to see them, but I understand they aren't here yet," Heather said.

"No, they're being bound. But I heard this morning they might be back in a day or so. Originally I heard it would be another week or more."

"Great. So about those magazines of yours, would you mind if I stopped by your house sometime and looked at them?" Heather asked.

"You're more than welcome to see them." Ginny glanced at her watch and then looked back at Heather. "In fact, I'm getting off in ten minutes. You could come to my house now if you want."

"Thanks for the offer, but I have to go back to work," Heather said glumly.

"When do you get off work?" Ginny asked.

"Five."

"Stop by then. I'll be home. Please do," Ginny insisted.

"LET ME GO WITH YOU," Chris offered after Heather returned to the office and told him what she intended to do.

"Why?" she asked.

"You've never helped a spirit move on before," Chris reminded her.

"Are you saying I can't do it?"

"No, but—"

"I can do this. Anyway, I can't just show up with you. And considering Caitlin's age, she might refuse to move on when she sees you, and instead of her haunting her old house, she'd be haunting my office, mooning over you. That would be so annoying."

"Don't be ridiculous," Chris scoffed.

"You aren't coming," Heather said before turning her attention back to the paperwork on her desk. Heather remained steadfast, and when she left work on Wednesday for Ginny's, she didn't take Chris with her, yet she talked him into dropping Bella off at her house on his way home.

When Heather arrived at Ginny's house, she was shown to the study. Bookshelves lined one wall, with a desk under the window on another wall, its blinds drawn. In the center of the room stood a card table, and on it, stacks of vintage magazines. The overhead ceiling fan along with a floor lamp provided ample lighting for the card table.

Ginny showed Heather to the stacks of vintage magazines. Heather sat on one of the two folding chairs at the card table, while Ginny sat across from her. Heather wasn't sure how this was going to play out. Would Caitlin's ghost simply show up, and if she did, how could she talk to her with Ginny in the room? Or would Heather need to make an excuse to look through the house in search of Caitlin?

While trying to work out the logistics in her head, Heather found herself distracted by Ginny, who prattled on, peppering Heather with questions about her recent abduction. Yet, by the questions, Ginny didn't seem that interested in the kidnappers or why or how Heather and the others had been taken captive. Ginny seemed intrigued about the mountains where they had been taken, and more interested in what they might have seen or discovered while up there.

"She knows you were there. Did you find it?" a woman's voice asked.

Startled by the unexpected sound, Heather looked in the voice's direction and saw Caitlin's spirit standing in front of the bookshelves. Heather stared at Caitlin a moment while Ginny, unaware of the ghost's presence, asked Heather another question.

"Ginny, could you get me a drink of water, please?" Heather blurted, her eyes never leaving Caitlin's.

"Yes, of course. I have to run to the bathroom too, so I'll be a few minutes." Ginny stood.

That would be perfect, Heather said to herself. She wanted Ginny out of the way so she could talk to Caitlin.

After Ginny left the room and was out of earshot, Heather asked, "You're Caitlin, aren't you?"

"Who are you?" Caitlin demanded. "I heard what she said. You were up there, weren't you? Did you find it? It's not yours. It's mine!"

Heather stood up, her gaze never leaving the ghost. "Did I find what?"

"I heard her talking to Cory about you coming over here. By their conversation, it's obvious you found something up in the mountains."

"Are you talking about Bud's treasure?" Heather asked.

Caitlin smiled. "So, you know. Did you find it?"

"No. Tell me about the treasure," Heather asked.

Caitlin laughed. "I'm not stupid. You're trying to find it for yourself. But you can't have it!"

The next moment the bookshelves shook while Caitlin's apparition slowly floated up toward the ceiling. Mesmerized by the sight,

Heather stood and stared, yet let out a scream a moment later and jumped to one side when one of the two bookshelves came crashing down, landing full force on the card table, sending it and the vintage magazines to the floor.

Now flat against one corner of the room, the fallen bookshelf blocking her way to the door, Heather felt her heart pounding in her chest as she looked warily at the remaining bookshelf still standing.

"What happened?" Ginny yelled from the doorway.

Instead of answering, Heather looked back to Caitlin still hovering by the last standing bookshelf. In the next moment, Caitlin vanished.

"BRIAN, Heather Donovan is here to see you," Joe announced when he walked into the break room.

Brian, who sat at the table, looked up from the coffee and frowned. "Heather's here?"

"She's up front. Said it was important, that you were the only one she wanted to talk to. I have to admit, I am curious."

Brian stood up and left his coffee sitting on the table. Leaving Joe in the break room, he stepped out to the hall and headed for the front lobby. When he got there, he found Heather, visibly shaken, pacing by the front desk.

"Heather? What's wrong?" Brian asked.

Heather resisted the temptation to jump into Brian's arms and instead glanced over his right shoulder and spied Joe walking down the hall in their direction.

"I need to talk to you, alone," Heather whispered.

With a nod, Brian took Heather by the arm and led her down the hallway, past Joe, and back to the break room. When they entered, he shut the door and locked it. The next moment Heather flew into his arms.

"I almost got killed by a freaking ghost!" Heather blurted, holding tightly to Brian.

"You what?" Brian asked, pulling away from Heather and placing his hands on her shoulders. He looked into her eyes.

"Caitlin. That crazy ghost tried to kill me with a bookshelf!"

Brian eased Heather into a chair at the table and urged her to calm down. He brought her a glass of water, and after a moment she took a deep breath and recounted what had happened to her since meeting Ginny at the museum.

"I almost went to Chris's house. I needed to tell someone. But I figured he would just say he told me so. He wanted to go with me. And I don't think Walt and Danielle are home yet."

"So I wasn't your first choice?" Brian gently teased. He now sat in a chair next to her, holding one of her hands.

Heather shrugged. "You were my first non-medium choice."

Brian smiled.

"But dang, does this mean I'm not an innocent? I thought I was a good person," Heather grumbled.

"What are you talking about?" Brian asked.

"Eva always said a ghost couldn't hurt an innocent."

"If you think about it, you didn't get hurt. Shaken up, but not hurt."

"Yeah, but only because I jumped out of the way at the last minute. I sprained my ankle." She looked down at her right ankle, stretched out her leg, and then turned her foot from side to side.

"You didn't sprain your ankle. You walked back here from the front without a problem," Brian reminded her.

"I was running on adrenaline," Heather argued.

Brian leaned forward and kissed Heather's nose.

"Joe might walk in," Heather noted.

"I locked the door."

"Oh." Heather leaned toward Brian and dropped a kiss on his mouth.

"You know, we can't stay in here and make out," Brian said.

"Why not?"

Brian grinned and then asked, "What did Ginny say when she saw the bookshelf on the floor?"

Heather leaned back in the chair, Brian no longer holding her hand. "She freaked, tried to figure out what had happened. At first, I'm sure she thought I had somehow done it, but I told her I saw it shaking, so I stood up and then jumped back just in time."

"So you lied?"

Heather shrugged. "What else was I going to do?"

"You should not go back there."

"I agree with you."

TWENTY-FIVE

W hen Brian unlocked and opened the break room door, he came face-to-face with Joe, who stood in the hallway as if ready to open the door.

"Thanks for your help, Brian," Heather said as she marched into the hall, giving Joe a perfunctory nod and a curt, "Goodbye, Joe."

Joe watched Heather walk down the hallway while Brian picked up his now cold cup of coffee from the table and carried it to the sink.

"What was that about?" Joe asked, walking into the room. "And why was the door closed?"

"Obviously we wanted some privacy," Brian said, rinsing out his cup.

"What's going on with you two?" Joe asked.

"I told you, we're friends. She had a problem and needed someone to talk to." Brian refilled his now rinsed cup.

"You mean like a bookshelf almost falling on her?" Joe asked.

Brian frowned to Joe. "How do you know about that?"

"I just talked to Kelly on the phone. Ginny called her all upset, said Heather was over at her house, and the bookshelf in her study fell over and could have killed someone. She said Heather claimed it fell over on its own. But Ginny doesn't see how that is possible."

"It could have been a minor earthquake," Brian suggested.

"We didn't have an earthquake," Joe said.

"I don't always feel earthquakes, but it doesn't mean there wasn't one nearby."

"Kelly checked after talking with Ginny. There were no reported earthquakes in the area."

"What does she think happened?" Brian asked.

"That Heather tried to move it for some reason. Why was Heather over there in the first place?" Joe asked.

"Ginny had invited her over to look at her vintage magazine collection."

"Which was destroyed when the bookshelf fell. She's sick about it," Joe said.

"Heather didn't say anything about the magazines being destroyed," Brian said.

"Probably because she raced out of there after the bookshelf fell over. I guess Heather had asked her for a drink of water, and when Ginny left to get it for her, the bookshelf fell. She's pretty upset."

"Yeah, well, Heather was upset too. Imagine minding your own business, reading some magazines, and you almost get killed when a bookshelf falls over. Ginny's just covering her butt since Heather hurt her ankle. She's probably afraid Heather might sue."

"Heather hurt her ankle?"

Brian shrugged. "She thought she sprained it, but I'm sure it's okay. But still, Ginny didn't know that."

"When did Heather get interested in vintage magazines?" Joe asked.

"Heather's interested in lots of different things."

WALKING to her car in the police station parking lot, Heather debated going straight home or stopping over at Chris's house. Now that she had calmed down after almost being squished under a bookshelf, she felt she could discuss the matter with Chris. Or perhaps she would see if Walt and Danielle had gotten home yet. At least with them, she could mention speaking to Brian about the incident. While Chris understood Brian knew about ghosts, she didn't feel he would understand her relationship with Brian. As she reached her car, she asked herself, *What is my relationship with Brian?*

While trying to answer the question, she dug around in her purse, looking for her car keys. Just as she found them, a voice said, "You could have been killed."

Heather turned to the voice and looked into the gray eyes of a scraggly-looking young man wearing worn jeans and a faded blue T-shirt.

"Excuse me?" Heather asked.

"If you found what I think you did in the mountains, it belongs to Caitlin," he said.

"You know about Caitlin?" Heather asked.

"I know she wouldn't be happy with you snooping around. Looking into things that are none of your business. Whatever you found, you can't have it. It's not right," he said. "It doesn't belong to you."

"Who are you?" Heather asked.

"I'm a friend who doesn't want to see anyone hurt." He turned and hurried away.

Heather watched him leave and noted the car he got into before he drove away. Shaken, she unlocked her car door, got into the vehicle, and locked the door. After shoving the key in the ignition, she pulled out her cellphone and dialed Brian.

"That was quick," Brian said when he answered the call. "You're not home yet, are you?"

"No. I'm still in the parking lot. I just had the strangest encounter." She told him about the young man who had approached her, describing him and his vehicle.

"That sounds like Cory Jones," Brian said.

"Why does that name sound familiar?" Heather asked.

"We were talking about him the other night. He lives next door to Ginny and was friends with Caitlin. Cory's the one who found the body."

"The way he talks, I wonder if he's like me," Heather asked.

"He is a little odd," Brian said.

"I didn't mean like me in that way," she said with a snort.

HEATHER WENT straight home from the police station and fed Bella. She called Danielle to see if she and Walt were back from Astoria.

"I was getting ready to call you and see if you were okay," Danielle said.

"What do you mean?" Heather asked.

"I just got off the phone with Lily, who said Kelly told Ian you were at Ginny Thomas's house, and a bookshelf about fell on you. You didn't do anything to the bookshelf, did you?"

"No. But Caitlin did," Heather said.

"Why don't you come over. Chris is here now, he worried about you going to Ginny's, and then I told him what Lily told me. Lily and Ian are on their way over here. We're ordering pizza."

"I'll be right there," Heather said.

THE BEACH DRIVE MEDIUMS, along with Lily and Ian, sat around the dining room table at Marlow House while Connor played on the floor nearby with Sadie. By the time the pizza arrived, Walt, Danielle, and Heather had each told the others about their recent ghostly encounters.

"That does not make me feel terrific about Caitlin almost killing Heather," Lily said.

"Thanks, I think," Heather grumbled.

Lily looked to Heather and said, "It's just that Eva is always telling us ghosts can't hurt innocents."

"We were talking about Heather, not an innocent," Chris teased.

"Oh, shut up," Heather snapped. "Anyway, like Brian said, she didn't hurt me, she just shook me up."

Chris and the others looked at Heather. Chris arched his brow. "Brian? When did you tell Brian about this?"

Heather shrugged. She figured bigmouth Joe would tell Kelly, who would tell Ian. "I sorta stopped by the police station after it happened. Like I said, I was shook up, and I needed someone to talk to, and the police station was close by."

"Brian?" Chris snickered.

"Anyway, when I was there, I had a strange encounter with someone named Cory Jones." Heather told them what Cory had said.

"That's weird. Is Cory a medium?" Danielle asked.

"Sounded like it," Heather said.

"What I'm wondering, is it safe for Ginny to be in the house with Caitlin?" Ian asked. "I sure don't like the idea of my sister going over there."

"Why, isn't Kelly an innocent?" Heather snarked.

Lily giggled, and Ian gave his wife a harsh look.

"Oh, come on, Ian, you have to admit that was funny," Lily teased.

"I don't call someone almost getting killed by a bookshelf funny," Ian said.

"Actually, that part wasn't too funny. Scared the crap out of me," Heather said.

"I wish Marie or Eva would show up," Danielle said. "Where are they?"

"One problem with ghosts, they lose track of time," Chris reminded her.

"Eva or Marie need to handle Caitlin. It doesn't sound like she's aware she's dead, and while I'm fairly certain the universe won't let her antics hurt Ginny, she can still do a lot of damage," Danielle said.

"Not trying to be funny, we really don't know if Ginny is an innocent or not. But if she isn't, then I guess it's the universe's call," Heather said.

"We need Eva and Marie to handle her and help her move on," Danielle said.

"I told you not to go over there alone," Chris told Heather. She responded with an eye roll.

"I suppose Marie or Eva can also figure out if Cory is a medium," Lily said.

"Or just creepy." Heather snorted. "By the way, according to Brian, Cory is the one who found Caitlin's body. Brian was on that call. He said he couldn't figure out who was more hysterical, her mother or Cory."

"You've sure been chatty with Brian a lot," Chris noted.

Heather glared at Chris. "So?"

"I don't know about the rest of you, but I'm curious to find out what happened to this Teddy guy," Lily said. "Are you planning to talk to his second wife's ghost again?"

"It was obvious she did not want to talk to us," Walt said. "She knows more about what happened that day, but I don't imagine she'll talk to us again. Maybe Eva or Marie can get her to open up."

"While she might know more about what happened that day, I

doubt she knows what happened to Teddy. I wish those old newspapers would get to the museum. It's supposed to be another week. If Teddy was from Frederickport, there may be something in those old papers that might tell us what happened to him. I've hit a block wall in my online research," Danielle said.

"Oh, about those newspapers," Heather said. "According to what Ginny told me this afternoon, it looks like the newspapers are going to get there sooner than they first said, perhaps a day or so."

"I would assume some old police records might shed a light on what happened to Teddy," Ian suggested. "If he pushed his wife down the stairs, I would imagine they arrested him. There has to be something about it."

"I'll talk to the chief tomorrow," Danielle said. "He might know where we should look."

Connor, who had been playing on the floor with Sadie, began to fuss.

Lily stood up. "We should probably get Connor home. Time for his bath."

IAN CARRIED Connor as he and Lily walked back to their house, Sadie by their side. As they crossed the street, Lily asked, "What do you think's going on between Brian and Heather?"

Ian chuckled. "I was wondering the same thing."

"They are such an unlikely pair," Lily said. "But now that I think about it, they are a perfect match."

"Why do you say that?" Ian asked as they headed up the walk to their front door.

"Heather irritated the heck out of me when we first met. But she did save my life. And I certainly wasn't a fan of Brian when I first moved to Frederickport. So maybe they are perfect for each other."

Ian chuckled and unlocked the door. Sadie ran in first, followed by Lily and then Ian and Connor. "You're talking like they're a couple."

"I'm just saying, if they are, it sort of makes sense. Considering how I used to feel about them."

"Heather still irritates you," Ian reminded her when he shut the door behind them.

"True. But I like her now. Anyway, she's awful good with Connor, and he adores her. Kinda hard not to like someone who is good to your kid."

TWENTY-SIX

Because of Heather's harrowing encounter at Ginny's house, Chris gave her Thursday morning off and told her to sleep in. She intended to take Chris up on his offer, but Bella had other ideas. Heather woke to the weight of Bella sitting on her chest, along with the sound of purring and the tickling sensation of loose cat hair floating by her nostrils.

Begrudgingly, Heather opened her eyes and stared into Bella's face. The cat didn't look remorseful for having intruded on its human's sleep. The cat looked annoyed despite the loud purring.

"Seriously, Bella?" Heather grumbled as she nudged the cat off her body and sat up. She glanced at the clock. In fairness to the cat, it was past Bella's breakfast hour.

Thirty minutes later Heather sat in her kitchen, drinking a cup of hot tea. She still hadn't bought coffee, but since she preferred tea, the purchase didn't seem urgent. Heather glanced down at Bella, who sat by her empty breakfast bowl, grooming herself.

"Well, at least you're happy now," Heather said, taking another sip of her tea. As she sat alone at the table, Heather considered yesterday's events and how she had raced out of Ginny's house with barely a word, leaving the room in shambles and Ginny vulnerable to the lingering spirit.

"I really need to find Marie or Eva and have one of them deal with Caitlin. That girl needs to move on," Heather said aloud.

Heather didn't just feel guilty about leaving Ginny alone with an agitated spirit, she felt guilty for running out of Ginny's house with little or no explanation, leaving the study in shambles.

I need to go apologize; Heather told herself. But then she remembered Caitlin's spirit. *I'll stay outside on the front porch. Chances are, I won't run into Caitlin there, and how much damage can she do on the front porch?* Heather thought.

Another thirty minutes later, Heather was dressed and on her way to Ginny's. But as she neared the house, she began having second thoughts. When she finally reached the house, Heather took a deep breath and pulled up into the driveway and parked, not getting immediately out of the car.

Heather sat there a moment, not yet turning off the ignition, when a knock at the driver's side window made her jump. She turned to see who was there. She came face-to-face with Cory Jones. Hesitantly, she rolled down the window.

"Ginny isn't here. She's at the museum," Cory told her. "You really shouldn't be here. Caitlin wouldn't like it."

Heather was about to ask Cory if he had seen Caitlin when motion from the house caught her attention. She looked and saw the ghost standing in the window, staring at her.

"Okay, I am out of here," Heather said abruptly. Putting her car in reverse, she stepped on the gas and backed out to the street, leaving Cory standing in the driveway, watching her, while Caitlin remained in Ginny's house, staring out the window.

Heather didn't go directly to work. She had a few hours before Chris expected her to show up, and she still wanted to talk to Ginny. She decided to go to the museum to see her. It would actually be better to see Ginny on neutral territory where an unruly spirit couldn't intrude. Heather would soon discover she had miscalculated.

WITH A SPRAY BOTTLE of glass cleaner in one hand and a rag in the other, Ginny wiped down one of the glass display cases in the gift shop. It was typically slow on Thursday mornings at the museum. Visitors didn't start trickling in until around eleven. Millie would be coming in then to watch the gift shop while Ginny greeted the visitors.

As she wiped down the cabinet, her mind considered yesterday's troubling events. She still did not understand what had happened, yet the more she thought about it, the more she became convinced Heather had caused the damage, but why?

Just as she asked herself that question, the bell to the front door rang, signifying a visitor had just entered the museum. Setting the rag and bottle of window cleaner down on the counter, she left to greet the visitor but stopped in her tracks when she saw who it was, Heather Donovan.

"Hello, Ginny," Heather greeted her. "I wanted to talk to you. Heard you were here."

"What do you mean you heard I was here? Who told you that?" Ginny looked warily at Heather.

"I... I stopped by your house and your neighbor Cory told me."

"I suppose I need to have a talk with Cory about minding his own business. My vintage magazines are all ruined."

"I'm really sorry about that, but it wasn't my fault," Heather said.

"And whose fault was it?" Ginny snapped. "I doubt the book-shelf just fell over by itself. What were you doing in there?"

"I came over here to see if you were okay, but I certainly didn't expect to be blamed for your bookshelf almost killing me! I hurt my ankle!"

"So that's what this is; you come into my home, knock over my bookshelf, and then sue me for damages? I've heard about people like you!" Feeling the anger surging up, Ginny turned from Heather and marched back into the museum gift shop.

HEATHER STARTED to leave when the space between her and Ginny swirled like a gray mist. Briefly, Heather imagined Eva was making an entrance, but the next moment it was not Eva who appeared, but Caitlin. Just as recognition dawned for Heather, Caitlin picked up the donation box sitting in the doorway leading to the gift shop and hurled it in Ginny's direction. It barely missed her.

Ginny, whose back was to Heather and Caitlin, hadn't seen the donation box flying her way, yet turned abruptly when it landed a few feet from her. She stared accusingly into Heather's face.

"Oh, my gawd, you are crazy!" Ginny shrieked. Speechless,

Heather watched as Ginny looked around in a panic and then grabbed something off the counter—one of the large paperweights the museum sold.

Heather's eyes widened when Ginny looked as if she was preparing to hurl the heavy object in her direction. While Caitlin might not hurt one of them with her antics, Heather was fairly certain if Ginny hit her with that paperweight, it would do actual damage.

"Are you going to throw that at me?" Heather asked incredulously.

"If I have to! You get out of here! I'm calling the police!" Ginny yelled as she ran from the gift shop, back into the lobby, and down the main exhibit hall toward the office. To Heather's horror, Caitlin followed Ginny, snatching objects from the various exhibits and hurling them after the terrified woman.

From Ginny's perspective, Heather threw the objects at her. Heather groaned, unsure what she should do now, and regretting coming to the museum. Warily, she made her way through the exhibit area and found Caitlin camped outside the now closed office door of the museum. For whatever reason, Caitlin had not followed Ginny into the office. The spirit sat by the closed door and looked up at Heather, a smirk on her face.

Heather attempted reasoning with the spirit, yet Caitlin just stared. By the ghost's expression, Heather didn't know if the spirit was ignoring her or couldn't hear what she was saying. Heather didn't want to shout, for fear of Ginny hearing her, and the ghost was some distance away.

"What the hell," a male's voice shouted from the archway leading from the main exhibit area to the entry. Heather turned and found herself facing Brian Henderson, his right hand on his gun.

"You aren't going to shoot me, are you?" she asked dryly.

"What the hell is going on?" Brian's hand was no longer touching his holstered gun as he walked towards Heather and glanced around. It looked like a war zone with parts of the exhibits strewn across the floor leading to the office.

"I assume you're the one responding to Ginny's call?" Heather asked.

"I was just driving by when I got it. They said you were here attacking Ginny."

Heather frowned. "They told you that, and you came in here with your hand on your gun? You were going to shoot me!"

"No... but..."

"Oh, please. I should smack you, but you would shoot me," Heather scoffed.

"What happened?" Brian asked, now standing by Heather's side.

Heather turned toward Caitlin and pointed. "She happened."

"She? Who?" Brian frowned.

"Oh, stupid me went over to Ginny's to check on her, and when Cory told me where she was, well, stupid me came here. But Caitlin saw me when I stopped by Ginny's, and she followed me. And for some reason, she's throwing stuff at Ginny. But Eva is right, a ghost really can't do damage."

"Are you saying Caitlin's ghost was here?" Brian asked.

"Not was, but is. She's right there, sitting in front of the office door."

Brian glanced around. "And she threw all this stuff at Ginny?"

"Well, I sure as hell didn't throw it," Heather snapped.

"Why do you think a ghost can't hurt someone?" Brian asked.

Heather rolled her eyes. "Ginny's in the office unscathed. Just shaken up. Nothing hit her. Heck, she was so unglued she ran through the museum to the office. Had it been me, I would have run out the front door or used the phone in the gift store and dialed 911. But since Caitlin couldn't really hurt her, I suppose she was lucky."

"Maybe Caitlin has poor aim," Brian suggested.

Crossing her arms stubbornly across her chest, Heather glared briefly at Brian and then looked at Caitlin.

"Hey, Caitlin," Heather called out, speaking louder than she had when trying to talk to her earlier. "I bet you can't hit me with one of those books." She nodded at a stack of books on a nearby table.

The next moment a book flew off the table in Heather's direction. Just before it hit her, the book veered to the right and landed on the floor without hitting her or Brian.

"Holy crap!" Brian cried.

"See. I told you," Heather said.

"We have to get Caitlin out of here," Brian said. "Ginny can't stay locked in the office forever."

Heather stepped aside and gave a little wave in Caitlin's direction. "Have at it. She's all yours."

"I can't even see her," Brian snapped.

Heather shrugged. "Welcome to my world."

"No. Not welcome to your world. You can see her."

"But you know she's there," Heather reminded him.

Brian groaned, and then his phone rang. He looked at it before answering.

"Yes, I'm at the museum. No, I don't need any backup. Heather Donovan?... Have the chief call me... Yes, the chief." Brian hung up.

Heather let out a sigh. "I'm sorry about this."

"Yeah, me too," Brian grumbled.

"I'm going now," Caitlin announced. "You stay away from us; do you hear me? I know you're trying to find the treasure, but it's not yours." The next moment she vanished.

"She's gone," Heather announced.

"Are you sure?" Brian asked.

Heather shrugged. "Pretty sure."

"I suppose we should tell Ginny she can come out of the office. But..." Brian groaned.

"First, let's clean up this mess," Heather said as she picked up the book Caitlin had hurled at her. Since Brian didn't know where the items on the floor belonged, he watched as Heather hurried around the room, picking up what Caitlin had attempted to weaponize and returning them to their places. Fortunately, the spirit had hurled sturdy items, and nothing had broken.

By the time Heather finished putting the museum back in order, she was out of breath and said, "Dang, it took me a lot longer to put everything back than it did that crazy ghost to throw it."

"Now can we tell Ginny she can come out?"

Heather considered the question and then said, "Wait, the donation box!" The next moment, Heather ran to the museum store, picked up the donation box, and set it in the front entry. She returned to Brian.

"Okay, I put everything back," Heather told him.

"You should leave before I have her come out," Brian said.

"Okay, but why?" Heather asked.

"You get out of here, and it will be her word against yours," Brian said.

Heather flashed Brian a grin, gave him a quick kiss, and then dashed from the museum.

TWENTY-SEVEN

B rian stood at the door to the museum office and glanced back down the exhibit area to the front entry. Fairly certain Heather had left the building, he took a deep breath and knocked on the door.

"Ginny Thomas? It's Officer Brian Henderson. You can come out."

He stepped back from the door, waiting and wondering what exactly he was going to say. He thought back to all those times Danielle had been put in an impossible situation and made to look guilty by no fault of her own. The incident that stood out was when Walt had thrown all Cheryl's clothes and open makeup into her suitcase before Cheryl had disappeared. Of course, Brian had assumed Danielle had done it, which was one reason he believed she had been responsible for her cousin's disappearance. At the time, he did not know Walt's ghost haunted Marlow House.

He was about to knock again when he heard the door unlock, and then it opened a few inches. Ginny peeked out.

"It's safe. You can come out," Brian said.

The door eased open, and Ginny looked around. Hesitantly, she stepped out from the office. "Did they arrest her? Is that where she is?"

"Um… arrest who?" Brian asked, hating himself for having to play dumb.

Frowning, Ginny marched all the way into the exhibit room and glanced around. Someone had returned the thrown items to their places. It appeared as if nothing had happened. She looked at Brian, "Heather Donovan, of course. Who cleaned this place up?"

"I'm not really sure what happened," Brian lied. "But there is no one here."

"Heather Donovan was here a minute ago. I heard you talking to her out here. What is going on?"

Brian looked dumbly at Ginny, his brain racing to come up with a logical explanation. "When I arrived, Heather was here. She told me you were upset and had locked yourself in the office. Heather said something about an incident at your house yesterday when a bookcase fell over. She said you seemed to believe she was responsible for the bookshelf falling, but insists she had nothing to do with it. She told me she came here to discuss it with you. I told her to leave, and I'd talk to you."

"The woman attacked me!" Ginny snapped.

"Are you injured?"

"No. I'm not injured. Fortunately, she has lousy aim. But it wasn't because she didn't try!"

"I'm sure there has been some sort of misunderstanding," Brian suggested.

"Misunderstanding?" Ginny shrieked, waving one hand. It still held the large paperweight she had picked up in the museum store. "What about all the things she threw at me! I'm not only outraged that she attacked me, but this is a museum; we do not throw items at a museum because we are angry!"

"What's that you're waving around?" Brian asked.

Having forgotten what she held, Ginny stopped waving her hand and looked at it a moment. Finally, she said, "It's a paperweight. The museum sells them. I... I thought I might need to protect myself."

"Are you saying you were going to throw that at Heather?" Brian asked.

Gritting her teeth and clutching the paperweight, she glared at Brian. "Only to protect myself."

"I'm sure you don't need protecting from Heather," Brian insisted. "This is just a misunderstanding."

She looked around the room again and back to Brian. "Did you put everything back?"

"Um… no… I'm not sure what you mean," Brian lied.

"Heather threw things at me. They landed on the floor. Who picked them up?"

"I certainly didn't." This time Brian didn't lie.

"I want to press charges against Heather Donovan," Ginny said.

"Um… exactly on what grounds?"

"She came into the museum and attacked me. I think that should be sufficient," Ginny said stubbornly.

"Do you have any proof?" Brian asked.

"Proof? I'm telling you, she came in here and attacked me!" Ginny shrieked.

"I don't know what happened here," Brian lied again. "But it will be your word against hers. And frankly, Heather is a respected member of the community."

"Are you serious? She looks like a vampire," Ginny snarked. "Are you suggesting they would take her word over mine?"

"Heather works for the Glandon Foundation, which is the museum's principal benefactor."

"And I'm sure the Glandon Foundation would like to know they have an unstable employee. When I'm done talking to them, I don't imagine she'll have a job for much longer."

"Like I said, it will be your word against hers. I promise, you have nothing to fear from Heather. But I will have a talk with her."

"Officer Henderson," Ginny said curtly, "I would appreciate it if you would just leave now. It is obvious you're not planning to do anything about this. Considering your recent experience with Ms. Donovan after they kidnapped you, you clearly have misplaced loyalty to her. I hope it's worth your career. Please leave."

Brian didn't bother arguing. He gave Ginny a nod and then turned and headed for the front exit. Just as he reached it, Millie Samson walked in. Brian gave Millie a brief hello and continued on his way.

"Why was Officer Henderson here?" Millie asked when she walked into the exhibit area and found Ginny standing alone.

Relieved to see Millie, Ginny broke into tears and ran to her, throwing her arms around the startled woman.

MILLIE SAT with Ginny in the museum gift shop, listening to Ginny recount the events with Heather. When she finished, Millie let out a sigh. "It's true, Heather can be an odd one. But I have never known her to be violent."

"Are you saying you don't believe me?" Ginny asked.

"No, dear. But it seems out of character. Perhaps the poor girl snapped. You know, she had a rather traumatic experience just days ago. Drugged, kidnapped and taken to the mountains and left to die."

"Are you suggesting Brian is protecting her because he feels she snapped?"

"Very possible. And he is right, it is your word against Heather's. And like he told you, she works for the Glandon Foundation."

"Yes, but I imagine it may not thrill the Glandon Foundation to keep someone unstable like her working for them."

Millie chuckled and then leaned forward and gave Ginny a condescending pat on the knee. "Dear, you really have not been here very long, have you? She is Chris Johnson's right-hand person."

"Who is Chris Johnson?" Ginny asked.

"Let's just say, he might as well be Chris Glandon. He runs the foundation, and he is well aware of all Heather's quirks. That entire group is quite tight."

"Group? What group?"

"That entire Beach Drive group," Millie said. "The Marlows, Heather Donovan, Chris Johnson, the Bartleys. They all live on Beach Drive."

"The Bartleys? Kelly's brother?" Ginny asked.

Millie gave a nod. "Yes. All close friends. And I imagine the community of Frederickport would be quick to throw their support behind them, considering how much they have all donated to local charities."

BRIAN SAT ALONE with the chief in his office. He had just told him what had happened at the museum. After listening to the entire story, the chief let out a long low whistle while he reclined in his desk chair, the back of his head cradled in his palms with his fingers laced together.

"Now you see what I've had to deal with since Danielle moved to Frederickport," the chief said only half in jest.

"I felt like I was gaslighting the poor woman." Brian groaned.

The chief let out a sigh and sat up in the chair, propping his elbows on the desk. "I get it. But what else can we do? I don't think either of us wants to arrest Heather for something a ghost did. Especially since Heather was trying to do the right thing."

"I understand that. But you should have seen how Ginny was looking at me."

"Yeah, I heard Kelly has been trying to hook you two up. I can't see that happening now." The chief snickered.

"It's not that," Brian scoffed.

"Yeah, I know. I guess I need to be prepared for Ginny Thomas."

The chief's desk phone rang. He picked it up and answered it. After a moment, he hung up the phone and looked at Brian. "And sooner than later."

"What?" Brian frowned.

"Ginny Thomas is here. She wants to talk to me. You should probably get out of here. I told them to wait a minute before they send her back. But let's stick with the story that if someone cleaned up the museum, Heather did it."

"She did."

"I meant before you got there," the chief said.

HEATHER AND CHRIS sat across from each other at a booth at Lucy's Diner. After Heather had arrived at work and told Chris what had happened at the museum, he insisted he take her out for lunch so they could talk away from the office. There were more employees working at the Glandon Foundation offices these days, and he would rather they continue the discussion away from his other employees.

"So does this mean I might need to get you bail money?" Chris asked after the server took their order and left the table.

"I'm glad you find this amusing," Heather grumbled.

"Well, just be grateful Brian knows about us, or my offer might not be so much in jest."

"I feel horrible about Ginny," Heather said as she absently

poked at the ice in the water the server had brought to their table when coming to take their order.

"Just stay away from her," Chris said. "At least until we know Caitlin has moved on," Chris warned.

"Yeah, yeah, I get it," Heather grumbled, giving her ice another poke with the tip of one finger.

CHRIS AND HEATHER had finished lunch and returned to the Glandon Foundation offices, when Kelly met Joe for a late lunch at Pier Café. The two had already placed their order and sat together at a booth.

"Ginny is so upset. I can't believe the chief's not going to do something," Kelly said.

"I don't think there is anything he can do. It's Ginny's word against Heather's."

"Well, I take Ginny's word," Kelly insisted. "I always thought Heather was a little weird, but I never imagined she would attack someone. Or that Brian would cover for her."

"I don't believe Brian covered for her," Joe insisted. "Brian is not like that. He will not cover for someone who breaks the law, not even a friend."

"How can you say that? He obviously helped Heather remove any evidence of her outburst," Kelly said.

"According to Brian, nothing was out of place when he got there. So if anyone put the place back together, it had to have been Heather before he got there."

"Yeah, that's pretty much what the chief told Ginny," Kelly said. "Not that Heather put the place together, but that when Brian got there, nothing was out of order. Millie suggested Heather had some sort of breakdown."

"Breakdown?" Joe frowned.

"Yes. That their time in the mountains was more traumatic than they let on, and that she snapped and just sort of lost it at the museum. I suppose that's possible. And that might explain why Brian is covering for her."

"I don't believe Brian would cover for Heather if he believed she broke the law."

"He might if he was trying to protect her because something

167

happened up on that mountain. Something that sent Heather over the edge," Kelly said. "And if that's the case, I just hope Brian knows what he's doing. What happens if Heather ends up hurting someone? She could have killed Ginny today if one of those things had hit her just right."

TWENTY-EIGHT

Thursday evening Eva Thorndike stood in the portrait wing of the Frederickport museum, admiring her painting. For security reasons, this area of the museum had limited hours and heightened security because of the valuable portraits on display. Yet at this hour of the night, they locked down the entire museum.

Eva, who had been a famous silent movie star during her lifetime, had also performed in the theater. She had met the artist of these paintings during her time in the theater. Many people had compared her likeness to the Gibson Girl, a pen-ink-illustration of Charles Dana Gibson. The artist had captured this resemblance in Eva's portrait.

She turned her attention to Walt's painting and smiled. It made her happy that her old friend no longer stumbled in the darkness but was back on the path to fulfil his destiny. With that thought, she decided to pop down to the cemetery. It had been the last place Walt had seen the spirit, and if the spirit had not moved on, perhaps she might find him there and learn what he hadn't told Walt.

A few moments later Eva stood in the Frederickport cemetery. The evening breeze rustled the treetops, while the crescent moon dimly lit the sky. She gravitated toward the older section of the cemetery, and that was where she found him, standing over the grave of Nanny Benson Becker. Or at least, she assumed it was him, considering his beard and manner of dress, the faded denim pants, worn flannel shirt, boots and floppy hat.

"Someone you know?" Eva asked.

The spirit of the man turned and faced her. He looked her up and down and said, "Yes. My sister, Nanny. Who are you?"

"I'm Eva Thorndike, a friend of Walt Marlow's. I would like to talk to you."

He shook his head. "I don't understand any of this. Is he a ghost? Are you? What am I?"

Eva reached out one hand and said, "Come, let's talk. I can help you. And you can help my friend."

TOGETHER BUD and Eva sat in the moonlight in the cemetery, close to his sister's headstone. After Eva explained his new reality—along with Walt's—she asked him to explain a few things. Before he did, he shook his head in confusion.

"I can understand about me. I think I've known for a long time but refused to accept the fact. And if I understand about me, then understanding about you is easy. But what you tell me about Walt Marlow, that I can't seem to fathom."

"I imagine when you move on, you'll have more clarity with what I've told you. I understand some things are easier to comprehend on the other side."

He studied her a moment and then asked, "Why aren't you there? Why are you here?"

Eva flashed him a soft smile. "Because, like Walt has his destiny, so do I. While there are common rules, common structure and order, there are no absolutes. Normally our path is to continue on, as I believe yours is. Yet for me, I still have things to do here."

"And for Walt?" he asked.

"His path was interrupted, and they gave him another chance."

"Why isn't everyone given a second chance? I didn't want my life to end when it did."

"Because your journey has not been interrupted in the same way as Walt's. Your personal journey continues on the other side."

He frowned. "I don't understand."

"You will, eventually. But for now, tell me about Walt's father and why you believe he is responsible for your death."

Bud told Eva what she asked of him, and when he finished, she said, "You need to go to Walt and tell him what you know. And I believe you will move on in your journey after you put your body to rest." She nodded at his sister's headstone. "I have a feeling this is where you want it to be, and then you can go."

WALT SAT on one end of the library sofa with Danielle. She leaned against him with her feet on the other end of the sofa. Each held a book in hand, but instead of reading, they discussed Heather's unfortunate incident in the museum.

"I don't know who to feel sorrier for, Heather or Ginny," Danielle said.

"What about poor Brian?" Walt asked.

"Brian? Ahh, that's payback for all the times he wanted to arrest me for murder," Danielle scoffed.

Walt chuckled.

"As soon as we see Marie or Eva, we need to have them go over to Ginny's house and try reasoning with Caitlin. And maybe find out what treasure she keeps referring to," Danielle suggested.

"You believe Cory can see her?" Walt asked.

"The things he's said to Heather, what other conclusion can I come to?" Danielle asked. "And if he can see Caitlin, well, there must be something special in the water here."

"What do you mean?" Walt asked.

"I have lived with this—gift—since I was a child. And until I moved to Oregon, I had never known another person who claimed to see or talk to spirits. But since moving here, I keep stumbling over one medium after another. What is it about this place?" Danielle asked.

Walt moved his right arm around Danielle's shoulder and brought her closer. "Perhaps you knew other mediums, but they never revealed themselves. Perhaps they were always there, but you never saw them."

Danielle shrugged. "I suppose that's possible."

"Walt Marlow, I would like to talk to you," a male voice interrupted.

Walt and Danielle looked up to see Bud standing in the middle of Marlow House's library.

"Bud?" Walt said, standing up from the sofa.

Bud looked at Danielle. "Can I talk alone with Walt, please?"

"Okay." Danielle stood up from the sofa. She walked toward the door, and before stepping into the hall, she glanced back at Walt and Bud and muttered under her breath, "My life's not weird at all."

WALT LEANED back on the sofa while Bud sat across from him in a chair.

"I met your friend Eva Thorndike. She explained things to me."

"Didn't I do that at the cemetery?" Walt asked.

"I thought you were a ghost then."

Walt smiled. "I guess she explained everything."

"I don't understand, not really. But Eva says I will, eventually."

"Sometimes I wake up, and I don't quite believe it." Walt grinned.

"Do you remember me?" Bud asked.

"Yes."

Bud leaned back in the chair and crossed one leg over his opposing knee. He studied Walt and said, "You used to call me Uncle Bud."

"Yes, I remember," Walt said. "Will you tell me now why you think my father was responsible for your death?"

"Will you do me a favor first?" Bud asked.

"What?"

"I want to be buried at the Frederickport Cemetery. My sister is there. Before I move on, I want my body brought down from the mountains."

I can't imagine there is much left, Walt thought to himself but instead said, "Do you know where you were buried?"

"Yes. I returned to the mountain after we talked in the cemetery and found my grave. I can show you."

"If I agree to this, will you explain about my father?" Walt asked.

"Yes. But not until you move my body to Frederickport."

"Can't you at least tell me after you show me where the body is?" Walt asked.

Bud considered the question and then said, "Let me think

about it."

"If you won't tell me about my father now, will you tell me about Teddy Newsome?" Walt asked.

Bud frowned. "What about him?"

"What do you know about Teddy? Was he my father's friend?"

Bud frowned. "Don't you remember?"

"Remember what?"

"You used to call him Uncle Teddy, like you called me Uncle Bud."

"I remember he used to sneak me candy," Walt said.

"That was like Ted, buying a person's affections," Bud scoffed.

Walt studied Bud quizzically. "You weren't friends with Teddy?"

Bud let out a sigh and said, "What do you want to know?"

"Everything you remember about Teddy, in relation to my parents."

"We all grew up together." Bud paused a moment and then asked, "Did you know your father's birthday was December 5?"

"Yes. Why?"

"That's the day Alexandre Dumas died. Your father used to say he was his reincarnation. He claimed that's why he'd been named Alexander." Bud chuckled.

"Are you talking about the French author?" Walt frowned.

Bud nodded. "Yes. Your father didn't really believe that, but he loved his books, and when he found out Dumas had died a few years before he was born, on the same day, your father liked to say he was his reincarnation. He also called us the three musketeers, which was his favorite of Dumas's works. But that's when we were boys, and I suppose it suited us back then. We were once close. Like brothers."

"Once?"

"Yes. None of us had brothers. I had my sister. But your father and Teddy didn't have siblings."

"What happened to the friendship?" Walt asked.

"I suppose it lasted longer than many friendships. Looking back, the unravelling began when girls came into our world."

"How so?" Walt asked.

"Your mother and Teddy's wife, Maddie, were best friends. When we met them, Teddy fell hopelessly in love with your mother."

"Teddy and my mother?" Walt choked out.

"Teddy never had a chance," Bud said with a snort. "Your

parents fell in love when they first met. And Maddie fell for me, but I wasn't paying attention. There was a friend of my sister who had caught my eye, and I refused to see Maddie for anything but a friend. When she failed to get my attention, she turned to Teddy. They married, which was a mistake. Neither one loved the other. But Maddie's parents had money, and they died in a boating accident, along with her three siblings, leaving her to inherit a sizable estate. She felt vulnerable, scared. That's when they married."

"Teddy married her for money?" Walt asked.

"Yes. And Maddie married out of grief and fear."

"And then she got sick?" Walt said.

"Yes. You remember that?" Bud asked.

"I remember my mother always going over there to take care of her, and how my grandmother resented the time my mother spent over there. Once I heard my grandmother saying Teddy should hire more people to help with Maddie and not rely so much on my mother."

"He couldn't. He could barely afford to pay their bills," Bud said.

Walt frowned. "I don't understand. You said Maddie inherited a fortune from her parents' estate?"

"Yes. Which Teddy went through, one get-rich scheme after another. Or should I say, get richer. Because they were wealthy with Maddie's inheritance until Teddy went through it. He liked to say I was always chasing foolish dreams, but at least I didn't do it with my sick wife's money. And then he got a girlfriend. I imagine she was taking any extra money he had."

"Girlfriend? Are you talking about Josephine?" Walt asked.

Bud cocked his brow. "So you know about her? When I found out, I went to your father. I assumed he agreed with me about what we should do. But I guess I was wrong."

"Agreed with you about what?" Walt asked.

Bud stood up. "I'll tell you the rest after. Do you remember where you saw me in the mountains?"

"Yes." Walt stood.

"Can you find it again?"

"I believe I can."

"When you're ready to hear the rest of the story—and learn how your father is responsible for my death, I'll be there. But come prepared to bring me down off the mountain." He disappeared.

TWENTY-NINE

"What was I thinking?" Walt said on Friday morning. He sat at the kitchen table with Danielle, each with a cup of coffee and a section of the morning newspaper.

Danielle looked up from the article she was reading to Walt. His attention was not on the newspaper in his hand. "What is it?" she asked.

"I realized I might not be able to find the spot where we saw him. We got lost a few times. Wandered around in loops. And what if I can't find it?"

"What if you get lost again?" Danielle asked. She folded her newspaper and set it on the table.

"If I don't find him, he might tire of waiting for me and move on. I'll never learn the truth."

"And if you get lost, I may never find you again," Danielle said.

Walt frowned at Danielle. "Are you listening to me?"

"Yes. But you keep talking about going up there alone, and that is foolish. You don't need to wander around in the mountains. At least now you admit you could get lost up there. If you go, don't go alone. Get Heather and Brian to come with us."

"Us?"

"Yes. I'm going with you. And Brian and Heather have been up there. I'm sure the three of you can figure out where this place is."

"If they remember," Walt said.

"Call Heather. Ask her."

Walt glanced at the clock. "I imagine she's at work already."

"Chris won't care if you call her at work."

A few minutes later Walt had Heather on the phone. He told her about his visitor last night and what he wanted to do.

"Well, what did she say?" Danielle asked when Walt got off the phone.

"She's pretty sure she can find it again. But she agrees Brian should go too."

"That's what I said," Danielle reminded him.

"She's going to call Brian," Walt said.

"HE WON FAIR AND SQUARE, CARLA," Earl Sweeney told the waitress as he flipped the ham steak on the flattop at Pier Café. He chewed on a toothpick, wishing it were a cigarette. Carla stood on the other side of the pass-through window with the busboy.

"Aw, come on, Earl; we probably shouldn't be placing bets at work anyway," Carla whined.

"I paid up to Earl when I lost yesterday's bet," the busboy reminded her.

"Then Earl can clean off the gum," Carla grumbled.

"I didn't make the bet," Earl reminded her. He glanced at his watch and said, "Your shift ends in ten minutes, Carla. Make sure you do it before you leave."

"Fine," Carla huffed. "But that is the last time I make one of those stupid bets." She turned abruptly and stomped from the window.

"Is she serious?" the busboy asked Earl.

"Nah. She's just a poor loser. But Carla's not a quitter."

CARLA CASHED out her last customer for the day and begrudgingly returned to the kitchen to grab some food handler's gloves. If she was going to spend the next hour peeling gum off the bottom of table six, she was going to do it wearing gloves.

Why did she make that stupid bet? Silly kitchen bets were common at Pier Café; it was one way to break up the mundane and routine. Last week, when one of the other servers had bet she could get Pearl Huckabee to change her normal pie order, Carla took the challenge. Carla won the bet, which meant she didn't have to refill the salt and pepper shakers that week.

Unfortunately, the stupid bet she made with the busboy over who was going to walk in the door next she lost, which meant she had to clean the gum off the bottom of table six. Every teenager in Frederickport wanted to deposit their used gum under table six. Only table six. They found it funny. She had too, when it was the busboy's job to clean it off.

Wearing food handler's gloves, Carla placed a clean plastic trash bag under table six to sit on. Grumbling, she disappeared under the table, putty knife and cup in hands. The putty knife to scrape off the gum, the paper cup to hold the gum.

BRIAN HENDERSON WALKED into Pier Café and glanced around, looking for somewhere to sit. The breakfast rush was over, and the lunch rush wouldn't be starting for another hour. Most of the tables were empty but needed cleaning, something the busboy and one server were currently doing.

The server looked up from an empty table, her hands filled with dirty dishes. She greeted Brian and told him to sit wherever he wanted. Since he didn't want to sit at a table with dirty dishes, he headed to the first clean table he saw, table five.

He glanced at his watch as he sat down. Walt was to meet him here in about five minutes. Brian picked up the menu and glanced over it, yet he didn't know why he bothered. He knew the menu by heart. The server brought him a cup of coffee without him asking and offered to take his order. After explaining he was waiting for someone, she filled two glasses with water, left his table, and returned to cleaning other tables in the diner.

Brian was halfway through the cup of coffee when Walt arrived.

"So Danielle didn't want to come with you?" Brian asked.

"No. She's baking this morning. Double fudge chocolate cake. I didn't want to disturb her." Walt sat down and picked up a menu.

Brian chuckled. "You and your chocolate cake."

"You go a hundred years without cake, and see how you do," Walt said.

Brian chuckled again and asked, "I understand you want to go back up to the mountains."

"Yes, about Uncle Bud," Walt said.

"Heather told me all about it. I still can't believe Heather's mountain man is this Uncle Bud."

"I assumed I could find the place again, but this morning I tried retracing in my mind how to get there, and now I'm not sure I can find it. Do you remember where it was?"

"I'm pretty sure I do," Brian said.

"Heather said she could probably find it again. I was hoping if you and Heather go with us, we could find it together. There will be some digging, but I can do that," Walt said.

"At least you won't break a sweat or get your hands dirty," Brian teased.

"So you'll go with me?" Walt asked.

"When do you want to go?" Brian asked.

"Are you working tomorrow?" Walt asked.

"Yes. But I have Sunday off."

"Can we do it on Sunday? Heather has the weekend off. We can all drive up together. Find my treasure and put this behind us."

"Treasure? So there is one?" Brian remembered Heather mentioning Caitlin's talk of a treasure.

Walt shrugged. "I'm more interested in learning what happened. And like William Penn once said, *'Knowledge is the treasure of a wise man.'*"

CARLA SAT UNDER THE TABLE, a paper cup in one hand and a putty knife in the other. She stopped prying gum from off the bottom of the table. Instead, she listened to Brian and Walt's odd conversation. She had recognized their voices immediately. Not wanting the men to find her eavesdropping, she remained still and didn't resume her cleaning detail until the pair left the restaurant. After that, she hurriedly scraped off the gum. When she crawled out from under the table, she moaned and stretched, telling herself she would never make a bet like that one again.

After showing Earl the filled cup to prove she'd honored her side of the bet, she tossed the gloves and cup in the trash and returned the trash bag to where she had found it. She went to the bathroom to wash her hands.

When she stepped out of the women's restroom, she spied Bill Jones sitting at a nearby table with his nephew, Cory. Bill waved her over to his table.

"We're ready to order, Carla," Bill told her when she walked up to the table.

Carla sat down at one of the empty chairs at his table. "Sorry, Bill, you'll have to find another server. I'm off for the rest of the day. I had the early shift."

The next moment another server came to the table to take Bill's order.

"Bring me a burger," Carla told the server. "I'm hungry, might as well grab something to eat before I go home."

"Should I put it on Bill's check?" the server joked, eliciting a frown from Bill as he handed her the menu he had been holding.

Carla laughed. "No. Tell Earl it's for me."

The server laughed and gave Bill a playful jab with the menu in her hand as Carla said, "Scared you for a moment, didn't we?"

"You always scare me, Carla." Bill snorted.

Bill and his nephew gave the server their order, and she left the table.

"I heard the most interesting conversation between Brian Henderson and Walt Marlow," Carla whispered.

"When did you see them?" Bill asked.

"They were in here a little while ago for lunch," she said.

"They seem like an unlikely pair," Bill said.

"You forget what they went through last week. They spent a few days with Heather Donovan lost in the forest," Carla reminded him.

"Yeah, I read about that. Crazy," Bill said.

"What did you hear?" Cory asked.

Carla flashed Cory a smile and told Bill, "See, someone is interested in what I heard."

"Go on, tell us," Bill said.

"I'd say more happened to them than what was in the paper," Carla said in a whisper.

"What do you mean?" Bill frowned.

"I think they found a treasure up there," Carla said. "And they're going back to dig it up on Sunday."

"Treasure?" Cory asked.

"I'd believe that if it was Boatman going back up there. She's the one who always finds treasures," Bill grumbled. "It's like she's some treasure savant."

"What's a treasure savant?" Cory asked.

"A phrase your uncle just made up," Carla said.

"Maybe I did, but it fits. Or perhaps treasure magnet?" Bill asked.

"She's probably going with them. And it hasn't been Boatman for ages. She's Danielle Marlow. And it's her husband who found this treasure. From what they said, it belonged to someone they called Uncle Bud," Carla said.

The glass of water Cory held slipped from his hand. It landed on the table and rolled off, hitting the floor and shattering into pieces after splashing water around the table.

"Cory, watch what you're doing," Bill grumbled, picking up a napkin and wiping off the table.

Carla stood up, careful not to step in any glass, and said, "I'll go get the broom and dustpan."

Cory remained frozen; he hadn't moved since dropping the glass.

"Are you okay?" Bill asked his nephew.

"Ahh… yeah… I think so," Cory muttered.

THIRTY

"What are you doing this afternoon?" Joe asked Kelly as she pulled into the parking lot of the Frederickport police station to drop him off for work. His shift started in fifteen minutes.

Kelly brought her car to a stop but did not turn off the engine. Hands still firmly on the steering wheel, she glanced to Joe. "I was thinking about stopping over at my brother's. I need to talk to him about Heather."

Joe groaned. "What are you going to do?"

Looking back out the windshield, her hands still clutching the steering wheel, Kelly said, "I don't like the idea of Heather watching Connor. That woman's crazy and has no business being around small children. Even if she wasn't nuts, they don't need her. They have me."

"Kelly, it's not like you're always free to watch Connor. And after we get married, we'll be starting our own family."

Kelly frowned and turned back to Joe. "We will?"

"Won't we? I thought you wanted kids," Joe asked.

"Yes, I want kids. But the way you said that, *starting our family*, it sounded like we'd be having kids right away."

"We aren't getting any younger," Joe reminded her.

Kelly arched her brows. "Are you calling me old?"

"I'm just saying I want kids and thought you did too, and when we get married, there is no reason to wait. So we should start right away. I'd like to have a big family."

Kelly narrowed her eyes and studied Joe. "How big?"

Joe shrugged. "I don't know. I figured once we got married, you would go off birth control, and we'd let nature take its course."

Kelly continued to stare at Joe. Finally, she said, "I don't want to talk about this now. You should go to work."

Joe let out a sigh, unfastened his seatbelt, leaned over, and kissed Kelly. After the kiss, he got out of the vehicle and slammed the door shut.

Kelly watched as Joe walked away. Abruptly she rolled down her window and shouted at him, "Give me a number!"

Joe stopped walking and turned to Kelly. "Number?"

"How many kids do you want? Give me a number."

Joe stared at Kelly a moment and then said, "Six?"

Kelly didn't respond; instead she rolled up her window and sped out of the parking lot.

As she pulled out into the street, Brian drove up, returning from his early lunch with Walt. Instead of going into the station, Joe waited for Brian on the sidewalk.

"Kelly's getting a little lead-footed there," Brian said when he reached Joe. "What's the hurry?"

Joe let out a sigh. "I'm a bad person, Brian." Joe turned to the entrance of the police station and started walking in that direction, Brian trailing after him.

"What are you talking about?" Brian asked.

"I just told Kelly I want six kids."

Brian came to a stop and stared at Joe. "You want six kids?"

Joe stopped walking and turned to Brian. With a frown, he said, "Oh hell no. Two at most."

"Then why did you tell Kelly you wanted six? No wonder she stormed out of here. Are you trying to get her to break off your engagement?"

"No. I don't want to break off the engagement. Do you think she's going to think that?" Joe glanced briefly to where Kelly had just driven off. A moment later he turned and started for the front door of the police station.

"Why would you tell her you wanted six kids?" Brian asked as he followed Joe.

Joe shrugged. "I love Kelly, but sometimes she gets too involved with people. And I just figured she needs to focus on her own life and stop trying to meddle in other people's lives."

"Is this about her trying to play matchmaker for me?" Brian asked.

"That and other things," Joe said, now at the front door. He reached out and grabbed hold of the door's handle and pulled it open.

"Well, you give her six babies, and she sure as hell isn't going to have time to worry about anyone else," Brian said with a snicker.

———————

LILY WAS CLEANING the kitchen after lunch, while Ian was in the nursery changing Connor's diaper, when Kelly rang the doorbell. Sadie reached the door before Lily, her tail wagging.

"Hi, Kelly," Lily greeted her a few moments later. "Just putting stuff away from lunch. You hungry? I have some tuna left."

"Thanks," Kelly said as she closed the front door behind her and followed Lily into the kitchen while giving Sadie some hello pats. "I already ate. Where's Ian?"

"Changing Connor's diaper," Lily said as she returned to the kitchen counter to put the bread back in the breadbox.

"I need to talk to you," Kelly announced, taking a seat at the breakfast bar. She sat up primly, folding her hands before her on the counter while she watched her sister-in-law.

"Sure, what's up?" Lily asked as she closed the bread box and turned to face Kelly.

"You can't let Heather watch Connor anymore," Kelly blurted.

Lily frowned. "I can't?"

"It's not safe."

"Is this about what happened at the museum?" Lily asked.

"You know about that?"

"Ian told me what you told him. So I suppose I know. At least, what you told him."

"Then you understand why you can't let her watch him anymore," Kelly said.

Lily let out a sigh. "I wasn't at the museum, and neither were you. Heather can be a little—quirky. Truth is, she and I had some issues when she first moved to Frederickport. But I've gotten to

183

know her better. I consider her a friend. And she loves Connor, and he adores her. He's perfectly safe with Heather."

"How can you say that?" Kelly asked, her voice getting higher in pitch. "The woman is clearly unstable and prone to violent outbursts. What happens when Connor does something that makes her mad, like spills a glass of milk or refuses to take a nap?"

"Heather is wonderful with Connor," Lily insisted.

"You have no idea what she does when you aren't here," Kelly said.

"I appreciate your concern, Kelly. But Connor is my son, and I think I know what is best for him."

"He's my nephew," Kelly snapped.

Lily arched her brows. "And?"

"He's Ian's son too."

"Obviously." Lily glanced toward the hallway, wondering when her husband would come and save her from this conversation with his sister.

"I would think Ian would have some say in who watches his son," Kelly said.

"Of course he does. But he agrees with me," Lily said.

"I can't imagine that. Heather attacked Ginny Thomas and could have killed her."

"I heard she didn't have a scratch on her," Lily said.

"That's only because Heather has lousy aim," Kelly said.

"I don't know about that. Have you ever seen her throw a ball or a Frisbee?" Lily asked.

"This isn't funny," Kelly snapped.

"Actually, I was serious. And Heather isn't dangerous."

"Lily, must you be so stubborn?" Kelly asked. "I'm only thinking of what's best for my nephew."

"What's going on in here?" Ian asked when he stepped into the kitchen.

"Where's Connor?" Lily asked.

"He's playing with some toys in his bedroom. What's going on in here? I could hear you two from Connor's room," Ian said.

Kelly turned to her brother. "It's your wife. She's not being reasonable."

Frowning—and looking ill at ease—Ian glanced from his sister to his wife.

"She doesn't want us to let Heather watch Connor anymore," Lily told him.

"Why?" Ian asked.

"What do you mean, why?" Kelly asked her brother. "I told you what Heather did."

"None of us were there. It's hearsay," Ian said.

"Are you suggesting Ginny is lying?" Kelly asked.

"No. I'm just saying that sometimes we don't know the whole story," Ian said calmly.

"If it were my son, I wouldn't need to know more," Kelly snapped.

"But he isn't your son," Lily reminded her.

Frustrated, Kelly looked from Lily to her brother and asked, "What is Mom going to say?"

"Mom?" Ian frowned.

"Yes. When I tell her what Heather did, and then let her know she's someone you leave alone with her grandson," Kelly asked.

"Do not tell Mom," Ian warned.

"Why?" Kelly snapped, no longer sitting at the breakfast bar, but standing, her fists resting on her hips.

Unbeknownst to the three people arguing in the kitchen, the spirit of Marie Nichols entered the outside wall into the nursery and was just greeting Connor when she heard raised voices coming from the open door.

"I'll be right back, Connor," Marie told the boy as she moved from the nursery to the kitchen. She found Kelly arguing with Ian and Lily about Heather babysitting Connor.

"Oh my, if Heather can't babysit, then I doubt Lily and Ian will feel comfortable letting me watch him," Marie muttered to herself, knowing they couldn't risk someone like Kelly stopping by and finding Connor seemingly alone. "Why doesn't Kelly want Heather to watch him?"

Over the next few minutes Marie learned the answer to the question when Kelly repeated the conversation she had already had with her brother regarding the events at the museum between Ginny and Heather.

"Heather attacked someone? No. That can't be true," Marie said aloud. Yet there were no mediums in the room to hear.

She listened a few more minutes and then realized, by Ian's and Lily's expressions, there was more to this story. *Another ghost?* she wondered. Marie knew Eva had seen Bud, but there had been no mention he could harness energy.

"There are some things you just don't understand," Ian told his sister.

Deciding to illustrate Ian's point, Marie focused her energy on a bowl sitting on the counter. Lily stood with her back to the bowl, while it was out of Ian's line of sight. Only Kelly could see it. The next moment it rose into the air, hovering for a moment.

Kelly didn't notice it at first, but when she did, she stopped talking and simply stared. When Lily turned to see what her sister-in-law was looking at, the bowl had already floated back down to the counter.

Kelly licked her lips nervously and swallowed. "Okay," she said, "I won't say anything to Mom. You're right. There are some things I don't understand. I have to go now." Without a word, she made a hasty exit out the front door.

"Wow. What just happened?" Lily asked when she heard the front door close.

"My work here is done," Marie chirped. Instead of returning to Connor, she headed for the Glandon Foundation. She wanted to ask Heather what had happened at the museum.

Ian groaned. "I wish I could explain things to my sister. I feel like a jerk," he said after Marie had gone.

"Yeah, I know." Lily walked over to Ian and wrapped her arms around his waist, pulling him into a hug.

"She only cares about Connor," Ian whispered as he rested his chin atop Lily's head.

"I understand. And maybe I was too harsh with her. But still…"

THIRTY-ONE

On Friday evening Danielle sat at her laptop in the parlor, taking another shot at research. Just as Walt walked into the room carrying two glasses, one filled with wine and the other with brandy, Danielle looked up and said, "I think I found him."

"Found who?" Walt asked, setting the glass of wine on the desk next to the laptop.

"Ted Newsome," Danielle said as she picked up the wine and took a sip.

"Where?" Walt asked, taking a seat in a nearby chair.

Danielle turned to face Walt, a glass of wine in hand. "It's an obituary in a Portland newspaper. For a Ted Newsome, age forty-seven. If it's him, he died the same year as you did." She took another sip of wine.

"It could be someone with the same name," Walt suggested.

"I don't think so, since it said he was born in Frederickport. According to the obituary, he didn't have any children. And it didn't mention any surviving nieces and nephews, which makes sense since your Teddy was an only child. Plus, it talks about his two wives who preceded him—who happen to have the same names as Uncle Teddy's two wives. I don't think he remarried. And I don't think they arrested him for pushing his second wife down the stairs."

"How did he die?" Walt asked.

Danielle shrugged. "It didn't say."

"Did it say what he was doing in Portland?" Walt sipped his brandy.

Danielle turned back to the computer and brought up the article. She quickly skimmed the obituary. "It said he was a driver for Kitterman's Laundry."

"You're kidding me," Walt said.

"Why?"

"George Hemming's cousin owned Kitterman's Laundry. I never met them, but they used to go to Portland and stay with them. George's cousin was actually Kitterman's wife. And George's wife and she were pretty close. That's who introduced George to Marie's mother."

"And Ted worked for them?" Danielle asked. "Wow, small world."

"Knock, knock," Marie's voice said just before she appeared in the parlor.

"We were just talking about you, sort of," Danielle said.

"I was with Heather earlier, and she told me what happened at the museum, and she said you might want to talk to me," Marie said.

"Yeah, that too. But we were actually talking about your Kitterman cousins," Danielle said.

"Goodness, I haven't thought about them in years. How did their name come up?" Marie asked, taking a seat on the chair next to Walt.

"It seems the Ted Newsome Walt knew worked for Kitterman's Laundry, according to a Portland newspaper. He died the same year as Walt."

"Do you know what he did for the laundry?" Marie asked.

"Driver, why?" Danielle asked.

"When I was a teenager, I remember one visit to the Kittermans. They had a daughter my age, Charlotte. Oh, we had so much fun. Anyway, during that visit, when our parents started talking about how 1925 had been a horrible year for all of them. For my parents, it was my father finding Walt hanging in the attic," Marie explained.

Walt cringed. "Please, I'd rather not think about that."

"Sorry, Walt," Marie said with a shrug and then continued. "And for the Kittermans, someone murdered their driver that year. Murdered while on the job. Horrible thing. They caught who did it, and there was a trial. It was probably this Ted if he died in 1925. They only had one driver at the time."

"The obituary said nothing about him being murdered," Danielle said.

"I remember something else Charlotte's mother told us. She once heard him bragging to one of the girls in the laundry about how he was coming into money. Some sort of inheritance. Charlotte's mother always wondered if there really had been an inheritance, and who got it after he was killed."

"Who would Teddy inherit money from?" Walt wondered.

Danielle shrugged. "Not his father?"

"From what my grandmother told me, he didn't have any family. His parents died before mine," Walt said.

They considered the question for a moment, and then Danielle suggested, "August Becker?"

"August Becker?" Walt asked.

"Yeah, wasn't he Teddy's uncle, and according to Ginny, he had a lot of money," Danielle said.

"Not a blood uncle," Walt reminded her. "His wife was Teddy's aunt. He had blood nieces and nephews to leave his money to."

"True, but he didn't get along with his family," Danielle reminded him.

"Who's August Becker?" Marie asked. "The name sounds a little familiar."

"His house used to be where Beach Taco is now," Danielle said. "He died in 1929."

"I suppose there is some poetic justice there," Walt said.

"What do you mean?" Danielle asked.

"If his second wife was telling us the truth, and he was responsible for my parents' death, it sounded like his life didn't quite work out for him. If he really believed August would leave him a substantial inheritance, he had the misfortune to die before cashing in on it."

"Plus, remember what Ginny told us," Danielle said.

"What?" Walt and Marie asked at the same time.

"Remember, according to her grandmother, August was perpetually on his deathbed. Doctors were always at his house. Sounded like he had people believing he had one foot in the grave," Danielle reminded.

"Then I suppose August didn't let Teddy know he had his feet firmly planted on this side, or I imagine he would have given him a shove like he did his second wife—and my parents and Maddie," Walt said.

"If someone hadn't murdered Teddy, and if he was waiting for an inheritance from August, according to Ginny, August lost his fortune just before he died, from the stock market crash. So it looks like it was never in the cards for Teddy to inherit," Danielle said.

"Does any of this help you find what you're looking for?" Marie asked.

"Not really. But I should have the answers to those questions when we see Bud again," Walt explained.

"Yes, Heather told me about that. She also told me what happened at the museum with Caitlin," Marie said.

"We were hoping you or Eva might try helping Caitlin adjust to her reality. Help her move on. She sounds too volatile for Heather, or even for Walt and me," Danielle said.

"I'm going to find Eva and see if she'll go over there with me tonight. I think it might be best if she comes too. She's better at this sort of thing," Marie said.

HEATHER WALKED SLOWLY down the grocery store aisle, paying scant attention to her surroundings as she looked down at her cellphone in her hands, her thumbs typing out a text message. She smiled when she hit send and then looked up, preparing to shove her phone in her purse, when she came to an abrupt stop. Walking in her direction was Kelly Bartley, who by her expression, had just noticed Heather.

Irrationally believing Kelly might see her text message and learn she had just been texting with Brian, Heather shoved her phone in her purse.

"Hello, Kelly," Heather said hesitantly.

"Hi," Kelly said curtly, preparing to step around Heather and continue on her way.

Heather stopped walking and looked at Kelly. "Can we talk, please?" Heather blurted.

Reluctantly Kelly stopped and turned to Heather. "About what?"

"You need to understand, I would never hurt Connor. You are

his aunt, and you love him. I get that. I would feel the same way if I thought some wacko was watching my nephew. Well... if I had a nephew. But since I don't, I would feel that way if they were watching Connor."

Kelly's eyes widened. "Did Lily tell you?"

"Lily? Um, no."

"Ian told you?" Kelly gasped.

Heather cringed. Actually, Marie had told her. "No, they didn't tell me. But, well, you know how things get around."

"Oh, I know. Lily told Danielle, and Danielle told you," Kelly grumbled.

"It doesn't really matter. I just wanted you to know Connor is safe with me. I would never hurt him."

Kelly stared at Heather, withholding comment.

"And I would never hurt your friend Ginny," Heather added.

"You threw things at her," Kelly accused.

"No, I didn't."

"Are you saying Ginny is lying about it?" Kelly asked.

"I'm saying Ginny is confused about what happened. But ask her this. Ask her if she actually saw me throw anything."

"I don't understand." Kelly frowned.

"It's a fairly simple question. Ask her if she actually saw me pick up anything and throw it at her."

"She saw things flying at her, but I assume she was trying to get away from you, so I don't imagine she stood around and watched you pick stuff up."

"And nothing hit her?" Heather asked.

"I guess it was lucky for Ginny that you don't have good aim."

Heather arched her brows. "I don't have good aim?"

Before Kelly answered, Heather snatched a small bag of rice from a shelf and called out to a teenage boy who was just coming down the aisle.

"Hey, kid, heads up!" Heather called out.

For a moment Kelly thought Heather was going to hit her with the bag of rice, but then it sailed down the aisle, over Kelly's head, landing in the teenage boy's hands.

"Wow," the boy muttered, looking down at the bag of rice in his hands. "Good throw!"

"Excuse me, I need to get my rice," Heather said and then added under her breath, "Poor aim, my butt."

THIRTY-TWO

Backing out of her driveway, Ginny Thomas glanced up at her house and didn't notice the two women standing on her rooftop under the quarter moon, watching her. One, an elderly-looking woman wearing a floral print dress and straw hat, the other a beautiful younger woman dressed in a long gown with her hair pulled into an elegant chignon. They had arrived just moments earlier and had intended to enter the house immediately but stopped when they heard the garage door opening. They waited for her to drive away.

It had been Eva who suggested they wait a few minutes to see if Ginny was leaving. If so, Eva reminded Marie the situation would be better handled without a non-medium lingering by, should Caitlin decide to throw things again.

"I suppose you're right," Marie agreed. "Caitlin was such a troubled girl when alive. It doesn't appear she's improved in death. She sounds worse. I don't recall her having violent outbursts when alive."

"She's obviously confused. But we can help her," Eva said.

They watched Ginny drive her car down the street and out of sight.

"Shall we go in now?" Eva asked.

A few minutes later, the two spirits stood in Ginny's living room.

"Caitlin!" Eva called out. "We've come to talk to you—to help you. Please show yourself!"

Silence.

When Caitlin did not respond, Eva and Marie moved through the house, looking for the troubled spirit. They searched every room, every closet, the basement and attic, and even went through the walls, but she was not at the house.

———————

OVERHEAD, the moon cast golden light along the water's surface. Together Caitlin and Cory sat on the end of the pier, their bare feet dangling over its side, while watching the seawater bounce and splash in a steady rhythm against the wooden pillars below.

Caitlin's long blond hair fell straight past her shoulders, wispy and as lifeless as herself. The plain shift she wore was the same one she'd been wearing when Cory had found her unconscious in her bedroom just minutes before her spirit had stepped from her mortal body.

Cory's disheveled yet clean dull brown hair spiked in random directions, the result of going to bed right after stepping from the shower. He wore just boxers, no shirt, but he wasn't cold.

Music played in the background, not blaring like he and Caitlin had liked to play their music, but faint and distant, as if coming from another world in a far-off place.

Cory had just finished telling Caitlin what Carla had told them at Pier Café.

"They found Uncle Bud's treasure," Caitlin said.

"It sounds like it," Cory agreed.

"And they haven't brought any down from the mountains yet?" Caitlin asked.

"No, at least not by what Carla overheard. She said they're going back for some on Sunday."

"It's our treasure!" Caitlin said. "This isn't fair. All those times we looked for it, and they find it?"

"I thought you would want to know," Cory said.

"You need to follow them up there," Caitlin said. "Which should be fairly easy since you know what day they're going."

"I don't know when they're going on Sunday," Cory pointed out.

Caitlin looked at Cory and narrowed her eyes. "Please don't make me do everything. You always do that."

"What do you mean?" Cory frowned.

"You know they're going up there on Sunday. I have to assume they'll want to get an early start to give them time to get up there, get what they can, and then return. So obviously, you need to camp out over by Marlow House early on Sunday morning. When they head up to the mountains, follow them. They'll lead us to the treasure."

"Then what?" Cory asked.

"I'll take over from there," Caitlin said.

Cory frowned. "I don't understand?"

"You don't have to understand, Cory. Just do as I say. Follow them up to the mountains."

"What are you going to do when we get there?" Cory asked.

"That treasure is rightfully mine." She paused a moment and then smiled at Cory and added, "Some of it is yours if you continue to help me like you always have. But they have no right to it."

"I don't understand what you plan to do when we get up there," Cory said.

"Just do as I say, remember that. Follow them up to the mountains!"

"But—" Before Cory could finish his question, Caitlin reached over and gave his back a shove, sending him tumbling off the pier into the water below.

CORY'S EYES FLEW OPEN, and he sat up in bed, the blanket falling off his bare chest. Darkness covered his bedroom, save for the moonlight slipping through his window, its blind open. Absently combing his right hand through his still damp hair, he sat there just a moment longer before climbing out of bed, barefoot and wearing just boxers. Cory stumbled to the window and looked out. Caitlin's house was dark. But it was not Caitlin's house anymore, it was Ginny's house. He continued to stare out the window when he noticed headlights coming up the street. Standing in the darkness of his bedroom, he peered out the window into the night. A moment later, the headlights turned into Ginny's driveway. He recognized the car. It was Ginny's. The garage door opened, and then the car disappeared inside before the garage door closed.

Cory turned from the window and went back to bed.

—————

JOE WORKED LATE ON FRIDAY, and instead of Kelly picking him up, he hitched a ride with one of his co-workers. When he arrived home, Kelly was already in bed, sleeping. After taking a shower and climbing into bed, he reached over to give her a kiss, but she groggily rolled away, apparently still asleep. With a sigh, Joe gave her a little pat, turned off the bedroom light, and then grabbed his pillow, giving it several punches with a fist before shoving it under his head.

He fell asleep quickly, but he didn't stay asleep long. Something woke him up, and when he reached out toward Kelly, she was no longer there. He glanced at the alarm clock on the nightstand and saw he had been sleeping less than an hour.

Rather than trying to go back to sleep, he lay quietly in bed, waiting for Kelly's return. The time ticked away. Eventually he looked back to the clock. Another hour had passed. With a sigh, Joe climbed out of bed.

He found Kelly in the study, curled up on the sofa with a blanket around her, the lamp on the end table on, but the overhead light off.

"Are you coming back to bed?" he asked in a soft voice.

Kelly looked up at the doorway. "In a while."

Joe frowned and walked over to the sofa and sat down with Kelly. "Is something wrong?"

Kelly shrugged.

Letting out a sigh, Joe leaned back on the sofa. "Are you mad at me?"

"I'm not mad at anyone," Kelly muttered unconvincingly.

They sat there in silence for a few minutes. Finally, Joe blurted, "I don't really want six kids."

Kelly frowned at Joe. "Excuse me?"

"I lied. I don't really want six kids. That's why you're out here, right?"

"Why would you lie about something like that?" Kelly asked. "Were you trying to scare me? Did you want me to break off the engagement? Are you having second thoughts?"

"No!" Joe groaned. "Brian said you'd think that."

"Brian? What does Brian have to do with this?" Kelly sat up straighter, the blanket no longer pulled tightly around her body.

"Brian has nothing to do with this. And I don't want to break off our engagement. I'm in love with you, Kelly. I want to marry you," Joe insisted.

"Do you love me as much as you loved Danielle?" Kelly blurted, immediately regretting the question. She hadn't meant to voice it, but it had been in her head.

"Danielle? I was never in love with Danielle," Joe said.

"Yes, you were," Kelly argued.

"I will admit I was infatuated. And I thought she needed me," Joe said.

"Needed you?" Kelly frowned.

"I don't want to talk about Danielle. She's not the one I want to marry."

"Okay, then what's this about six kids? Wanting them and then not. What was that all about?"

"I do want kids someday. And I will admit that I have been thinking maybe we shouldn't wait to start a family, considering—"

"My age?" Kelly finished for him.

"No, actually, my age," Joe grumbled.

Kelly sat up even straighter and leaned toward Joe. "Your age? Guys can be fathers when they're a hundred."

"That's not what I'm talking about. I just realize I'm getting pretty set in my ways, comfortable. And if we wait much longer, maybe I won't want kids."

"So that's why you said you wanted six kids?" Kelly frowned.

"No. I said that because…" Joe let out a sigh and reached out and took Kelly's hand. "I was just trying to get your mind off everyone else's business."

"What do you mean everyone else's business?"

"Just sometimes you get a little overinvested in other people's lives. Like wanting to play matchmaker for Brian or worrying about who's babysitting for Connor."

"It's just that I care," Kelly insisted.

"I know. But sometimes…" Joe didn't finish the sentence.

Kelly slumped back on the sofa, Joe no longer holding her hand. "Sometimes it's annoying?"

"Well, I wouldn't say annoying, exactly."

"And you thought giving me six kids would take care of it?"

Joe shrugged. "I really wasn't going to give you six kids."

They sat there for a few moments. Suddenly, Kelly laughed.

Confused, Joe asked, "What's so funny?"

"Oh, I totally missed my chance."

"Chance for what?" Joe asked.

"When you said you wanted six kids, I should have…" Kelly flew into Joe's arms and squealed, "Oh yes! Six kids! I am so glad you said that! That's what I want too!" She peppered his face with kisses before abruptly stopping and sitting back on the sofa.

"You want six kids?" Joe squeaked.

Kelly frowned. "Oh, hell no."

Joe chuckled and put his arm around Kelly, pulling her closer. They sat in silence for a moment before Kelly asked in a quiet voice, "You really weren't trying to get me to break off the engagement?"

"Absolutely not. I want to marry you," Joe insisted.

"I wasn't really sure of that. Even before you said you wanted six kids."

Joe pulled away from Kelly for a moment and looked at her. "Why did you think that?"

Kelly shrugged and said, "We've been together for over three years, and you never really talked about marriage before. And I was the one who first suggested us moving in together."

Joe let out a sigh and pulled Kelly back closer to him. "It's what I was talking about. I was comfortable."

Leaning against Joe, Kelly said, "I don't understand."

"I was comfortable with our relationship. Comfortable living together. Real comfortable. And I was afraid I might get too comfortable, and I might decide I want nothing to mess up what we have."

"You think kids will mess up what we have?" Kelly asked.

Joe shrugged. "It will change things."

They sat in silence for a few minutes. Finally, Kelly said, "I ran into Heather at the grocery store."

"And?"

"She knows I talked to Lily and Ian about her babysitting."

"They told her?" Joe asked.

"She said they didn't. I assume Lily said something to Danielle, who told Heather," Kelly said.

"Was she mad?"

"Actually, no. She said she understood and that if the situation were reversed, she would probably feel the same way."

"Really?"

"And you know what else?"

"What?"

"If Heather had wanted to hit Ginny, she could have."

THIRTY-THREE

S tretched out leisurely on the tree branch, his tail swishing back and forth, Max the cat looked down at Sadie, who raced across the side yard of Marlow House in eager pursuit of the tennis ball Walt had just pitched. Max didn't get it. What was this fascination dogs had with balls? Yarn he understood—but a ball? And to make it more perplexing, once Sadie caught that ball, she would give it back to Walt. Why? What was the point? If Max ever managed to snag the yarn, he certainly wasn't going to drop it at Walt's feet. After all, it wasn't a dead mouse.

He looked toward the house and spied Lily sitting with Danielle, chatting. With a yawn, he closed his eyes and rested his head on the branch for a nap.

"MAYBE CAITLIN MOVED ON," Lily suggested after Danielle told her how Marie and Eva had gone over to Ginny's the night before but hadn't found the restless spirit.

"I suppose it's possible, but considering her tantrum at the museum, I suspect she wandered off somewhere else. I don't see her moving to the other side in her state."

"Maybe she stayed at the museum?" Lily suggested.

"Eva wondered that too. They headed over there after leaving

Ginny's but couldn't find her," Danielle said. "Plus, Eva had stopped by the museum after Caitlin's outburst and hadn't seen her. Of course, at the time she wasn't aware of what had happened at the museum earlier that day."

Lily glanced out at the yard and watched Walt and Sadie. "I'm not sure who's enjoying that more. Walt or Sadie?"

"Good exercise," Danielle said as she sipped her tea.

"Now I feel guilty just sitting here," Lily grumbled.

"Meh, you get plenty of exercise running around after Connor."

"I keep waiting for you to join me," Lily said with a grin.

"We are trying. Walt is especially enthusiastic about the project."

Lily laughed and said, "He always was a good sport."

Danielle giggled.

Lily picked up her tea and asked, "So you guys going up there tomorrow?"

"Yeah. Walt wanted to go today, but Brian has to work this afternoon. I really don't want Walt wandering around in the mountains and getting lost again. I suppose we could get Marie or Eva to go with him, but if they want to find the spot where they first ran into Bud, it'll be easier having Brian and Heather there. Together they should be able to find it."

"What does he hope to accomplish?" Lily asked.

"It's about Bud's accusations regarding Walt's father. It's bad enough for Walt to learn his parents were probably murdered. Murdered by someone they considered a close family friend. Now, another close friend is accusing Walt's father of murder. But we don't see how that is possible. Even if Bud didn't die in the mountains, someone obviously buried him up there, if he's right about finding his body. We need a better understanding of the timeline. If Bud talked to Teddy hours before Walt saw him at Marlow House, there was no way Alex had time to kill Bud, take his body to the mountains, bury him, and get back to Teddy's house. It took hours to get from Frederickport to where Bud was by horseback."

"I still don't understand. Why did Teddy murder Walt's parents? Assuming he did," Lily asked.

"Bud told Walt that when he found out about Teddy's girlfriend, he discussed it with Alex, and they decided what to do about it. Yet Bud claims that instead of doing whatever that was, Alex murdered Bud."

"What did they decide?" Lily asked.

"Bud left before he could explain. But Walt's sure it has something to do with his father saying he was going to bring Maddie back with him and Anna to Marlow House the night of the fire."

"I'm sorry, Dani," Lily said.

"We need clarity on the timeline and on what Bud thinks he knows."

Danielle's cellphone rang. She picked it up and answered it. A moment later she hung up and told Lily, "That was Millie Samson. She wanted to let me know the newspapers arrived yesterday, and they'll be on display today, if I wanted to come down and look at them."

"I KNEW how anxious you were to see those newspapers," Millie told Walt and Danielle as she led them to the far end of the exhibit room on Saturday afternoon. "We're so excited to have a complete collection of the *Frederickport Press*. And the Glandon Foundation paid to have them digitalized, so if something were to happen, like another fire, God forbid, they won't be lost."

"Heather mentioned that," Danielle said.

"Oh, Heather, did you hear?" Millie asked. "Not that I've been telling people, but I know you and Heather are friends."

"I assume you're referring to the incident between Heather and Ginny," Danielle said.

Now standing by the table with the newspapers, Millie shook her head and sighed. "I really don't understand what happened. I like Ginny Thomas, and she has been most generous with the museum, but I don't know her well. Yet she seemed sincerely upset, considering the way she clung to me the other day. It was right after Brian Henderson left and not long after the supposed incident."

"Sorry you had to be put in the middle of this," Danielle said, because she didn't know what else to say.

"Yet, if I'm totally honest, Heather can get a little snippy. And it wouldn't surprise me to hear she lost her temper and threw something. After all, I have seen her punch Chris's arm a few times when he annoyed her. And he's her boss," Millie said.

"Heather has been working to break that habit," Walt said, resisting the urge to smirk.

"But the thing is, I find it hard to believe Heather would throw something that belonged to the museum," Millie said. "She used to be a docent, and she was always respectful of the displays and would get quite annoyed when someone came in and picked something up." Millie lowered her voice and added, "Frankly, a couple of times I thought she was going to smack one of our visitors who picked something up when there was a no-touching sign posted. It's one reason I was rather relieved when she said she couldn't docent anymore. We really can't have our docents hitting visitors."

"What you're saying, you can imagine Heather throwing something at Ginny if she annoyed her, yet just not throwing something from an exhibit?" Walt asked.

"Exactly!" Millie chirped. "Plus, she's been instrumental in getting the Glandon Foundation to fund many of our projects."

THERE HAD BEEN changes made to the newspaper section of the museum that Danielle hadn't noticed before today. Along the back wall, behind the table, they had installed a new bookshelf to store the additional volumes of newspapers, and no longer were any of the volumes stacked on the table. The table, now bare, provided a space for researchers to set volumes they wanted to read.

After Millie left Walt and Danielle alone, they located the volumes with issues from 1904 and set them on the table. Danielle sat down on a chair, while Walt took the second one.

They each spent the next twenty minutes looking through the newspapers and reading the various articles.

"Oh my," Danielle muttered, looking down at the newspaper before her. "I found the article on the fire. There's a picture of the house. Burned to the ground."

Walt stood up and walked around the table to Danielle's side. He looked down at the newspaper and its grainy black-and-white photograph.

"I remember that article," Walt said as he returned to his seat across the table from Danielle.

"You do?" Danielle frowned.

"Yes. It tells about the furnace exploding, and how my parents were attempting to carry Maddie out when a beam fell, trapping them."

"You were just a little boy when this article came out," Danielle said.

"My grandmother kept a copy of it. I found it later in her things, after she died. I remember reading it. It gave me nightmares for days. Such a hellish way to die. But perhaps they were already dead. While no one wants to hear someone might have murdered his parents, I suppose it comforts me to think that perhaps their death wasn't as horrific as I imagined. Oh, still horrific, but you know what I mean."

Danielle looked down at the article and reread it. She flipped the page and found another article discussing the victims. "There's a picture of your parents with Maddie, taken at a picnic. Maddie was a tiny little thing."

"I don't remember. My only memories of her are going to visit their house with my mother, but she was always in bed."

"Your father, he was a tall man," Danielle said.

"Yes, I remember that. Of course, I suppose from the perspective of most small boys their fathers are large."

Danielle looked up at Walt and said, "I suspect someone staged the scene of the fire."

"Why do you say that?"

"Think about it. Let's say you don't have your telekinesis powers. But we are in a fire with Lily. Lily has a broken leg. Would you and I carry her out?"

Walt frowned. "No. I would tell you to run for it and then carry Lily out myself."

"Exactly," Danielle said.

They skimmed through the rest of the newspapers for that year yet found no news stories that hinted at any conflict between Alex and either of his two friends. When they finished going through the papers for 1904, they started on 1905.

"I found an article on Teddy's second wife," Walt told Danielle.

She looked up from the paper she was reading and asked, "What does it say?"

"It paints Teddy as a most tragic figure," Walt told her.

"How so?"

"Their maid found Josephine at the bottom of the stairs when she came in that morning. Supposedly, Teddy was in town at the barber when it happened. They claim he had left the house just minutes before his wife fell to her death. Poor man, to lose both wives under such tragic circumstances," Walt scoffed.

"Really? How convenient for him," Danielle said.

Walt closed the book and looked up at Danielle. "Let's go. I don't think we're going to find anything here. Perhaps I'll learn what I need to know tomorrow from Bud."

Just as Walt and Danielle stood up from the table, Millie scurried over to them. "Did you find anything interesting?"

"A few things," Danielle said. "I'm just glad Ginny didn't dump all the old newspapers in the recycle bin."

"So true! And she has some wonderful old photographs. People thought Emily was a hoarder, but she actually had some very interesting things."

"The museum's gain, that's for sure," Danielle said.

"I don't imagine you've heard about the gold nugget Emily donated before her death," Millie said.

Danielle frowned. "Gold nugget?"

"Yes. Actually, it belonged to Emily's daughter, Caitlin. Poor girl, died of a drug overdose. Always was a troubled child. They had passed it down in the family, a rather interesting story. According to Emily, what makes it so intriguing, it comes from a gold mine in one of the local mountains."

"I don't recall any mines in this area," Walt said.

"No, most are south or east of here. But according to Emily, she had a great-uncle who prospected in the local mountains and hit gold. He didn't tell anyone where his mine was; he was very secretive. He only told his sister. But she didn't believe him, so to prove he had actually hit gold, he gave his sister one of his nuggets. That's the one that was passed down to Caitlin. Although this is all a little awkward, especially with Ginny being one of our new docents."

"Awkward, how?" Danielle asked.

"The board didn't see any reason to make a press release until after the display case we ordered arrives and we schedule the official opening for the new exhibit. We thought a little luncheon would be nice. But when I mentioned something to Ginny about it the other day, she didn't seem to know anything about the donation her cousin had made."

"Did she know about the gold nugget?" Danielle asked.

Millie shrugged. "I'm not really sure."

"What happened to this uncle?" Danielle asked.

"According to Emily, he disappeared. And his gold mine—and whatever gold he took from it—was lost forever. It will make a wonderful exhibit, don't you think?" Millie grinned.

"You don't know this uncle's name, do you?" Walt asked.

"Of course. His name was Bud Benson," Millie said.

THIRTY-FOUR

"A gold mine makes more sense," Danielle told Walt as he held the door open for her. Early afternoon sunlight flooded the museum's entry as Danielle stepped outside, followed by Walt. He let the door close behind them as they walked down the steps to the sidewalk.

"More sense than a pirate treasure?" Walt teased. He took her right hand in his, and together they walked toward the Packard parked nearby.

Danielle let out a sigh and said, "He was up in those mountains doing something. And considering how he looked, I'd say he was up there for a while. A hidden pirate treasure made no sense to me, because why would they take it up there and leave it? My bet, whoever stole the carriage and horses took off on the horses after they left the carriage in the mountains, with whatever they brought with them."

"That's what I always assumed. I'd heard the carriage had a broken wheel when they found it, which would explain why they abandoned it. But the gold mine story, that's a new one for me," Walt said.

When they reached the Packard, Walt opened the passenger door for Danielle. Just as she was about to get in, she stopped and said, "Tomorrow's Sunday."

Walt frowned. "Um… yes."

Danielle cringed. "Remember, Adam invited us to his house on Sunday for a barbecue."

"We should be back by then," Walt said.

"I don't remember getting the time." Danielle glanced at her watch and then looked back at Walt. "Since we're over here anyway, why don't we stop by his office. He should be there. We can find out what time we're supposed to be at his place. I hope it's not early."

CORY'S INTENTION had been to cruise by Marlow House to see if they were home. He worried they might decide to go up to the mountains on Saturday instead of Sunday. When he followed them up to the mountains—today or tomorrow—he wasn't sure what he planned to do next.

He spied their Packard parked by the museum as he drove through town. Instead of continuing to Marlow House, he parked down the street from the museum and watched.

Sitting in his parked car, slumped low in the driver's seat, Cory peered over his steering wheel and watched as Walt and Danielle got into the Packard. A moment later they drove down the street. Just as Cory was about to turn on his ignition, the Packard drove by Lucy's Diner and then pulled over and parked again. He watched as Walt and Danielle got out of the car and then walked up to the front door of Frederickport Vacation Properties' office. A moment later, they went inside. Instead of turning on his motor, Cory settled back in his seat and continued to wait and watch.

"AFTERNOON, are you here to see Adam?" Adam's assistant, Leslie, greeted Walt and Danielle when they walked into the front office of Frederickport Vacation Properties.

"Yeah, is he here?" Danielle asked.

"He's in his office." Leslie glanced down at the phone; the line to Adam's phone was not lit. She looked back up and smiled. "He was on the phone, but he just got off. Go on back."

"Thanks, Leslie," Danielle said as Walt gave the assistant a smile and nod.

When they reached Adam's office a few moments later, they

found the door open. Instead of walking in, they stopped by the doorway while Danielle knocked on the doorjamb and called out, "Hello?"

Adam looked up, and immediately his smile turned to a frown. "How dare you show yourself," he called out.

Danielle walked into the office, Walt trailing behind her. "What did we do?"

"Trying to sabotage my barbecue?" Adam asked, sounding as if he was only half joking. "I just got off the phone with Chris. He asked when he was supposed to be there, and that he would get back to me after talking to you if he could still make it."

"What time did you want us over there?" Danielle asked, now all the way in the office, Walt by her side.

"I was thinking of five. What's going on? You having a party without me?" Adam asked.

Danielle glanced at Walt, who gave her a nod and said, "That will work."

She looked back to Adam. "Chris will be there. So will we. In fact, that's why we stopped by."

Walt stepped toward Adam, who now stood behind his desk. Walt put out his hand and greeted Adam, who accepted the gesture. A moment later they all sat down, Adam at his desk, and Walt and Danielle in two chairs facing him.

"So what's going on tomorrow? What was I not invited to?" Adam asked.

"We're driving up to where the kidnappers took Walt. But we're only going up and coming right back down. Nothing particularly fun or social, I promise," Danielle said.

Adam glanced at Walt and then looked back at Danielle. "Holy crap, you really found a treasure?"

Danielle and Walt exchanged quick glances, and Danielle asked, "What are you talking about?"

"I had breakfast with Bill this morning," Adam began. He then recounted what Bill had said about a conversation Carla claimed to overhear.

"A treasure? She said they found a treasure?" Danielle looked at Walt.

"I think I know where that came from," Walt said. "I quoted William Penn."

Both Danielle and Adam looked to Walt, waiting for him to further elaborate.

"Brian and I were talking about our time in the mountains, and I said, 'Knowledge is the treasure of a wise man.' It's a quote by Penn."

Danielle and Adam continued to stare at Walt.

"You would have had to have been there," Walt said with a shrug.

"So you didn't find a treasure?" Adam asked.

"No," Walt said.

"Then why are you going back up there? I would think you've all had enough of the wilderness for a while."

After a moment of silence, Danielle blurted, "Pictures."

"Pictures?" Adam frowned.

"If you think about it, what happened to them was a rather monumental event in their lives. And they didn't have their phones with them, obviously. And when we picked them up, we didn't stick around to take any pictures."

"I don't know about you, but when something horrible happens in my life, I sure don't want to capture the memories in pictures," Adam snarked.

"It wasn't all horrible," Walt said. Adam and Danielle turned to him. "It was something of an adventure. Extreme camping," Walt said with a grin. "And we'd like to get some pictures of the place. Where we camped, where we got water. The mountains change with every season, and before we get into fall, we'd like to get some pictures showing what it was like when we were up there."

Adam nodded. "I get that. Yeah, makes sense."

"One reason we wanted to go tomorrow, both Brian and Heather have the day off," Danielle added.

"And Chris is going too?" Adam asked.

"He's taking the pictures," Danielle lied. "He has that really nice camera they use for the foundation."

"I'll be curious to see the pictures," Adam said. "Make sure you bring them with you."

"Um… I will…" Danielle muttered.

"And don't forget to make the brownies," Adam reminded her. "After all, that is the only reason I invited you."

Danielle rolled her eyes and said, "I won't forget."

"By the way, I heard what happened at the museum with

Heather and Ginny Thomas," Adam said with a chuckle. "I always told Mel I wouldn't want to piss off Heather." He chuckled again.

"Who told you?" Danielle asked.

"Ginny told Cory, Bill's nephew. You know they're neighbors, and he's been doing some odd jobs for her. Cory told Bill, and Bill told me this morning when we had breakfast together. What set Heather off?"

"I think it was just a misunderstanding. And if Heather had thrown anything, she didn't hit Ginny," Danielle said.

"Yeah, I heard that. About her not getting hit. Which made little sense to me. I've seen Heather throw the ball for Hunny. That girl had to have been on a softball team. She has a good arm and good aim," Adam said. "And we've all played Frisbee with her. She doesn't throw like a girl."

"I think I'm offended," Danielle muttered.

Adam shrugged and then asked, "So what happened?"

"It was a misunderstanding," Danielle reiterated without going into details.

"Is anything going to happen to Heather? Cory told Bill Ginny went to the police station to file charges against Heather, but the chief wouldn't do anything."

"I think that's because it was Ginny's word against Heather's. There wasn't any proof that Heather threw anything."

Adam arched his brow. "So Ginny lied?"

"I don't think she lied," Walt said. "There is just probably more to the story than any of us know. Frankly, I wouldn't be too hard on Heather or Ginny. Hopefully, they'll work out whatever differences they have."

"AND WHAT DIFFERENCES ARE THOSE?" Danielle smirked when she and Walt walked out to the Packard after leaving Adam's office.

Walt shrugged. "I feel bad for both of them."

"I'd better call Chris and the others," Danielle said when they reached the car. Walt opened the door for her, but instead of getting in the Packard, she took her phone out of her purse.

"Reminding him to bring his camera?" Walt teased as he waited for her to get into the car.

"Something like that," Danielle said as she stepped into the passenger side of the vehicle, the cellphone by her ear.

By the time Walt got to his side of the car, Danielle was no longer talking to Chris, but ringing up Heather. Walt waited for her to finish her calls before starting the ignition.

"Okay, that's taken care of," Danielle said as she dropped her phone back in her purse. "I told them both what I told Adam. Heather is going to call Brian and give him the heads-up so we're all on the same page."

"Now that I think about it, I wouldn't mind taking some pictures when we're up there," Walt said. "That's not a bad idea."

"Yeah, Chris thought that too. He's bringing his camera," Danielle said.

FROM DOWN THE STREET, Cory sat in his car, watching Walt and Danielle. They had been sitting in their vehicle for a few minutes and didn't seem to be in a rush to leave. Cory glanced at his watch and then looked back at the Packard. A moment later, it pulled out into the street and headed south, toward Beach Drive. After they drove away, Cory turned on his ignition and headed up the street.

ADAM LOOKED up from his desk when Cory walked into his office.

"Hi, Cory, what can I do for you?" Adam asked.

Cory stood there a moment, absently chewing his lower lip when he asked, "Um, have you seen my uncle?"

"Yeah, I had breakfast with him. Why?"

"Um, I was looking for him," Cory lied.

"Isn't he answering his phone?" Adam asked. "Maybe he's in the middle of a job and can't answer. He said something about replacing shingles on one of the rentals."

"Yeah, I guess that's it," Cory said, walking all the way into the office.

Adam frowned at Cory. "Is there something else?"

"Are you friends with the Marlows?"

211

"Yeah, why?" Adam asked.

"I saw them drive off. I just think they have a really cool car. That thing must be worth a fortune."

"From what I understand, it used to belong to the original Walt Marlow. It ended up with Ben Smith's father. Remember Ben?"

Cory shrugged. "Yeah. Old dude who used to work at the museum."

Adam nodded. "When he died, he left it to Danielle. That girl is always falling into money."

THIRTY-FIVE

A woman should be able to feel safe in her own home, Pearl Huckabee told herself as she parked her car in the driveway behind her house. But how is one to do that with homicidal neighbors? she asked herself. Pearl turned off the ignition, but instead of getting out of the vehicle, she looked over at Heather Donovan's house and glared.

This afternoon at her quilting group, the women had been talking about how her neighbor had attacked a woman at the museum. From what they said, Heather had gone berserk and left the place in shambles. No charges were filed, probably because Heather's boss paid for all the damages with a little something extra to keep Heather out of jail. According to the women in the group, those two had a thing going on.

The next minute headlights pulled up the alley and turned into Heather's driveway. A back porch light turned on a moment later, enabling Pearl to see the vehicle. It belonged to Officer Henderson. He got out of his car and headed toward the house, not looking Pearl's way.

"That's one busy girl," Pearl muttered. "And dangerous."

HEATHER HELD the door open for Brian as he walked in her back door carrying a paper sack, its contents jingled.

"Thanks for turning the light on for me," Brian said as Heather shut the door behind him and turned off the outside light.

"Did you say hi to Pearl?" Heather smirked.

"Pearl?" Brian frowned, following Heather into the kitchen.

"Yeah, she pulled into her driveway a few minutes before you got here. She's just sitting there. I was watching for you so I could turn on the light. Saw her still sitting in her car when you pulled up."

"Really? I didn't notice." Brian handed Heather the sack he had been holding. It jingled again.

"Oh, thanks," Heather muttered, taking the sack and looking inside. Glass jars—empty pickle jars, jelly jars and mayonnaise jars once destined for the recycle bin filled the sack.

"What do you need all those for?" Brian asked. Before Heather could answer the question, he looked over to the kitchen counter and noticed more than a dozen jars lined up, each filled with something that looked like paste.

"What are you doing?" Brian asked, walking over to the jars.

"Um… well… it's my sourdough starter," Heather said, sounding slightly embarrassed.

He counted the jars. "Sixteen? You need sixteen jars of starter? What are you going to do, open a bakery?"

"Yeah, I know it's lame. But I just thought it was so wasteful to throw half away, like Lily told me to do. So I just figured I would move the discard into another jar, feed it, and then I'd have another jar of starter."

"That's why you needed the jars?" Brian asked, glancing at the sack he had handed her.

"Yeah, well," Heather stammered, looking into the bag. Dejected, she set the sack on the kitchen table and groaned. "I am such an idiot."

"I wouldn't say idiot, exactly," Brian said.

"Do you know how much flour I've used, and I haven't even baked any bread yet?"

"No, how much?"

"I've gone through a five-pound bag already and have a second bag opened. And if I feed all the starter I have, I'm going to need more flour." She groaned again.

Brian laughed and said, "I don't think this is how it's done."

ON SUNDAY MORNING Pearl hurried down her walkway toward her car, on her way to church. She had forgotten to set her alarm clock the night before and was running late. While unlocking her car, she looked over to Heather's house and noticed Brian Henderson's car still parked behind Heather's house.

She shook her head at the sight and then unlocked her car door when a van came down the alley and turned into Heather's driveway, parking behind Brian Henderson's car. When the driver got out of the vehicle, she recognized him. It was Chris Johnson. Pearl paused a minute, looking for Hunny. Yet the pit bull was not with Chris.

"Good morning, Pearl," Chris called out cheerfully as he made his way up to Heather's house.

"HEY, BRIAN, YOU'RE HERE ALREADY," Chris said after Heather let him in the house and showed him to the kitchen. Brian sat at the kitchen table with a cup of coffee and a cinnamon roll from Old Salts Bakery.

"Morning, Chris," Brian said.

"He got here early," Heather explained. "Want some coffee?"

"Sure. You have an extra cinnamon roll?" Chris asked.

"Of course," Heather said as she went to get him a cup of coffee. "Where's Hunny?"

"She's staying with Ian and Lily while we're gone today." Chris glanced over to the counter and noticed all the jars. "Hey, what's with all the jars?"

"Don't ask." Brian chuckled.

"Oh, shut up," Heather grumbled, bringing Chris a cup of coffee and a cinnamon roll.

CORY PARKED in the alley a few doors down behind Marlow House, hoping to stay inconspicuous and then follow the Marlows from a safe distance when they left for the mountains. But so far it was like Grand Central Station around here, he thought. Some old lady just took off, and another car pulled up. He considered driving around to the front, but then the guy who had parked next door to the old lady's house came back outside, this time with two other people.

"Oh crap," Cory muttered, recognizing one of the people. It was Officer Brian Henderson. He slumped down in his car seat, hoping no one would notice him. The three walked over to the gate leading into the Marlows' backyard. He watched them go through the gate; it closed behind them.

Nervous someone might come back into the alley and see him parked along the bushes, he started his engine and decided to move his car somewhere less conspicuous.

CHRIS HAD OFFERED to drive them all to the mountains on Sunday morning in the Glandon Foundation's van. He had intended to pull in behind Marlow House, but when he noticed Brian's car over at Heather's, he thought he would stop over and let them know he was there and to be ready to leave. Instead of driving over to Marlow House, he just left the car behind Heather's, and the three of them walked over to get Walt and Danielle.

When they got into the van later that morning, preparing to drive up to the mountains, Chris asked Brian to sit up front in the passenger seat next to him. "Walt can sit in the back with Danielle, where they can get all mushy. Heather can chaperon," Chris said as he got into the van.

"Mushy, do we get mushy, Walt?" Danielle asked as she climbed into the vehicle.

"Chris is just jealous," Walt said as he waited for Heather to get into the van. He flashed her a smile and glanced up to Brian, who seemed reluctant to sit up front.

Twenty minutes later, the van moved down the highway heading to the mountains, Chris driving the vehicle while Brian sat in the passenger seat next to him. With the radio on, and the van size, those in the back seat could not easily hear the conversation in the front of the vehicle, and vice versa.

"Heather tells me you have accepted all this," Chris said, glancing at Brian and then back down the highway.

"What else did she tell you?" Brian asked.

"What else is there?" Chris asked.

Brian turned to Chris. "Remember when you first moved to Frederickport?"

Chris chuckled. "And you thought I murdered Trudy."

Brian frowned. "Trudy?"

"You knew her as Anna," Chris said.

"And she was a ghost."

"I didn't make her a ghost," Chris added.

"You know, the chief told us she went into witness protection," Brian said.

Chris grinned, his eyes still focused on the highway. "Yeah, I know. That was when I invited everyone to go to the dude ranch, and Joe wasn't thrilled spending a vacation with a killer."

"Joe might have been better off if the chief had let him believe you were a killer," Brian teased.

"No kidding," Chris scoffed. "Absolutely worst vacation ever."

"Like our trip to the mountains," Brian said. "Although we hadn't planned to go camping, and when I think about it, I would probably do it again."

"I certainly would not want to go through our kidnapping." Chris glanced briefly at Brian and then looked back down the highway. "Wow, we've both been kidnapped during our lives. Who else can say that?"

"I don't think most people would want to," Brian said.

"True, but you just said you'd do it over," Chris reminded him.

Brian leaned back in his seat, attempting to stretch out his legs while he looked out the side window and watched the scenery move by. "I never would have learned the truth about Walt—and everything else. I always knew there was something going on, but I never could pin it down."

"Yeah, witnessing things and not knowing can be confusing. But sometimes it's worse when you know, but those around you don't. Like with what happened between Heather and Ginny. I feel sorry for both of them," Chris said as he glanced up in the rearview mirror. He saw Heather's face staring at him, her expression unreadable.

THEY DIDN'T NOTICE the car following them since leaving Fred-erickport. It followed behind at a discreet distance, speeding up and slowing down when necessary. And since Cory, the driver of the car, knew the general direction they headed, he didn't feel it necessary to get too close behind the vehicle.

When the van finally reached the mountains and grew close to its ultimate destination, it made a right turn onto a dirt road. Instead of turning down the dirt road when he reached it, Cory pulled along the side of the highway and parked. Unsure what to do, Cory sat there a moment.

I can't just pull up behind them, Cory told himself. He waited a few more minutes, trying to decide what to do.

"What are you doing just sitting here?" Caitlin asked from the passenger seat of Cory's car. "Come on, follow them!"

Cory took a deep breath and put his car in gear. He stepped on the gas and pulled back onto the road, heading for the dirt road the van had taken. After driving for a few minutes, he came to a fork in the road.

"Should I keep straight or go right?" Cory said aloud.

"Go right," Caitlin insisted.

Cory turned right, driving slowly down the road. He came to another turnoff, but then noticed the van had pulled off the dirt road just around the next curve. He could see a section of the van through the brush. Instead of continuing on, he turned at the fork in the road and parked his car under the limbs of the trees, obscuring it from view.

"Why did you park here?" Caitlin asked.

Cory glanced briefly Caitlin's way and then turned off his igni-tion and got out of the car.

Annoyed, Caitlin followed Cory, but when he refused to talk to her, she muttered, "I hate when you get like this!"

Instead of walking with Cory, Caitlin made her way to where she had seen the van parked. Hiding in the bushes, she watched as the van's occupants headed down a trail. Determined, she returned to Cory to tell him where they had headed.

THIRTY-SIX

D anielle didn't leave breadcrumbs as they stumbled through the forest, attempting to retrace Walt, Brian and Heather's steps from the last time they had been on the mountain. But she didn't want to get lost, so she snapped photos with her phone to help them retrace their steps when the time came to head back to the van.

Had Marie or Eva accompanied them, she would not have been as concerned, but the ghosts had stayed back in Frederickport, looking for Caitlin's spirit. Eva didn't believe the unsettled spirit had moved on. Considering the energy Caitlin had harnessed, they felt uncomfortable letting her go unchecked. Perhaps the universe saw to it she could not hurt an innocent. It didn't mean there might not be collateral damage, which could have been the case had Ginny hurled the paperweight at Heather.

It had been almost twenty minutes since leaving the van when Heather called out, "Over here!" She hurried ahead of her friends to lead the way. "I recognize this place, around that bend. It's where I first saw him."

"And if he was telling the truth, it's where he'll be waiting," Walt added.

They followed Heather, none of them realizing they were also being followed. When they rounded the turn, Heather let out a little yelp in surprise. Yet she should have expected to find him standing there. He had told Walt this was where he would be waiting.

"You came," Bud said. He still wore his denims, flannel shirt and boots. Gone was the hat and beard. Without the beard Bud no longer looked like an old man.

The others caught up with Heather, with Chris and Brian to her right, and Walt and Danielle on her left. In the nearby shrubs, Cory and Caitlin watched.

"We did what you asked," Walt told him.

Bud looked over the group. "Can you all see me?"

"No, Brian can't." Heather nodded to Brian.

Bud glanced to Brian and back to Heather. "I remember him. He wasn't afraid when I shot at him."

"Pretend bullets aren't that scary," Heather snarked. "Especially when you can't see them."

Bud smiled at Heather. "I suppose you're right. And I'm weary of pretend bullets and being up here alone. I want to move on. I'll take you to where Alex put me."

"I don't believe my father killed you, much less buried you," Walt blurted.

Bud looked at Walt and said, "You were just a child."

"Do you remember seeing Alex bury you?" Danielle asked.

Bud cocked his head to one side, his expression quizzical, and then said, "I would assume someone had to have buried me. It makes sense it was my killer."

Brian frowned and said, "Can someone tell me what is going on?"

Heather reached out and patted Brian's wrist. "Bud's going to take us to his grave."

Bud turned his back to the group and headed down the trail. They followed. The trail ended along a hillside. Bud pointed to a pile of small boulders pushed against the base of the hill. The boulders' arrangement might have been placed by nature or by the intervention of man. Yet if they covered Bud's grave, the latter was more likely.

"You'll find me there, under those rocks," Bud announced.

Walt looked to the pile, and his energy lifted one boulder-size rock and moved it five feet away before dropping it to the ground. Yet instead of moving another boulder, Walt asked, "When was the last time you saw Teddy?"

"Why do you want to ask me about this now?" Bud asked.

"I'll be happy to do what you want. But we came all the way out here. The least you can do is answer a few questions," Walt said.

"It was in the morning in Frederickport. After I spoke to Teddy, I came up here. The next morning, your father murdered me."

"How do you know it was my father?" Walt asked.

"Because he shot me. I saw him. There, I told you. Are you still going to help me move down to Frederickport so I can be with my sister, or will you betray me like your father did?" Bud asked.

"What did you and Teddy talk about the last time you saw him?" Danielle asked.

Bud looked at Danielle. "We argued. I told him I knew about his girlfriend."

"Can you tell us more about that?" Danielle asked.

When Bud did not respond and just stared, Danielle added, "Please?"

Bud let out a sigh and said, "Ted had started a business in Astoria, and he hired a woman to work in the office. That's one reason Anna was always staying with Maddie, because Ted would spend days in Astoria. He told everyone he couldn't move Maddie down there, she was too ill, and made everyone think he was doing this for her. But I found out Teddy was seeing the woman he hired. She was far more than just an employee."

"Did you tell him you were going to tell Maddie?" Danielle asked.

"No. I told him I had already told Alex. I thought Alex had a right to know, since Anna spent so much time with Maddie. When I told Alex, he was furious. Alex claimed he was going to tell Maddie, convince her to move to Marlow House and leave Teddy. I thought it was a good idea."

"And that would mean Teddy would lose Maddie's inheritance," Danielle asked.

Bud shook his head. "No. It didn't matter at that point. There wasn't much left. Ted had burned through Maddie's money. But even if she had money and left him, Ted still controlled it under the terms of her parents' will. Yet at that point there was not much left."

Danielle frowned. "So basically, Alex taking Maddie off his hands should thrill Teddy. Free him to be with his mistress, not have to deal with an invalid wife he didn't love."

"Yes, if it weren't for Ted's uncle August. August was leaving his estate to Ted. But only because he adored Maddie. Had a thing for her, if you ask me. The old guy was sickly, ready to go any minute. I suspected Teddy planned to leave Maddie once the old man died and the inheritance was his. But if she left him before he died—and she left him because he was seeing someone else, it was a good possibility August would change his will and leave it all to Maddie. After all, Teddy was not his blood nephew. Teddy's mother was his wife's sister," Bud explained.

"And if Maddie were to die first?" Walt asked.

Bud looked at Walt. "Then I guess Ted would have hit the jackpot."

Danielle started to say something when Bud said, "No more questions. I told you everything. Please do what I asked." He stepped back from his grave. "Keep your bargain."

"I'll keep my bargain," Walt said solemnly. "Let's see if you're here."

BRIAN FELT as if he were listening to one side of a phone conversation, where you did not know what the person on the other side of the line was saying. Yet in this case, there were no phones involved, just a ghost. He remembered Lily recently telling him how one-sided conversations were one of the more annoying aspects of being a non-medium in the know. Brian now understood what she had been talking about.

Both Walt and Danielle had asked a series of questions, and Brian hoped Heather would remember enough of the conversation to fill him in on the missing parts. Brian wondered if Walt got the answers he sought. But that would have to wait.

They had arrived at what supposedly was Bud's gravesite. Brian silently watched as Walt focused his energy, moving large boulders, reminding him of their time up here, when Walt had cleaned up the campfires without getting his hands dirty.

Boulder-size rocks shifted and slid, leaving grooves in the ground as they moved away from the mountain's wall, revealing the gravesite. After clearing the area, dirt and smaller rocks floated up, drifting off to one side before falling to the ground, gradually forming a pile. A hole emerged where the boulders had been. Fascinated by the sight, they all stepped closer and watched the hole deepen, revealing its secrets.

"Is that a skull?" Heather asked.

"I think that's Bud," Chris said.

"Maybe we should stop now," Brian said when more dirt moved from the hole.

They all looked to Brian, and Bud said, "No, he can't stop now."

"Why?" Heather asked Brian, since he couldn't hear Bud's plea.

"I suspect Brian is suggesting we need to call someone up here. Someone more official," Walt said.

"This is a crime scene," Brian reminded them.

"An old crime scene," Danielle muttered.

"And there are no statutes of limitations on murder," Chris reminded them.

"True, but considering the age of this case, I doubt they will put much time into investigating it," Heather said.

Brian pulled out his cellphone. While he made his phone call, Bud demanded to know why Walt had stopped digging up his grave.

"As Brian said, this is a crime scene. Brian is a police officer, so it's understandable he would prefer to go through proper channels," Danielle explained.

"I want to be buried in the Frederickport Cemetery," Bud said. "That's why I wanted you to handle this!"

"Seriously?" Heather looked at Bud and rolled her eyes. "What did you expect, Walt would dig up your bones, shove them in a gunny sack, and then bury them himself at the cemetery in the dead of night?"

Bud frowned at Heather.

"Ahh, Heather, that's a little cold," Chris said.

"I'm sorry. But lately I just don't have patience for ghost demands," Heather huffed.

"You never have patience," Chris countered.

"Oh, shut up," Heather snapped.

"See!" Chris said.

"I don't understand. Does this mean I won't be buried with my sister? Did you lie to me?" Bud demanded of Walt.

"No, I didn't lie," Walt insisted, shooting Heather an admonishing glare, to which she responded with a shrug.

"Bud, we will bury you at Frederickport cemetery even if we have to pay for the burial. I promise you. But we have to do this legally," Danielle told him.

223

CORY CROUCHED behind the pine tree, looking out at the five people he had been following. It seemed he had been hiding behind bushes and trees ever since he got to the mountains, moving from one place to the next to keep up with the five.

They stood along the base of a hill, their backs facing him, but he couldn't see what they were doing, nor could he hear what they were saying. Some words he could make out, but none of it made sense.

"They're digging up the treasure," Caitlin announced. "We need to move now before they take it."

Cory pulled his phone from his back pocket and looked at the time. He then cringed when he realized he had forgotten to turn off the phone's ringer. Hastily he turned off the ringer, grateful he had received no calls.

"Cory, are you just going to sit there playing with your phone? They are digging up the treasure!"

He shoved the phone back in the pocket and muttered, "What am I going to do?"

Frustrated, Caitlin gave Cory a shove. He stumbled from behind the tree out into the clearing, landing on the trail, backside first. The five people he had been tracking turned around abruptly and saw him sprawled on the ground.

Cory regained his composure and got to his feet. "I believe you have something that belongs to Caitlin," he announced.

THIRTY-SEVEN

B rian Henderson had just finished his phone call to report the discovery of a grave when Cory Jones came rolling out of the trees and into the clearing.

"What are you doing here, Cory?" Brian demanded while stuffing his cellphone back into his pocket.

"We've come to claim what's ours!" came a shout from Caitlin, who stepped out from behind the trees and took her place next to Cory.

"Oh, terrific, that crazy teen ghost again," Heather muttered.

Confused, Bud stared at Caitlin and Cory. The mediums looked from ghost to ghost, while Brian, who hadn't heard Heather's comment, didn't realize Cory had company.

"If you found the treasure, it belongs to Caitlin. It's hers," Cory announced.

"What's he talking about?" Bud and Brian asked at the same time.

"I suspect they're talking about Bud's gold mine," Danielle explained.

"How did you know about that?" Bud demanded.

"What do you mean *they*?" Brian asked.

"The crazy teen ghost is here too," Heather told Brian. "She showed up right after Cory did."

Brian glanced around, looking for a ghost that he couldn't see even if she stood inches in front of him. Heather rolled her eyes at his futile attempt and pointed to where Caitlin stood.

When hiding in the trees and watching, Cory had assumed they gathered around the treasure. But their backs had been to him, obscuring from his view the movement of the boulders. Ignoring their questions, Cory moved closer to what they had all been staring at, and in doing so, he stumbled mindlessly through Bud. The ghost let out a howl at the unexpected intrusion.

Oblivious to Bud's presence, Cory stared into the partially exposed grave and asked, "Is that a skull?"

"You walked right through me!" Bud cursed. He gave Cory a punch, unnoticed by the young man staring down at the skull. Bud cursed again, and the next moment a rifle appeared in his hands. He took a shot at Cory, who remained unaware of the attack, still looking down at the skull.

"You can't shoot my friend!" Caitlin ranted at Bud. She picked up a rock and hurled it at the other ghost. It flew through his body, landing next to Cory.

Cory jumped back and looked down at the rock. He turned abruptly and asked, "Who threw that?"

"Is she throwing things again?" Brian asked Heather.

"Yep," Heather answered, her arms now crossed over her chest as she watched the ghosts.

Mesmerized by the unfolding drama, all the mediums watched, while Brian looked around nervously, waiting for another missile to fly by, and Cory waited for an answer to his question.

Nose to nose the two ghosts shouted at each other, Bud telling Caitlin he had never hit a girl before, but he had no problem turning her over his knee and giving her a good spanking, while Caitlin dared him to give it his best shot but warned she would kick him so hard he would roll up like a pill bug, and then she'd squish him like one.

"Who threw that rock?" Cory asked again. He turned to the others and started walking toward them, stepping right through the arguing ghosts. When he did, Bud and Caitlin stopped shouting at each other and looked incredulously at Cory, his back now to them.

"You walked through me!" Caitlin shouted at Cory.

"What's going on?" Brian asked Heather.

Heather shushed Brian and told him to hold on a minute, her attention on the dueling ghosts.

"How do you think I feel?" Bud asked Caitlin. "He walked through me twice!"

Having seen enough, Chris whistled. The ghosts and Cory looked at Chris, while Danielle arched her brows at Chris and said, "Wow, impressive. I didn't know you could whistle that loud."

"Sometimes it comes in handy," Chris said. He looked at Cory, pointed at the ghosts, and asked, "Can you see them?"

"Who?" Cory asked.

"Are you saying you can't see Caitlin?" Danielle asked.

"That's a silly question," Caitlin snapped. "Of course he can!"

Cory frowned. "What are you talking about?"

"You can't see Caitlin, can you, Cory?" Walt asked.

Cory looked at Walt. "What are you talking about? Caitlin is dead."

"No!" Caitlin wailed before disappearing.

"She was annoying," Bud muttered.

"Well, you are sort of related." Heather shrugged. "So there is that."

"What do you mean we're related? I've never seen her before," Bud snapped.

"Who are you talking to?" Cory asked Heather.

Cory now stood with his back to Danielle, Walt and Bud, his attention on Heather. Seizing the opportunity, Danielle stepped closer to Bud and whispered softly, "He can't see you. Please don't leave; let us find out why he's here."

"I would like to find that out myself," Bud said.

"Who are you talking to?" Cory again asked Heather.

"Cory," Danielle called out. He turned and faced her. "Why did you follow us up here? You knew we were coming here today. Carla told you. Your uncle told Adam about what she said, and Adam told us."

Cory looked around sheepishly, shuffling his feet as he glanced over to Officer Henderson. "Is this going to get me arrested?"

"I guess it depends how you answer the questions," Brian said.

"When Carla told us you were coming up here today because of Uncle Bud's treasure, I didn't have a choice, because it's rightfully Caitlin's," Cory explained.

"What does he mean, Uncle Bud's treasure?" Bud asked.

"What is this treasure?" Danielle asked after hearing Bud's question.

Cory frowned at Danielle. "Why are you asking me that? You just said it a minute ago. His gold mine."

"But why do you keep calling it a treasure?" Danielle asked. "While a gold mine can be valuable like a treasure, it sounds funny calling it that."

"All the gold he took out of the mine and never brought off the mountain." Cory looked at Walt and said, "You obviously found it. Carla heard you talking about the treasure and coming up here to bring it back."

"That's what happens when someone eavesdrops and passes a story on," Danielle said.

"Are you saying they didn't find the treasure?" Cory asked.

Danielle nodded to the partially open grave. "Does that look like a treasure?"

Cory walked back closer to the grave. Bud quickly stepped to one side to avoid being walked through again. Cory looked down and frowned. "It looks like a skull."

"How did he know about my gold mine?" Bud asked.

Danielle looked to Bud and asked, "Did you remove gold from the mine and hide it somewhere up here?"

Bud shrugged. "Maybe."

Cory frowned. "Who are you talking to?"

"I like to think out loud," Danielle lied. "Why did you think Bud had a treasure up here?"

"It was a story in Caitlin's family, about some great-uncle Bud, a prospector who struck gold up here. He brought back a gold nugget. Caitlin showed it to me, but her mother gave it to the museum. That was wrong. She shouldn't have given away the nugget. And now that the museum has it, pretty soon everyone is going to find out about the gold mine up here."

"How does he know any of this? And who is he?" Bud demanded.

"Cory," Walt said, "tell us what you know about Uncle Bud. I assume Caitlin told you?"

"Who is Caitlin?" Bud asked.

"I told you, a relative of yours. Shush so we can hear what he says," Heather told Bud.

Cory turned to Heather and frowned. "What?"

Heather shrugged. "Danielle is not the only one who thinks out loud. Go ahead, answer Walt's question."

Cory looked from Heather to Danielle and then to Walt. Brian cleared his throat, getting Cory's attention. When Cory looked at Brian, the police officer flashed him a stern look, as if saying, *go on, answer Walt's question.*

Cory let out a sigh and hesitantly said, "There was a story in Caitlin's family about a great-uncle Bud who had gone prospecting up here and struck gold. His sister didn't believe him, so he brought back a gold nugget and gave it to her. She wanted him to file a claim, but he was afraid to do that, worried that someone would follow him back up here and kill him for his gold."

"But that is why you file a claim, to protect your interest," Chris argued.

"No one knew there was gold up here," Bud interjected. "The minute I filed a claim, these hills would be swarming with people. I just wanted to remove as much gold as possible first, and I could file my claim later."

Cory shrugged at Chris's comment. "I don't know about that. Caitlin just said he never filed a claim, but he got a lot of gold out. And then he disappeared. Caitlin never believed he just took off or that anyone killed him. She figured he did something stupid like got bit by a rattlesnake, and then some mountain lion ate him. Leaving behind his treasure."

"This Caitlin has a morbid imagination," Bud grumbled.

"If that grave belongs to Uncle Bud, then Caitlin was wrong. Someone did kill him," Brian said, nodding to the grave.

Cory furrowed his brows, looking from the grave back to Brian. "Are you saying that is Uncle Bud?"

"What's left of him," Brian said.

"Hey, I am right here!" Bud shouted.

"And someone already found the treasure, and they killed him?" Cory asked.

"Why did Caitlin say pirates kidnapped Uncle Bud?" Danielle asked.

"Pirates?" Bud frowned.

"Who told you about the pirates?" Cory asked.

"A friend told me," Danielle said.

"Oh, Adam," Cory grumbled. He shrugged and said, "When Caitlin's mom was a kid, she heard a story about pirates hiding in the mountains or something like that. Caitlin liked to say pirates kidnapped Uncle Bud, like the story her mom told her, but she figured he probably just died a boring death by doing something stupid."

"Boring death?" Bud squeaked. "Death is death!"

"What did you hope to accomplish following us here?" Danielle asked.

Cory shrugged. "I'm not sure. Not really. I had a dream, and Caitlin told me to follow you up here. Figured, if I came up here, the dreams might stop. I didn't really have a plan for once I got up here. But then when I was watching from behind the trees, I felt something push me, and suddenly I am standing here, in front of all of you. So I did the only thing that I could do; I made a declaration for the treasure, for Caitlin. Because it really should be hers."

"You've been dreaming about Caitlin?" Danielle asked.

Cory nodded. "Yes. Ever since she died. It upset her when her mother donated the gold nugget to the museum. It had belonged to her."

"Do you believe Caitlin's spirit really visited your dreams?" Danielle asked softly.

Cory shrugged again. "I don't know. It felt real. But I want the dreams to stop. Not because I don't want to see Caitlin, but I don't like the way they make me feel. She's always so angry. I just want them to stop."

"I don't understand any of this," Bud said.

Danielle looked at Brian and asked, "Um… when are they supposed to get here? We really need to talk to Bud before they do."

"Cory, where's your car?" Brian asked.

"What did she mean she needs to talk to Bud?" Cory asked.

"I'll explain it to you, but let's walk to your car and do it there. When they get here, I have to show them where the grave is," Brian explained. "We'll talk down by your car." Brian looked at the others and asked, "Is there anything else you want to ask Cory before we go?"

Danielle glanced at her fellow mediums before answering. They all shook their heads in a silent no. She looked back to Brian and said, "No, nothing now."

"Am I under arrest?" Cory asked.

"You don't seem to be armed and dangerous, perhaps a little confused," Brian said.

"His ghost friend was the one who was armed and dangerous," Heather muttered.

"Heather, why don't we go with Brian in case she's still hanging around. And let Walt and Danielle handle the situation here," Chris suggested.

"In case who's hanging around?" Cory asked.

"Don't worry about it," Brian muttered, giving Cory a gentle nudge to get him walking back to the road.

THIRTY-EIGHT

"Who exactly is this Caitlin you were talking about?" Bud asked after Cory left with Brian, Heather, and Chris.

"She was the one who threw a rock at you," Danielle explained.

"And she's dead too?" Bud asked.

"Yes. But I don't think she completely understands. There is a lot of anger there," Danielle said.

"She looks so young. I should have dealt with her differently. But it all happened so fast."

"Caitlin is volatile," Danielle said.

"That's an understatement," Walt muttered.

"Who is she?" Bud asked. "Is she really related to me?"

"Yes, distantly." Danielle explained the family connection between Bud and Caitlin.

"So you did give your sister a gold nugget from your mine?" Walt asked.

"Yes. She didn't believe me when I told her I'd struck gold."

"They passed the gold nugget down in your family, and it ended up with Caitlin until her mother donated it to the local museum after she died. I believe the museum was rather excited to learn of a possible undiscovered gold mine in one of the local mountains," Danielle explained.

Bud frowned at Danielle and then looked to Walt. "I don't understand. I would assume everyone knew about the gold mine by now. Last night I realized that had to be the reason your father killed me. He was the only one other than my sister I told about the gold, and the only one who actually knew where the mine was and where I hid the gold I had already removed. I hadn't filed the claim yet. I was planning to do it when I came back down from the mountains the last time I came up here. Your father knew that. Why would he kill me and not claim the mine?"

"And you saw Walt's father shoot you?" Danielle asked.

"It had to have been Alex. The only ones who knew I had been prospecting up here were Walt and Teddy. Teddy had no reason to want me dead; I never told him I'd struck gold. Teddy would have been the last person I would tell. I saw Alex that day. He was standing over there, on that ridge." Bud pointed off in the distance.

"That's rather far off. How did you see his face?" Walt asked.

"I'd recognize that hat and coat Alex wore anywhere, and it was his horse."

Walt frowned. "I remember Teddy's horse; he looked almost identical to my father's gelding. My father used to call them a matching set."

"True, but that wasn't Teddy I saw. Whoever it was, he was wearing Alex's hat and jacket," Bud insisted.

"What do you remember after he shot you?" Danielle asked.

Bud considered the question a minute and then said, "Everything went dark, and then I woke up, and I thought I'd gotten away from him. But I felt I couldn't go home. I thought he was going to kill me."

"You were dead already," Danielle said. "And confused."

"I realize that now."

"Let me get this straight, you told my father about Teddy and the woman who worked for him, and that morning you came up here?" Walt asked.

"Yes. Anna was with Maddie that day, and Alex told me he was going to stop home and tell his mother that he might bring Maddie home with him and Anna that night. I left for the mountains. But he obviously had other plans and showed up here the next day."

"Do you remember what day that was?" Danielle asked.

When Bud told them the date, Walt and Danielle looked at each other for a moment.

Danielle looked back to Bud and said, "I know without a doubt that Walt's father was not responsible for your death."

"How can you say that? You weren't even born yet," Bud said.

"Because," Danielle let out a sigh before saying, "Walt's parents were already dead. We're fairly certain Teddy killed them, and then he probably came up here and murdered you."

THEY SAT on the boulders Walt had moved from the gravesite, waiting for the authorities to arrive for Bud's remains. They told Bud all they knew about Alex's and Anna's deaths.

"All this time I thought Alex had shot me that day, and all this time he was already dead before it ever happened."

"I'm just trying to understand why Teddy came up here and killed you," Danielle said.

"It was all my fault," Bud groaned. He buried his face in his palms, as if blocking out the world while trying to come to terms with what he had caused.

After a few minutes of silence, Walt asked Bud, "What do you think happened?"

Bud lifted his face from his palms and looked at Walt. "I walked in on Teddy and Josephine. Teddy had claimed she just worked for him, but she was obviously more than an employee. I didn't realize Teddy had seen me. I went straight to Alex."

"Why to my father?" Walt asked.

"Maddie's illness had so disrupted your family because your mother spent so much time there, with Teddy gone so often, not willing to move Maddie to Astoria, saying it wasn't fair for her. But it was that he didn't want her there, I realized that day. Alex had told me he wished he could move Maddie to Marlow House to live. It would have made things so much easier on everyone. Alex even suggested it to Teddy, but he refused."

"Why would he refuse?" Danielle asked. "I'd think that would have made his life easier. He could have spent more time with his girlfriend."

"It's because of his uncle August. August and Frederick Marlow did not get along. If Maddie moved under the Marlow roof, Teddy worried his uncle would change his will."

"After you told Alex about Teddy's girlfriend, what happened?" Danielle asked.

"Alex told me he planned to tell Maddie the truth and get her to move to Marlow House. After all, Alex knew Maddie was not in love with her husband, so he understood she would not be heartbroken. She had only stayed with Ted out of a sense of loyalty."

"And Teddy knew Alex was going to talk to her?" Danielle asked.

"After I spoke to Alex that day, right before I left for here, Teddy showed up and tried to make excuses for what I saw—or, as he said, what I thought I saw. I told him I had no intention of telling anyone —other than Alex. He begged me not to tell Alex, and I said it was too late, I had already talked to him, but that he could probably catch him at Marlow House and tell his side of the story before he told Maddie."

"I saw him that afternoon," Walt muttered. "When he stopped by Marlow House."

"I can't imagine what happened that day between Teddy and your parents. I believe when Teddy left me, he only intended to talk to Alex. I'm sure he thought he could convince him not to tell Maddie. If he intended to kill them, I think he would have killed me first instead of letting me return here. But whatever went wrong at Teddy's house that day, he obviously worried that because of our conversation that morning, I could incriminate him in your parents' and Maddie's deaths, so he came up here looking for me."

"He obviously took Walt's father's coat and hat, which he wore up here," Danielle mused.

"I imagine he wanted Bud to think it was my father riding up," Walt said.

"Yes. Not that I would have assumed he was going to shoot me, but Teddy rarely came up here," Bud said.

"While Walt and I will always wonder what really happened the day of the fire, I imagine once you move on, you'll find out," Danielle said.

"Will I see them again?" Bud asked.

"I'd be surprised if you don't. Not sure about Teddy, but I imagine you'll see Walt's parents and Maddie," Danielle said.

"I don't want to see Ted," Bud grumbled.

"I don't blame you," Danielle said.

"Can I ask you one question?" Walt asked.

"What's that?" Bud asked.

"Where exactly is this gold mine of yours? And where is the gold you've already removed?"

WHEN THEY WERE ABOUT twenty feet from Cory's car, Heather saw her, Caitlin. The teenage ghost sat in the passenger seat, waiting for Cory. Heather stopped abruptly and turned to Brian. She whispered something in his ear. Afterwards, Brian nodded and looked to Cory and said, "We're going to walk down there and wait for the responders by the van while you and I have a little talk." Brian pointed down the dirt road in the opposite direction from Cory's car.

Cory gave Brian a nod and started down the road with him. They had walked just six feet when Chris let out a whistle while shoving his hand in one pocket. When Brian stopped and turned to Chris, Chris pulled something from his pocket and tossed it to Brian while saying, "Here's the keys, if you want to wait in the van until they arrive."

Brian caught the keys in midair and gave Chris a nod before turning with Cory and heading down the dirt road.

"Do you want to do this alone?" Chris asked Heather as they stood in the middle of the dirt road, looking at Cory's car and its ghostly occupant.

"No. If she sees you, she might stick around long enough to understand she's dead," Heather said.

Together Heather and Chris approached the car.

"Caitlin, we would like to talk to you," Heather called out.

"Go away. I don't want to talk to you." Caitlin wrapped her arms around her chest and slumped down in the car seat.

"We just want to help you," Chris called out, now by the hood of the car.

Caitlin looked up at Chris. "Who are you?"

"I'm Chris. I just want to help you." Chris smiled, showing off his straight white teeth.

She turned to Heather and glared. "I don't want to talk to her. I don't like her!"

Heather stopped in her tracks and looked from Caitlin to Chris.

"Will you talk to me?" Chris practically cooed.

Sticking her lower lip out in a pout, Caitlin looked at Chris and gave a nod.

Heather rolled her eyes. "Oh, brother. I'm going back to Walt and Danielle. Good luck, pretty boy."

CAITLIN no longer sat in the passenger seat of Cory's car. Instead, she sat with Chris in the back seat.

"Am I really dead?" Caitlin asked.

"You sort of already knew, didn't you?" Chris asked.

Caitlin nodded. "I guess. But sometimes I could get Cory to talk to me, and I figured I couldn't be dead. I mean, Cory can't see ghosts, can he?" She looked eagerly at Chris, waiting for an answer.

"I suspect Cory talked to you in his dreams," Chris suggested.

"Is that what I am, a ghost?" Caitlin asked.

"You are now until you move on. I'm sure your mother is eager to see you," Chris said.

Caitlin shook her head. "No. She's mad at me. I told her I didn't take drugs anymore. I promised. But I lied."

"I don't think she's mad at you. Heartbroken, maybe," Chris said.

"She's mad. She gave away my gold nugget," Caitlin said.

"You were gone, Caitlin. When people die, people left behind often give away some of their belongings. It's how it works. If your mom had died first, you would have probably given away some of your mother's things."

"I suppose." Caitlin let out a sigh. "I really don't want to be dead."

"So you didn't mean to kill yourself?" Chris asked.

Caitlin frowned at Chris. "Gosh, no. Why would you say that?"

"You took a lot of drugs that last time," Chris said.

Caitlin shook her head and looked out the window, staring at nothing in particular. "I regret everything."

"Time to forgive yourself, Caitlin. Time to move on. Your mother is waiting."

Caitlin looked at Chris. "Promise?"

Chris smiled softly. "Promise."

The next moment Caitlin vanished.

THIRTY-NINE

I t had been almost a week since they brought Bud's remains down from the mountains. Because of the personal effects buried with the body that had survived all those years, authorities were fairly confident of his identity. Danielle discovered she didn't need to buy a cemetery plot for Bud to keep her promise. They learned through Ginny that Bud's sister had purchased a plot for him, and it remained empty.

To quell some skeptics, they ordered a DNA test of the remains. Chris paid to put a rush on the order, knowing Bud would not move on until they laid his remains to rest near his sister. Danielle understood the DNA results might not prove his identity, since they relied on his family's DNA already on file. Fortunately, the results showed the remains likely belonged to Bud, and on the last Saturday in August, a group stood in the Frederickport cemetery for a gravesite service.

"Why are there so many people here?" Bud asked Danielle as he looked around. "I'm flattered, but I've been dead for a hundred and fourteen years."

"The museum decided to move the official opening for the gold nugget exhibit to this afternoon," Danielle told him in a whisper. "Finding you, well, it sort of plays into that rather nicely."

Bud frowned. "I'm not sure how I feel about that." He looked back to the open grave and watched as they lowered his casket. He found the sight unsettling, so he turned his attention to the surrounding crowd.

Danielle stood to his right, with Walt next to her. On his left stood Chris and Heather. Brian, the man he had once shot at and who couldn't see or hear him, yet had helped bring him down from the mountains, stood some distance away, standing with the police officer he had encountered when first returning to Marlow House, along with two little boys. He remembered one of the little boys could see and hear him. Brian continually looked their way, and since Bud knew he couldn't see him, he wondered what Brian kept looking at.

The young man named Cory, who'd rudely walked through him several times, was also there. He stood with a woman who, according to Danielle, was also a relative of his, named Ginny Thomas. Standing with their little group were two other couples, with one man holding a small child.

After they lowered the casket into the ground, the minister said a few more words, and then the crowd dispersed. Bud watched as Brian and the people he had been standing with headed their way.

A moment later, Brian stood talking to Chris and Heather while the other police officer stood talking to Danielle and Walt. The taller of the two boys who had been standing with the police officer wandered closer to the open grave, looking down curiously at the coffin. The smallest of the two boys stood directly in front of him, staring up at his face. Bud looked down at him. The boy smiled.

"I wanted to say goodbye," the boy whispered. "Danielle says you're moving on after your funeral. Would you do me a favor?"

Bud arched his brow at the boy and leaned down toward him. "What kind of favor could I possibly do for you?"

"Would you say hi to my mom for me?" the boy asked. "Tell her I love her."

Bud's smile vanished. "Your mother, she's on the other side?"

The boy nodded.

"Evan, what are you doing?" the taller boy, who had just wandered over from the open grave, asked. "You look goofy talking to yourself."

"I was just thinking out loud," Evan said, flashing a smile to Bud.

Bud's smile returned, and he gave Evan a wink while saying, "I'll find your mom and give her your message. I promise."

THEY STOOD by the Packard in the cemetery parking lot, Walt, Danielle and Bud.

"Are you sure you don't want to go to the museum with us before you move on?" Danielle asked. "The exhibit is about you."

Bud shook his head and sighed. "No. I'm ready to move on. There is nothing left for me here. And I'm anxious to see Alex. I need to apologize to him for what I thought all this time." Bud looked at Walt and asked, "Do you want me to give your parents a message?"

Walt considered the question a minute and then said, "Tell my parents I'm sorry I've kept them waiting so long to see me again. I hope they understand."

Bud smiled at Walt, reached out as if to touch his wrist and said, "I'm sure they do." He disappeared.

"It's too bad Bud couldn't remember where his gold mine was, or where he stored all that gold he took out of it," Walt mused.

"Why? The last thing we need is to find another treasure," Danielle said.

WHEN WALT and Danielle arrived at the museum, people were already milling around, some looking at exhibits while waiting for the formal unveiling of the newest one, while others chatted with friends or helped themselves to the refreshments offered in the lobby.

Millie Samson greeted Walt and Danielle when they stepped into the museum.

Giddy with the response to today's program, Millie said, "If you hadn't found Bud Benson's remains up in those mountains, I can't imagine we'd have this sort of response. Already we've received two nice donations and several new members to the historical society."

"I'm glad it's worked out for the museum," Danielle said, glancing around.

"There are refreshments. Help yourself," Millie said, pointing to one table set up in the lobby. "The program doesn't start for another twenty minutes."

"What is that?" Walt asked, pointing to another table in the

240

lobby, this one filled with an odd assortment of glass jars, each half filled with a cream-colored substance.

Millie glanced at the table and then laughed. "Oh, that's Heather's donation. It's sourdough starter. Gold miners would often take sourdough starter with them, which they'd used to leaven their bread. According to an article Heather showed me, some of them actually slept with the starter to keep it warm. She thought it would be a fun gimmick to give away sourdough starter at the exhibit opening. A clever idea—a little odd, perhaps." Millie paused a moment, shrugged, and then added, "But the Glandon Foundation does so much for the museum."

After Millie walked away, Walt and Danielle wandered to the table with the sourdough starter. Each jar sported a twine bow. Danielle picked up one jar and turned it in her hand. She looked at Walt and said, "This is one of the jars I gave Heather."

"Planning to make sourdough bread?" a voice behind Danielle asked. Danielle turned around and found Lily standing behind her, Ian by her side, with Connor in Ian's arms.

"Not really," Danielle said, placing the jar back on the table.

"I guess Heather ignored the part in my instructions where I told her to just toss the discard the first week. Instead, she fed it." Lily chuckled. "I need to give her some discard recipes or Frederickport's going to face a flour shortage before long."

"I don't understand," Walt asked.

"Think about it. If you start with one jar of starter, divide it, feed each jar, and then repeat the next day…" Lily began.

Walt cringed. "It doubles every day."

Lily nodded. "Exactly."

Danielle glanced at the table. "You have to give Heather credit. It's a clever way to get rid of it."

"Yeah, well, giving away starter is sort of like giving away a puppy," Lily said.

"A puppy?" Danielle frowned.

"It's a living thing, and you have to feed it every day," Lily reminded her.

HEATHER STOOD by the doorway leading to the portrait exhibits. She looked out at the main exhibit area where today's program would take place. The spirit of Eva Thorndike stood by her side, watching the gathering crowd.

"Why are you standing here by yourself?" Eva asked.

"I'm not alone. You're here," Heather reminded her.

"There is a handsome gentleman who keeps looking your way. A rather dashing-looking one with gray hair. Sometimes a mature man can be rather appealing," Eva purred.

Heather shrugged. She looked over at Chris, who stood on the other side of the room talking to an attractive woman. From Chris she looked over to Brian, who stood with Joe and Kelly, talking. Occasionally he would look over at her, as if waiting for some signal. Ginny Thomas walked up to the small group and started talking to Kelly.

"Eva, did Caitlin move on for sure?" Heather asked.

"You asked me to check, so I did. From my sources, yes. She moved on."

Heather looked over at Eva and frowned. "What are your sources?"

Eva smiled at Heather and vanished.

Heather let out a sigh and looked over at Brian and the others. Ginny no longer stood with them. She had moved over to the newspaper section, inspecting the newest additions.

Glancing around, Heather took a deep breath and headed toward Ginny.

Ginny didn't see Heather coming. Her back was to her. She stood by the rack holding the bound editions of the *Frederickport Press*.

"Ginny, can we talk?" Heather asked.

Upon hearing Heather's voice, Ginny twirled around, facing Heather, her eyes wide.

"What do you want?" Ginny demanded in a whisper.

"I've come to apologize. Please accept my apology," Heather asked.

Confused, Ginny furrowed her brows. "You admit what you did?"

Heather took another deep breath and said, "Please hear me out."

Ginny studied her and then nodded.

"I did not touch your bookshelf. When it fell, it scared the crap out of me. It almost crushed me. I had no reason to push it over. Why would I?"

"You threw things at me. I saw you," Ginny accused.

"I felt bad about rushing out of your house, and I came to talk to you about it. And then you accused me of knocking your bookshelf down. Why would I do that? And I was already stressed from what happened just days before. You have no idea how terrifying that was, being drugged, and then waking up in the middle of the forest, tied to a tree, defenseless to any wild animal, and it was almost nightfall."

"You really had nothing to do with the bookshelf?" Ginny asked in a whisper.

"No, I didn't. And I admit, I sometimes have a temper. But if I did throw something, I never would try to hit you. I would never do that. Well, maybe I would with a Nerf ball. But there are no Nerf balls in the museum."

Ginny stared at Heather for a moment. Finally, she said, "I'm sorry if I falsely accused you. And I appreciate your help in bringing Bud home. Danielle told me you were the one who found him up there."

"I'm glad we could identify who it was. Everyone deserves that," Heather said.

When Ginny walked away a moment later, Eva appeared by Heather's side and asked, "Why did you confess to something you didn't do?"

Heather shrugged. "I didn't confess exactly."

"I SAW YOU TALKING TO HEATHER," Kelly whispered to Ginny a short time after she left Heather by the newspaper display.

"She apologized to me," Ginny said.

Kelly arched her brows. "She admitted what she'd done?"

"Not exactly." Ginny then repeated to Kelly what Heather had said.

Looking over to Heather, who now stood on the other side of the room, chatting with her brother and Lily, Kelly said, "I think she was telling the truth."

"You mean about not pushing the bookcase over?" Ginny asked.

"That and the fact she never intended to hit you," Kelly said. "If Heather had wanted to hit you with something, she could have."

FORTY

R unning the brush through her damp hair and wearing just an extra-long T-shirt, Danielle stepped from the bathroom into the bedroom. She found Walt already in bed, sitting up, reading a book, the covers pulled up to his bare chest. Upon hearing her approach, he looked over the book and smiled.

"That was an interesting day," Danielle noted as she tossed her brush on the dresser. "But rather exhausting."

"I felt a little sorry for Heather, having to take most of that starter home with her," Walt said as he closed his book and set it on the end table.

"I don't think many people in Frederickport are interested in baking sourdough bread. Not when they can get it from Old Salts." Danielle pulled back the covers on her side of the bed and climbed in.

"What is she going to do with all of it? Keep feeding it?" Walt asked.

Danielle chuckled and pulled the covers over her. "Lily told her to just put it all in one big jar, stick it in the refrigerator, don't feed it, and tomorrow she's going to give her some recipes she can use it up in. I have a feeling Heather is going to stick to feeding just one jar of starter from now on—if she keeps any at all."

Walt reached over and turned the lamp sitting on his nightstand off, sending the bedroom into darkness. He wrapped an arm around Danielle and pulled her close.

"I wonder where Max is," Danielle whispered, snuggling closer to Walt.

"He's sleeping in the parlor," Walt said, pulling her even closer.

"Walt, how are you doing with all this?" Danielle asked after a few minutes of silence.

"What do you mean?" he asked.

"This has been the most insane month," Danielle said. "First the kidnapping and then finding out about your parents. I just can't imagine how you're processing all this."

"After this last week, the kidnapping almost seems like a lifetime ago. I never believed my father had anything to do with Bud's death. But I feel a sense of relief knowing why Bud believed that and knowing he now has the truth. As for my parents' death, in some ways, it's like losing them all over again. And these what-ifs keep running through my head."

"What-ifs?" Danielle asked.

"What if I'd come out of those bushes when Teddy had come here to talk to my father? I could have stalled him just long enough that when he got back to his house, my parents would already be gone."

"That's a big what-if," Danielle said.

"Or what if I had pretended to be sick that morning instead of throwing a tantrum? Maybe my mother wouldn't have gone over that day. She would have stayed with me."

"Unfortunately, we don't get do-overs," Danielle reminded him.

"Are you sure about that?"

Danielle laughed. "You have a point. Sometimes we do get do-overs. For which I am most grateful." She gave him a kiss.

When the kiss ended, Walt said, "As to your question, how am I processing all this? It's much easier with you by my side."

BLISSFULLY RELAXED, Walt reluctantly opened his eyes. He must have fallen asleep, he told himself. For a moment he thought he was in bed, but then he looked around. He sat in the side yard at Marlow House. Yawning, he sat up straighter in the chair. Something was different, he told himself.

No longer slumped back in the chair, he took in his surroundings. The landscaping had changed—lusher yet with smaller trees. Different, yet familiar. And what had happened to the outdoor kitchen? Frowning, Walt looked at the yard furniture—wicker. Marlow House hadn't had wicker furniture since he was a child.

"Good, you're here!" a woman's voice called out.

Walt turned in the chair and looked at a beautiful young woman, a man at her side. A man—who could be Walt's double.

"You look surprised," she said softly.

Walt's eyes widened as recognition dawned. He tried to stand yet felt physically incapable of motion. The woman—his mother—rushed to him, taking his face in her hands and giving first his right, then his left cheek a kiss. "You look wonderful," she whispered and then kissed him again. "So much like your father."

Speechless, Walt remained in the chair while his mother sat down next to him in a chair that hadn't been there a moment ago. His father, still standing, held out his hand. Walt managed to stand up and accepted the handshake.

"You do look wonderful," Alexander said. When the handshake ended, Alexander impulsively threw his arms around Walt, giving him an enthusiastic hug and pat on his back. Before releasing him, he kissed his son's cheek and then took a seat in a chair that appeared on the other side of the one Walt had been using. Walt sat down.

Walt looked to his mother and then his father, who sat grinning at him, as if waiting for him to say something.

"This is a dream hop," Walt finally announced, his voice calm yet his mind reeling.

Anna smiled. "We heard Danielle called these a dream hop. She's a clever girl."

"You know about Danielle?" Walt asked.

"Of course we do. We knew about her before you did," Alexander said with a chuckle.

Confused, Walt frowned at his father.

Anna reached out and patted Walt's knee. "Bud told us we needed to talk to you."

Walt turned to his mother. "You've seen Bud?"

"Yes. He told us what happened, but of course we already knew. Unfortunately, there was nothing we could do about it. At least not directly," Anna said.

"But we knew we could count on you," Alexander said.

Still confused, Walt looked from his mother to his father. "I hope you can understand why I decided not to move on yet. It's not that I didn't want to see you," Walt began.

"We understand, and we also knew it wasn't your time. You had to wait for Danielle," Anna told him.

Walt stared at his mother. "But I missed you. Why didn't you come before—in a dream?"

Anna smiled at her son and gave his knee another pat. "We did a few times. I'm sure you'll remember when you think about it. But just like Evan's mother understood it was not in Evan's best interest to stay on your side—even though he could see her—we realized visiting your dreams often was not in your best interest."

"You know about Evan?" Walt asked.

"Certainly. His mother is a friend. A wonderful woman. She and I have a lot in common. And she asked me to have you tell Evan she got his message, and that she loves him too. Of course, she realizes he already knows that, but just like she loves hearing it, she knows he does too."

Walt looked from his mother to his father and said, "I'm so sorry for what happened to you both. I can't believe Teddy was responsible."

"You need to stop thinking about it," Alexander said. "It was a long time ago, and your mother and I are at peace."

"Can you at least tell me what happened that day?" Walt asked.

"In Teddy's defense, he didn't plan to kill us. And I suppose his penance would not have been as severe had he not made certain choices. But he did and now must deal with the consequences," Alexander said.

"What happened? You say he didn't plan to kill you, but why did he?" Walt asked.

"When Teddy arrived that day, I had already told Maddie, and we were packing her things so she could come with us. Teddy was furious, and he and I argued. Afraid we were going to throw punches, and worried we were upsetting Maddie, your mother got between us, and Teddy pushed her away."

"I fell, hit my head. One minute I'm trying to stop Teddy and Alex from fighting, and the next I'm standing outside my body, trying to figure out what had just happened. When your father saw what Teddy had done, he went crazy. Teddy tried to push your father away."

"I fell, hit my head, but unlike your mother, I was just unconscious," Alexander explained.

"Teddy, at that point, didn't know what to do. Maddie managed to get out of bed and made her way into the room, and she was horrified at what she saw," Anna said.

"And he just killed his wife?" Walt asked.

"Teddy tried to calm Maddie down, got her back in her bed, but she was hysterical. I think he just wanted to stop her from yelling, so he covered her head with a pillow, begging her to just be quiet so he could think. Until she was… quiet. And standing with me, watching him," Anna explained.

"He didn't mean to kill her?" Walt asked.

"No more than he meant to kill me," Anna said.

"Bud and I were a different story. Teddy made the decision to kill us," Alex said.

"He set the fire after he killed Maddie?" Walt asked numbly.

"Yes. Fortunately, your father was unconscious, and the smoke killed him before the flames ever got to us. Alex was with Maddie and me, watching the fire as Teddy rode away."

"Had we followed Teddy that day," Alex said, "after he left us, we would have seen him kill Bud, and instead of Bud spending all those years in confusion, he would have moved on long ago. But we came back here, to Marlow House. In fact, your mother and I stayed many years before we moved on. You were a teenager when we finally did."

"You were with me all those years?" Walt asked.

"We've been with you the entire time," Anna said.

"I think someone is going to wake you up in a minute, so before they do, please understand that when your loved ones move to the other side, they never really leave you. And we understand why you chose not to move on. In fact, it was not your time to move on," Alex said.

"I have some advice for you. You might want to get stocked up on chocolate," Anna suggested.

"Chocolate?" Walt frowned.

"Danielle's going to be craving chocolate. And we're so excited about our grandchild!" Anna burst.

"Grandchild?" Walt frowned.

"One advantage to being on this side, just like we knew about Danielle before you did, we got to meet our grandchild before you. And I'm so happy for you both!" Anna said.

"You've met our child?" Walt sputtered.

"Don't get too jealous. You'll meet the sweet babe in about nine months… or less," Anna said.

MAX WOKE both Walt and Danielle when he jumped on their bed and started walking up Danielle's body.

"Oh, Max," Danielle groaned sleepily, nudging him to the mattress.

"I just had a dream hop," Walt announced, reaching to the nightstand and turning on the light.

Max, not deterred by Danielle's scolding, curled up between her and Walt and purred.

Absently stroking Max with one hand and rubbing her eyes with the other, she asked, "Dream hop? With whom?"

"My parents. My parents were here!" Walt beamed.

Blinking her eyes several times, she turned to Walt. "Wow. Really?"

"Yes! I think they came because Bud crossed over. They understood I needed to know what happened that night."

"So what happened?" Danielle asked.

Walt quickly told Danielle what had happened the night of the fire.

"I'm so happy for you, Walt. I treasure the memory of the Christmas dream hop you arranged for me with my family. By the way you're smiling, it looks like your visit was just as wonderful."

Walt grinned at Danielle. "Guess what else they told me."

"What?"

Walt's grin broadened. "First tell me, have you been craving chocolate? More than normal?"

Danielle frowned at Walt. "How did you know that?"

THE GHOST AND THE BIRTHDAY BOY

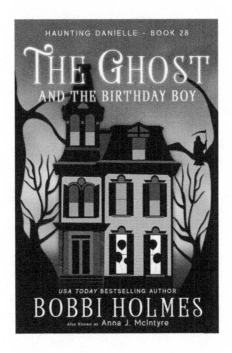

RETURN TO MARLOW HOUSE IN

THE GHOST AND THE BIRTHDAY BOY

HAUNTING DANIELLE, BOOK 28

Lily and Ian's families come to Frederickport to celebrate Connor's first Birthday.

Bringing the in-laws together is not always easy, especially when uninvited guests from the spirit realm show up.

NON-FICTION BY

BOBBI ANN JOHNSON HOLMES

HAVASU PALMS, A HOSTILE TAKEOVER

WHERE THE ROAD ENDS, RECIPES & REMEMBRANCES

MOTHERHOOD, A BOOK OF POETRY

THE STORY OF THE CHRISTMAS VILLAGE

BOOKS BY ANNA J. MCINTYRE

COULSON FAMILY SAGA

COULSON'S WIFE

COULSON'S CRUCIBLE

COULSON'S LESSONS

COULSON'S SECRET

COULSON'S RECKONING

Now available in Audiobook Format

UNLOCKED ♥ HEARTS

SUNDERED HEARTS

AFTER SUNDOWN

WHILE SNOWBOUND

SUGAR RUSH

Made in the USA
Monee, IL
31 March 2021